MW01134069

Woven Web

VALDA DRACOPOULOS

Suite 300 - 990 Fort St
Victoria, BC, V8V 3K2
Canada

www.friesenpress.com

First Edition — 2021

ISBN
978-1-5255-9395-6 (Hardcover)
978-1-5255-9394-9 (Paperback)
978-1-5255-9396-3 (eBook)

1. FICTION, MYSTERY & DETECTIVE, WOMEN SLEUTHS

Distributed to the trade by The Ingram Book Company

Chapter 1

I wake up and jump out of bed, rushing to the window. Outside, there's nothing except a barbed-wire fence and grass that sways with the wind.

I stop, looking at a spider that's outside on the window ledge, working away. The sunlight reflects off its web. Then I turn to the clock on the nightstand; it's after seven. My parents should be awake. All of a sudden, I panic. Something isn't right.

I quickly throw on a pair of jeans and T-shirt and pull my long curly red hair into a ponytail. Bruiser barked last night, but I didn't get up.

The house is quiet. When I oversleep, usually my parents call me to get up and do my chores. We are typically up early and have our tasks done before seven. I turn to examine my room, making sure nothing is out of place, and that my bed is neatly made.

I walk down the hall to the kitchen—my usual morning routine—and sniff the air, but there's no smell of coffee or bacon. The coffee maker hasn't been touched. The kitchen is clean. Where are my parents? Did they go somewhere without me? A chill rushes down my spine. Why did they not wake me?

I rush to the back door, and all is quiet. There is a slight breeze, and the sun is bright. It's almost too warm for seven in the morning. I look up at the tree limbs that protect the yard from the heat of the sun. The barn is a hundred yards away, but I can see that the barn door is closed. The truck is parked in its usual place. I stop in the middle of the yard.

Where should I look first? Do I go back inside and see if they overslept, or go to the barn? Do I get my chores done and wait for them? Maybe I should go back to the house and see if they overslept.

I turn back to the house and rush to their bedroom. I open their bedroom door, hoping to find them asleep, only to stop in my tracks when the bed is unmade and empty. Startled, I turn and run out of the house and to the barn.

I reach for the barn door; it's a large wooden door made of thick wood, and it takes all my strength to push the heavy door to the side. Catching my breath, I step inside to the scent of fresh hay and dust. The warmth and moisture of the enclosed barn cause me to fan myself. I walk further into the vast open area, moving cautiously because it's dark inside. The only light is the sun penetrating through the cracks of the boards at the back of the barn. The smell of something metallic or coppery overpowers me. I walk further into the barn and stop in horror. My parents are sprawled out on a thick mound of hay.

I fall to my knees and blink, my mind racing. *This can't be real—I must be dreaming. Why are they here and in their pajamas?*

I quickly turn and look around. *Was this an accident?* I lean over Dad, since he is the one closest to me. "Dad, why are you here?" I touch his arm, and there is a thick gooey substance on my hands. It's too dark to make out any details. I bring my hands closer to my face and see a dark, thick liquid. I know that it's blood. I quickly hold his wrist and try to get a pulse, but it's useless. My heart is pounding against my chest.

Maybe they're still alive—I have to help them!

I reach for Mother, and there is a gaping hole in her chest. Every minute counts. I place my hands over the hole in Dad's chest, trying to stop the bleeding. I hear a shuffling sound in the attic.

Is someone else in here?

The blood isn't pumping. I reach over and place my hand on Mother, but her heart is still. "What do I do?" I cry out. "How can I help?" I hope that I'm not too late.

I rush back to the house and grab the phone, punching in the number to the sheriff's office. Lucille, the dispatcher at the police station, answers the phone. Lucille also plays the piano for the church services on Sunday.

"It's Rebecca Wild—I just found my parents in the barn, and they're all bloody—I don't know what happened—I need an ambulance and the sheriff," I say all in one breathe.

"Becca, is this a joke?" Lucille replies.

"No," my voice cracks as I choke back a sob, "it's not a joke." How could she think I would joke about something so serious? My voice shakes as I yell, "Get the ambulance and the sheriff—now!"

"Was this some kind of accident?" Lucille asks.

"I don't know what happened. Stop asking questions, and send the sheriff! My parents are in their pajamas. I didn't see anything that would have caused an accident. I rushed to the phone to get help." I lean against the wall because my legs are shaking.

"You said your parents are hurt. How badly are they hurt? Are they conscious? You said you couldn't get a pulse. The sheriff is on the way. Lock the door and wait for him. Do you understand?" Lucille says, and I can hear a commotion and people shouting on her end of the line.

"My parents are a bloody mess," I answer. "They're in the barn, and I ran back to the house. I didn't see anything, and no, they aren't conscious. I can't get a pulse. I tried, but my heart is beating so hard that that was all I could feel. I'll lock the door and wait. I know that every minute counts. What can I do to help them?"

"Becca, you need to lock the back door and just wait for the sheriff."

I hang up the phone and rush to lock the door.

My eyes widen with horror when I realize something: whoever harmed my parents might still be in the house, or perhaps the barn. My hands shake as I grab the butcher knife; I stand at the kitchen sink and look out the kitchen window with my eyes fixed on the barn door.

Fear creeps over me. *Why did something so terrible happen to my parents?* I ask myself. *They're kind and gentle people . . . They would do anything for anyone.*

My parents could still be alive, I remind myself, and I begin to pray for God to save them and keep them alive. I'm crying and gasping for air, but I'll not leave my post. My eyes are fixed on the barn door.

I tremble as I realize Bruiser didn't greet me at the door or follow me to the barn. *Where is he?* I got that cute golden retriever pup a little over a year ago. He was playful and grew so fast. He is a smart dog; maybe he's hiding. I swallow and keep my eyes on the opened barn.

The wind blows a limb against the house, and the creaking of the boards causes me to jump. I keep my eyes on the barn, but I have an eerie feeling that someone could be in the house. I imagine that someone's eyes are peering through my back, but I won't turn around. Maybe they have a knife and are going to plunge it into my back. My knees feel weak, and I grab the edge of the counter to stabilize.

My thoughts shift back to my parents. Could I have done more? I didn't know what to do. I feel like I've failed them. "Please, God, let them be alive," I say.

The wail of sirens breaks the silence, and I strain to see flashing lights on the main road. I release a big sigh; I must have been holding my breath. The emergency vehicles turn onto the lane, and I stand firm until they are parked and out of the car.

I rush to the back door, open it, and run out to the sheriff's car.

"Sheriff, they're in the barn," I shout as tears stream down my cheeks.

The sheriff seems stiff as he gets out of the car and eyes me with a strange look. His eyes survey my bloody shirt.

"Rebecca, stay here by the car. I don't want you getting in the way. Did you move or touch anything?" He sounds harsh as he barks orders.

"The only thing I touched was the door to the barn when I opened it. My parents were lying there on a mound of hay. I checked them for a pulse." I burst into tears, and my body shakes.

"Stay here, and I'll take a look." He walks into the barn and motions for the paramedics to follow him. I stand next to his car and wait for the news that my parents are alive.

I grow weary of waiting, and I lean against the car. I shift my feet. I pace back and forth and swallow; my mouth is dry. I look around in all directions for any signs of Bruiser, but I don't see him. I keep waiting with no sign of the paramedics moving my parents to the ambulance.

What is taking so long?

The sheriff comes back to the squad car and radios for help. My heart sinks. Why are they not moving my parents? I'm only sixteen. If my parents are dead, what will happen to me now?

"Why don't you tell me what happened?" the sheriff asks, leaning beside me.

"I got up and dressed. It was after seven. I was shocked that my parents hadn't woken me. I rushed to the kitchen, but they weren't there, and then I rushed to the barn. It was a struggle to open that heavy door, but I got it open, and I saw them just lying there. I checked for a pulse before running to the house to call the station. What happened to them? Was it an accident?"

"Did you hear anything? Did you notice any unusual sounds during the night?" the sheriff asks with a stern voice and questioning look.

"I heard Bruiser bark. I turned to the clock on my nightstand; it was around two. I figured that he had seen a possum and had it cornered. I fell back to sleep. I heard a shuffling noise, but thought nothing of it. I didn't even wake up enough to think about the sound. I heard the sound of gunshots, but I thought Dad must have shot the possum. How are my parents? Are they going to be okay?" I ask, looking at the sheriff, hoping for good news.

"Rebecca, do you know anyone who would want to hurt your parents?"

"No—I know that Mr. Carson and Dad always seem to get in an argument, but I never heard Dad speak badly about anyone."

"Do you know how to shoot a rifle?" The sheriff crosses his arms and gives me a stern look.

"Well, yes—doesn't everyone? You have to know out in the country, because of the wild animals."

"Do you have a rifle?" The sheriff looks deeply into my eyes.

"No—there is a rifle in the house, but I don't have one," I say, thinking he must think I shot my parents. "Were my parents shot?"

"Maybe. You should show me that rifle and let me look around." The sheriff nods at the house. I lead him inside, and we walk to my parent's bedroom. I go to the closet, open the door, and reach for the rifle.

"I'll take that," the sheriff says. "Is that the only gun in the house?"

"The only one I know anything about," I say, turning to look at the unmade bed. "You see, my dad didn't care for guns. That gun was only to shoot unwanted critters."

"Someone woke your parents. Who do you think would have done that?"

"I don't know, Sheriff. I only know that someone harmed them, and I'm terrified to be without them. Why would someone come to our house and harm my parents and leave me?" I say, shivering.

"Get your things—you're going to the station with me," the sheriff orders, and I walk to my room. Why is he being so cruel? Doesn't he realize I've just lost everything?

He follows me, and I pick up my purse and look around at my bedroom. *What will happen to me now?*

Chapter 2

I walk to the squad car, and the sheriff follows me. It feels like I'm floating, and my feet never touch the ground. I'm numb, like I'm in a dream—or maybe a nightmare. I swallow hard and clutch my black purse to my chest. My eyes dart about the house as if I'm looking at my home for the last time. *I must be having a nightmare,* I tell myself, *and Mother will wake me at any moment.*

I reach for the door handle, but the sheriff comes around me and opens it. My eyes search the surroundings, looking for Bruiser and the ambulance. Other people have arrived and are walking to the barn. The ambulance is gone, but I didn't hear the siren. The sheriff wraps me in a blanket, and I slide into the back seat.

I ask the sheriff, "Will you please lock the back door and close the barn door?" I want to protect the little bit of my life I have left. I'm panicking; I should have fed the animals. I draw my purse even tighter into my chest.

"Someone will secure everything. One of the deputies will feed the animals," the sheriff says, locking the rifle I'd given him in the trunk and sliding in behind the wheel.

"What are you going to do with me?" I ask. Does he think I hurt my parents? Will I ever see them again?

"I'm going to check out this rifle and then ask you more questions. The questions will trigger something in your mind," the sheriff says as he glares at me through his rearview mirror.

I close my eyes, reliving the last time I'd seen my parents. We'd sat together in the den. I had popped popcorn in the microwave, and then we watched a movie: *The Blind Side*. We paused the movie because someone banged on the back door. Mother and I waited as Dad answered the door. I heard him shouting, and then he slammed the door. He'd looked angry when he came back to the room, but he didn't say anything.

I'm jarred from my thoughts when the sheriff starts the car and turns around to leave. I turn and look back at the house for any signs of Bruiser. Out of the corner of my eye, I spot a movement in the field. I look again.

"Sheriff, please stop. I think I see something in the grass."

The sheriff stops the car, and I see Bruiser limping towards us.

"It's Bruiser!" I shout.

The sheriff and I jump out of the car. A muddy and bloody Bruiser limps over to me. The sheriff rushes over to Bruiser.

"I don't know if he's hurt or covered in evidence," the sheriff says. "Let's put him in the car. Don't touch him."

"Come on, Bruiser, let's go. Get in the car," I say, wanting to hug Bruiser and make sure that he isn't hurt, but I hold back. I'm so glad that I have Bruiser because I'm all alone in this big world right now.

"Sheriff, how are my parents? When will I see them?"

"Your parents are at the hospital. You'll see them later," he responds in a rough voice, frowning at me in the rearview mirror.

Bruiser climbs into the car and tries to lick my face, but I push him away. "Bruiser, you need to sit. We will play in a little while," I tell him.

"We'll have the lab get samples from him, and then we'll see if he's hurt," the sheriff responds.

It's a good thing that the car has leather seats, because Bruiser is a mess. Most of the blood is dry, but around his mouth looks like fresh blood. I close my eyes and lean back in the seat. My mind returns to last night. When we'd finished the movie, I washed the popcorn bowl and our glasses and put them away. Then I got ready for bed, and Mother came to my room to say goodnight. She kissed my cheek and told me that we'd drive into town the next day—today—for groceries. She closed my door, and I fell asleep.

Oddly, Dad hadn't said goodnight; he went to his room without saying anything. I thought nothing of this last night, but it seems strange to me now.

I open my eyes and watch as the small town of Clark Creek appears ahead. Bruiser has fallen asleep and is lying on the seat. I look at my purse in my lap and wonder why my bag seemed so important at the time. It doesn't contain anything of value.

"Almost there," the sheriff says.

The sheriff parks the car in front of the station. I want to grab the door handle and jump out, but I sit still.

"Now, I want you to wait until I get back," the sheriff says as he gets out of the car. I sit back and wait for him to return. A few minutes later, he comes out with two deputies. The sheriff opens my door for me, and the deputies get Bruiser on a leash. They take Bruiser inside, and the sheriff and I follow.

He leads me into a small room with a table in the center and four chairs, two chairs on each side. I sit down and he closes the door, leaving me here. I look at the walls—a light shade of green—and notice how dim the light in the room seems. The chair I'm sitting in is just like the other chairs: made of solid wood, and very uncomfortable. The wooden table is scarred from years of use.

There is a knock on the door, and it opens. Lucille, a plump woman in her fifties, steps inside carrying a paper cup and something folded in a napkin.

"Rebecca, I thought you might need some hot chocolate and donuts. I bet you didn't have breakfast," Lucille says as she places the cup and donuts in front of me.

"Lucille, thank you. I didn't eat, but I'm not hungry," I say. The sheriff has been so harsh with me, and Lucille's kindness softens my heart.

"You eat it anyway. I think you're in shock and don't realize how hungry you are." Lucille sits across from me. She plans to watch me until I eat. I reach for the cup and take a sip of hot chocolate, and it soothes my parched mouth. I close my eyes and swallow, feeling the warm liquid slide down my throat. I reach for the cake donut and take a bite; I don't tell her I prefer glazed donuts. When I finish, I wipe my hands and mouth on the napkin, and she picks up the trash and leaves without a word.

I wait for the sheriff to return, and it seems like hours. I lay my head on the table and start to doze off.

"Well, I have some news about Bruiser," the sheriff says, entering the room. He looks so professional in his starched uniform, but now there is softness in his eyes.

I lift my head off the table. I don't say anything but wait for him to tell me what he knows. "It seems there are three types of blood on Bruiser," he tells me.

"What does that mean?" I ask.

"The blood on his body is dry, and it belongs to your parents. The blood on his mouth is fresh, and it belongs to a third person."

"A third person? I didn't see anyone in the barn except my parents," I say.

"I think Bruiser had a run-in with the person who attacked your parents."

"How are my parents? When can I see them?" I ask.

They're not dead, I tell myself. *They can't be dead. But there was so much blood . . . No—the paramedics must have gotten to them in time.*

The sheriff shakes his head and looks down at the table, "Rebecca, your parents didn't make it. They were dead when you found them." The sheriff reaches for my hand. I sit there, stunned.

"What happened to them? Why were they in the barn in their pajamas? Was it an accident?" I ask as I begin to cry.

"Rebecca, someone shot your parents. Do you know anyone who would want them dead?"

"No—my parents were good people." My crying gets louder, and the tears now have my entire face wet, and I can taste the salt on my lips. The sheriff sits silently, watching me as I cry. He looks at his notepad and back at me.

"Did your parents see anyone last night?"

"Someone came to the back door when we were watching a movie. Dad went to the door, and I heard shouting. He slammed the door and came back into the room, but he never said anything."

"So you don't know who the visitor was?"

"No, I don't," I sniffle.

"Maybe they hung around until the middle of the night," the sheriff says, watching my reaction.

"I don't know. I didn't see anything." I'm still crying and gasping for breath. Sheriff Webster can see that I'm in distress, and he quietly leaves the room.

Lucille comes back in with wet paper towels. She wipes my face and hugs me.

"I know how hard this is, Rebecca. It's bad losing your family. I saw how happy you and your family were at church. They loved you so much," Lucille says, holding me tightly. I'm thankful for her kindness.

Lucille sits down across from me. "Rebecca, do you have any other family? Someone we can call?"

"No, there's no family. Except my mom has a sister in California. I have only seen her once in my life." I wipe my face with the damp towel and look at Lucille. "What will happen to me?"

"Now you don't worry your pretty little head about that for a minute. Here in this town, we take care of our own. Normally we would call Child Protective Services, but we have the people at church, and we can call your aunt. What's her name?"

"Her name is Amanda . . . I can remember the return address on the envelope she sent to Mother. It's Amanda Gordon, and she lives on Williams Court in Bakersfield. I always wondered why we never saw her and only received occasional mail."

"So, she was close to your mother?"

"No, I don't think so. They sent cards to each other, but that's all. I saw Amanda once."

"We'll get in touch with her. Someone will need to help you with funeral arrangements. Do you have any friends you could stay with? Maybe you can stay with one of them tonight," Lucille says.

"That would be nice. I have a good friend named Erica—Erica Ward."

"Oh, the Wards are lovely people. I'll give Mrs. Ward a call," Lucille says, standing to leave.

"How did my parents die?" I ask her. "The sheriff just told me they'd been shot . . ."

"Honey, someone did shoot them," Lucille says, patting my hand.

"Why?" I ask, starting to cry again.

"We don't know," Lucille says.

"Why did they shoot my parents and leave me?" I ask.

"We can't answer that just now," Lucille says, and then she walks out of the room.

Chapter 3

I'm still waiting in this dreadful room with no clock or window as time drags on; it seems like I've been here for an eternity. I can't erase the picture of my parents' blood-splattered bodies. Maybe I should have tried harder to do something instead of, out of fear and panic, calling for help. Maybe if I had checked on Bruiser last night, when I heard him bark, none of this would have happened. What was that shuffling sound I'd heard in the house? Why didn't I get up then? If I'd gotten up when I heard the noise, would I be dead too?

I need to clear my head.

I bend down and take off my shoes. I roll up the leg of my jeans, and then unroll them again. For lack of anything else to do, I unlace my tennis shoes and re-lace them. I put my sneakers back on and lay my head on the table.

What'll happen to me now? My thoughts are racing. *I'm alone in this world. They called my aunt to come, but I don't even know her. Who is she? Will she even come? Does she even want to?* Tears pour out of my eyes and onto the table. I cry for what seems like the hundredth time.

"Lord," I say aloud, "I just studied the Beatitudes. What about, "Blessed are they who mourn, for they will be comforted?" Where is my comfort? Lord, why are you doing this to me?" I lift my head from the table, wiping away the tears.

There's a sound at the door, and I turn as the sheriff and a deputy step inside. The sheriff walks over to the table and sits down across from me, and the deputy leans against the wall, watching me.

Sheriff Webster leans forward in his chair. "Rebecca," he says, "the Wards are unable to take you for the night. I have even tried the juvenile detention center, but they don't have any space available. We're still waiting for test results, and it could take a few days. We need you to stay here in town for more questions."

"Where will I go?" I reply. "My parents were everything to me . . ."

"Then you shouldn't have anything to worry about if you're telling the truth," the deputy says as he approaches and places his palms on the table, leaning in.

Webster turns and looks at the deputy, shaking his head in disapproval of the deputy but the deputy ignores him.

"I'm telling the truth," I say, upset and wondering why no one believes me. "I loved my parents, and we were close."

"So close that they didn't want you to date, and you were angry about it," the deputy says, leaning even further over the table.

I jump from my chair. Facing the deputy, I yell, "I have no interest in dating. I love animals, and I enjoy taking care of them. My parents and I took care of our animals together. I enjoyed every minute. How can anyone think I could do such a thing?" I'm fuming; my grief has now turned to rage.

"Lucille is talking to the members of the church to see if someone will take you. She's calling everyone who has children around your age," Sheriff Webster says, standing up. I take it that he's trying to defuse the situation.

The deputy gives me a strange look and walks out of the room; the sheriff follows him out. I shake my head.

How can anyone think I'd kill my family? Why would I hurt my parents? I should have taken care of the animals before I left. Dad would be so upset with me.

I lay my head down on the table; I guessed I would be here until my aunt came to pick me up. She's never been to Clark Creek, to my knowledge.

"Lord," I say, "please comfort me. I need my parents. Why were they taken from me?"

The only thing I like better than animals is singing. I begin to hum a few lines of a hymn we often sing at church. Somehow the sweet melody gives me a bit of comfort.

There is a tap on the door, and Lucille comes in with her hands full.

"Are you hungry?" Lucille asks. She sets a paper bag before me. Inside are fries, a burger, and a Coke. She sits across from me, leaning back in her chair and crossing her arms. It's apparent that she's not going to leave me anytime soon. I recognize the scent of the food; it's from the diner across the way. I'm not hungry. I'm nauseous—the smell of the food is making my stomach churn—but I don't want to be rude. I fumble with the burger wrapper.

Lucille clears her throat. "I . . . well, I have some good news," she begins.

I take a bite of the hamburger, but the smell and the stress of everything that's happened cause my stomach to flip. I choke as I try to swallow. Fearful that it might not stay down, I lean back in my chair and push the food away from me.

"I think I might be sick," I say, looking at Lucille.

"Follow me," Lucille says, jumping from her chair and leading me down the hall to the restroom.

I make it just in time to empty the contents of my stomach into the toilet. I wipe my mouth with toilet paper and then go to the sink to wash my face and hands.

"Poor girl, I guess today has just been too much for you. You know that folks don't kill each other in our little town. Who do you think wanted your parents dead?" Lucille asks with her arms crossed in front of her.

"How would I know? I'm just sixteen with no parents. My life as I know it ended when I found them in the barn. I can't imagine why anyone would want to harm them." The cool water feels soothing against my skin. I reach for a paper towel.

"I found someone willing to let you stay with them. Mrs. Mosley is on her way to pick you up."

"Do you mean Maggie Mosley's mother?" I ask, stunned that the rich in town would be interested in taking in the poor little farm girl.

"Well, yes, Mrs. Mosley. I'm sure you'll be comfortable in their lovely home."

"Yes, as comfortable as possible under the circumstances. Is my aunt coming?"

"The sheriff said he spoke to her, and she's coming. It might be a day or two," Lucille says as we exit the bathroom and return to the dungeon room.

"You might try to eat a little. Your stomach must be empty now. Just nibble a little and sip on your cold drink," Lucille says, leaving me alone again in the room.

My thoughts begin to spiral again. *Why of all people are the Mosleys coming for me? Even Mother mentioned how snobbish they are, and that she felt uncomfortable around them. I'm sure I'll be an embarrassment to them.*

I remembered how Mrs. Mosley had made fun of our old pickup truck when she'd gotten a new BMW.

I take a small bite of my food and chew it slowly, surveying the room. I knew that this dreadful room would forever mark the memory of my parent's death.

I eat about a fourth of the hamburger. My stomach is still in knots, and I don't want to force anything down. I sip on the soda, and the cold liquid is soothing to my throat.

The door opens, and Lucille steps inside. She's all smiles. "The Mosleys are here. Have you finished eating?"

"I'm sorry, but I didn't eat all of it—my stomach is too upset." I feel bad that Lucille had purchased the food for me.

"I understand. I'm sure that you'll eat later at the Mosleys. They will take good care of you. Now come on, you shouldn't keep them waiting." She turns to walk out, and I jump up and follow. I've never felt more alone than I do at this very moment. I feel like a little stray dog looking for a new home.

I walk into the main office, and Mrs. Mosley and Maggie are standing in front of Lucille's desk. Mrs. Mosley smiles, but it doesn't look genuine, and Maggie has the same look. I think about my blood-stained T-shirt and their designer fashions, and I'm entirely out of place.

"I'm sorry about your parents, Rebecca," Mrs. Mosley says.

"Thank you, Mrs. Mosley," I say, wanting to run in the opposite direction.

"Come, we should go. I don't like standing around in this nasty place." Mrs. Mosley turns toward the exit.

Without a word, I follow behind her and Maggie to the car. I want to run, but where would I go? "Thank you for agreeing to take me," I say as we ride the few blocks to their big two-story house.

"I'm just glad we can be of help. I understand you weren't able to take anything with you. Maggie has some discarded things I'm sure you'll be able to wear," Mrs. Mosley says as she turns onto the driveway.

I swallow hard and look at the back of Mrs. Mosley's and Maggie's neatly coiffure heads. What thoughts are going through their pretty little minds?

"Come, Rebecca. I'll show you to the room, and we'll get you some clothes to wear. We're having a cookout tonight," Maggie says with a sincere smile as we get out of the car.

So far, they have been kind, I note. *A bit cold, but kind. Hopefully the clothes they lend me will be appropriate to wear in this beautiful home.*

We walk inside. I immediately notice that the carpet is thick and plush, and the large, expensive furniture makes me feel like I just stepped into the pages of a home decorating magazine.

Maggie and I have attended church together for our entire lives. We are friends, but not that close.

Maggie leads me upstairs to a bedroom and places two large bags of clothes on the bed. "I think you'll be able to find something nice in these bags. Why don't you change clothes and then come downstairs? There's the bathroom if you care to shower." Maggie points to the bathroom door and then leaves the room. I spin around, looking at the large room and its beautiful furnishings. I sit on the side of the bed and take it all in.

After a few moments, I reach into the bag and begin emptying it, one item at a time.

Maggie is a bit taller, and a year older—so will any of these things fit? I wonder.

My fingers delicately flutter over each garment. The quality of the fabric is beyond anything I've ever had. Since Maggie is wearing shorts, I select a pair of white shorts and a pink shirt.

My hands feel dry, and there is dried blood under my nails. Perhaps a shower would lift my spirits. I turn on the shower and wait for the water to warm up. The faucet provides a lot of water pressure, and I enjoy the feeling of the warm spray. The floral-scented soap transports my thoughts to a garden scene. I enjoy the spacious shower and bathroom. The shampoo has the same scent as the soap.

I quickly rinse off and dry with a fluffy pink towel. Then I dress in the clothes I'd selected. They are a bit loose, but they fit.

I hurry downstairs, but I stop when I hear Maggie and her mother talking.

"The sheriff says her aunt won't be here for several days. They have no idea who might have killed them. The poor child—she lived in horrid conditions, out in the middle of nowhere. She has such innocence about her, a sweetness that is so appealing," Mrs. Mosley says.

"This all leaves her alone at sixteen," Maggie replies. "Did you see her face? She has cried all day."

"You know the Wards refused to take her in. I thought Rebecca and Erica were good friends," Mrs. Mosley says.

I approach the kitchen and begin to speak as I get near to announce my arrival. "Where is everyone?"

Maggie turns around as I enter the room. She smiles when she sees me wearing her old clothes. "Rebecca, you look so nice in those clothes. Look, Mother, isn't she pretty?"

"Well, yes, she's pretty," Mrs. Mosley says, turning to inspect me.

They're taking care of me, but after hearing them talk, I want to run out the door and find my way back to the farm.

Chapter 4

Lying in bed at the Mosleys, the soft light reflects from the streetlight below. My room at the farm was always dark except for the light of the moon shining in through the blinds. I used to creep to the window and watch as the wild animals came out of hiding. I would laugh and joke about Bruiser chasing them. Now there's no reason to smile. My life changed in an instant.

A tear leaks from my eye; I let it fall on the pillow. No one tells me, "Goodnight, and sleep well." I allow the tears to wet the pillow.

The reality sets in. I'm homeless and alone.

Unable to sleep, I toss and turn.

Why did they kill my parents and leave me? I fret. *Was there something I could have done to help them? Could I have saved their lives? It's too late to think about now.*

The day replays in my mind. I remember how I'd opened the barn door and walked inside. My parents were there in their pajamas, faces frozen with a stunned look—with shock, upon realizing their lives were at their end. I'd stood there in disbelief, feeling like someone was watching me. Had someone been watching, or had it been an animal? I remembered seeing sprigs of hay that had fallen from the loft. I remembered hearing a shuffle. Had that someone still been in that barn? I hadn't told the sheriff that detail; I had forgotten all about it. Would it make a difference if I told him?

I toss and turn in the bed, but sleep won't come.

Then I remember sitting alone in that dreadful room at the police station while the police spoke in low tones that I couldn't comprehend. They must have been discussing what they were going to do with me. I close my eyes and think about Bruiser. *Where is he?* I wonder. *Whose blood did they find on him?*

Has someone fed the horses, Farrow and Velvet? Will Velvet eat if a stranger feeds her? What will happen to the farm? Will I ever see it again?

At last my mind quiets down and my body surrenders to the softness of the bed.

I awaken to the sounds of footsteps and people talking.

I inhale, expecting to smell the bacon cooking, but I'm not at home. I've survived my first night without my parents. Now I'm an orphan with no one and nowhere to go. I hurry out of bed and rush to the bathroom.

I jump in the shower and allow the water to wash away my thoughts. The floral scent of the soap transports me to a better place. I pretend that I'm a princess living in a castle and the people in the house are my servants.

I dress quickly in another of Maggie's old outfits: denim shorts and a pale-yellow blouse. I make the bed before rushing downstairs. Thinking of the conversation between Mrs. Mosley and Maggie the day before, I creep softly, hoping to hear what they be might saying and what they might know.

"Why did Dad rush off on a fishing trip before the cookout he planned?" I heard Maggie saying.

"I don't know," Mrs. Mosley replied. "I guess the opportunity became available, and he jumped on it. I was angry yesterday that he left me to do the cookout alone."

"That was inconsiderate of Dad. I'm sorry he did that to you."

"I'm over it now. Frank was nice to cook the burgers, and no one seemed to mind that your dad wasn't here. I had a good time chatting with everyone."

There's a pause, and then Maggie says, "I can't imagine ever being without you and Dad. Can you imagine how lost she must feel? Her whole world has been torn away from her. She is a sweet girl, and I've always liked her."

"Her parents were good people. They were just farmers, struggling to make ends meet. Farming isn't the best occupation right now because of the economy," Mrs. Mosley responds.

I know that I should enter the kitchen and not be eavesdropping, but I want to hear what they have to say.

"I'm glad that we have plenty of money. Rebecca looks so pretty in those clothes I gave her. I'm going to teach her how to wear makeup and give her some of mine. School starts on Tuesday, and I want her to be ready," Maggie says.

I take a few steps closer to the kitchen, but I'm still out of sight.

"Maggie, it's good of you to want to help her," Mrs. Mosley replies.

"I'm only doing what I feel is right. Rebecca needs a friend right now. I can't believe that the Wards wouldn't take her. Erica is her best friend—or at least I thought she was."

The sheriff said the Wards couldn't take me, but he didn't mention why, I thought. *Do they think I killed my parents? I can't believe that Erica would think I'd do such a thing . . .*

"The Wards are protecting themselves."

"Mother, you don't think we need protection?"

"I think what happened was a freak thing. I don't think there is a killer on the loose. Just that someone—maybe a disturbed person—killed them by accident."

"Mother, even I know that what you just said doesn't make any sense. Whoever killed Rebecca's parents is still out there somewhere, and if they killed once, they might do it again. We have to realize that there's a murderer in our area. All of us need to take extra precautions."

"Good morning. Where is everyone?" I say as I round the corner and enter the kitchen.

"Good morning. How did you sleep?" Mrs. Mosley asks as she turns to me. She's standing at the counter, mixing something in a bowl.

"I slept well. The bed is very comfortable. Thanks again for allowing me to stay here with you," I say, sitting down at the counter next to Maggie. Maggie is now my friend after overhearing her kind comments.

"Did you wash your hair?" Maggie asks.

"Yes, I took a shower. Is my hair a mess?"

"No, you have beautiful hair. I love the light-red color with golden highlights. Did you curl your hair, or are those soft curls natural? I thought—if you don't mind—I could help you with some makeup today," Maggie says.

"That would be nice. I've never worn any makeup. There isn't a need for makeup on the farm. Have you heard anything about the farm?" I ask, still concerned about the animals and Bruiser.

"Mr. Stark is tending the animals, and Sheriff Webster took Bruiser to his house last night," Mrs. Mosley tells me as she hands me a plate of fruit and yogurt.

"What is this?" I ask.

"This is the kind of breakfast we eat. What do you eat on the farm?" Maggie asks.

"Usually eggs and bacon with biscuits or pancakes," I say.

"Oh, that isn't good for the figure—too many carbs and calories," Mrs. Mosley pipes in.

"I guess I have some things to learn." I take a bite of fruit, wishing I was eating at home with my parents, laughing and talking around the table.

"You need to eat quickly. The sheriff is on his way over to talk to you. He thinks that maybe you might remember something that you forgot about yesterday," Mrs. Mosley says.

The doorbell rings; it must be the sheriff.

"I'll answer the door. When you finish, put your plate in the sink," Mrs. Mosley says, leaving the room.

Maggie looks at me, and there's pity in her eyes. I swallow hard, knowing that's the look I'll be getting from people for now on.

"Go ahead and see the sheriff," Maggie says. "I'll put your plate in the sink." I walk into the living room where Mrs. Mosley and the sheriff are waiting.

"Did you bring Bruiser?" I ask.

"No, he's resting at my house. He had a hectic day yesterday. It seems he chased the killer, and thanks to Bruiser, we have the killer's blood sample."

"So, you know who killed them?" I say, sitting down in the chair across from the sofa where the sheriff is sitting. Mrs. Mosley is perched on a chair next to me.

"No, it isn't quite that easy. The labs are checking the DNA, and we should know something soon, but it'll take a while. So, is there anything that you forgot to tell me yesterday?"

"Did I tell you that someone came to the house last night and knocked on the back door? No one comes to our house at night, and if they do, they would go to the front door. So it seemed very odd to me. My dad got up and went to the door. He stepped outside and talked to whoever it was. When he came back, he looked unhappy, but he didn't mention anything."

"Your mother didn't ask him about the visitor?" Webster asks.

"No, but we were watching a movie, and we paused it to wait for him; when he returned, we continued the movie, so there wasn't any talking."

"How long do you think he was outside?"

"Five or ten minutes, it couldn't have been any longer than that."

"So, it was a brief talk," Webster says.

"Yes, it was short," I say; maybe that visitor has nothing to do with their death. "There's something that I forgot to mention yesterday. When I found my parents in the barn, I was in shock and just stood there looking at them. It felt like someone was watching me—maybe not watching, but like there were eyes on me. I was terrified and I backed out of the barn. Just as I got to the door, I saw pieces of hay fall from the loft, and I heard a shuffle. That's when I ran back to the house."

"So you think someone could have still been there in the barn with the door closed?" the sheriff asks.

"Well, I'm just telling you what I remember. It could've been an animal, but I was scared," I say, swallowing hard and trying to hold back my tears.

"Who would want to harm your parents?" the sheriff asks.

"I can't think of anyone."

"Who was the visitor that came the night before?"

"I told you, I don't know. I didn't see the person." I think for a moment. "But I did hear my dad and a man shouting."

"So, there was an argument," the sheriff says.

"I don't know if it was an argument, but it sounded like shouting." The sheriff stares at me.

"Did your dad mention having problems with anyone?"

"No, only Mr. Carson, but I think I would have recognized his voice."

"What time was it when the visitor knocked on the back door?" he asks.

"I don't know . . . I would say halfway through the movie. Dad said, 'Pause it. I'll be right back.' Maybe he was expecting the visitor—I don't know."

"Did your mother seem curious?"

"She gave me a puzzled look. So I think it was a surprise to her," I say, wishing the sheriff would stop with the questions.

"That's all I have for now. If you remember anything, please call my office." He stands up to leave.

"I will," I say, getting up and walking back to the kitchen.

Did anything I just told the sheriff help? I wondered. *Will they ever find the killer?*

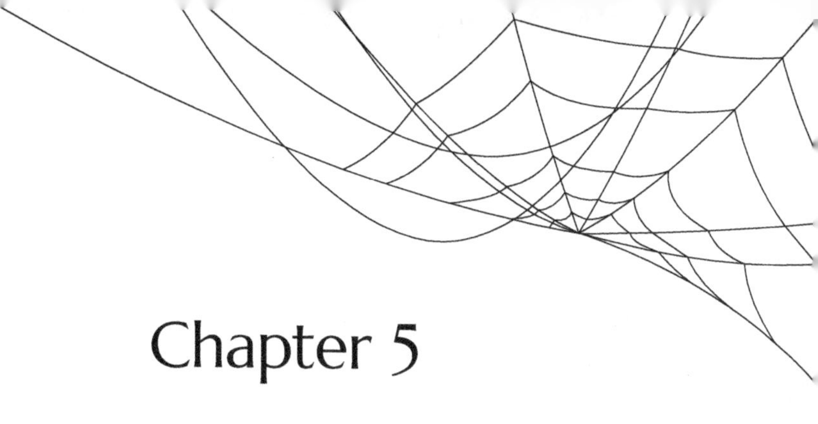

Chapter 5

I've been at the Mosleys for three days. It's hard to believe that I've survived for three days without my parents. I miss them so much. I miss playing card games, and Mother brushing my hair, and grooming the horses together. I miss the little things, like Mother telling me goodnight, and the warmth of her hugs. The way Dad always teased me and would give me a wink. Today I was going to plan the funeral with my aunt.

Despite all that's happened, I have enjoyed my time with Maggie. She taught me what it's like to be a teenager. She's shown me that life isn't all about working, but you can also have fun. But I'd trade the pretty house, the makeup, and the beautiful clothes to be back on the farm with my parents.

I've noticed that there's something strange about Mrs. Mosley. She seems distant and cold. I hate the way she gives me a disapproving look. I often catch her staring at me or frowning in my direction. I don't think she likes me.

I straighten my room and make the bed. I grab my old jeans and my T-shirt and put them on. The bloodstain is now gone, as though it had never existed. At first, I don't want to wear these clothes after wearing Maggie's things because of how tacky and worn my old clothes look. But now that I have them on, there's comfort in wearing them.

My aunt, Amanda Gordon, is coming for me today. *I wonder what she's like.* I wonder as I put on my sneakers. *Will she be kind and know how to cook? Will she love animals and want to live on the farm? I hope she's like Mother.*

A knock on the door startles me.

"Rebecca, your aunt will be here soon. Come and help us with lunch," Mrs. Mosley says through the closed door. I turn around and make sure everything is neat and orderly. Then I rush to the door and hurry down the stairs.

"Why are you wearing those clothes?" Mrs. Mosley asks me with a disgusted look on her face.

"I thought my aunt was coming for me today. These are the only clothes that I own," I respond, looking down at my worn and faded jeans. At this moment, however, my old clothes provide a shield of protection, forming a barrier between me and Mrs. Mosley's judgment of me.

"We gave you those clothes," Mrs. Mosley continues. "Now go and change into something suitable for meeting your aunt."

She doesn't like the poor farm girl, I think to myself. *Will Amanda like the poor farm girl, because that's who I am?*

Maggie is standing behind Mrs. Mosley, rolling her eyes. It's all I can do not to laugh. To hide my smile, I turn quickly, run up the stairs, and go through the bags of clothes, looking for a dress or something more suitable. I find a sleeveless sundress, just straight and simple. Its pale green with tiny little sunglasses embroidered all over it. I put it on and then look for a pair of shoes at the bottom of the bag. It's good that Maggie and I wear the same size shoe; the only shoes I have here are my tennis shoes. I find a cute pair of pink flats and put them on. Nervous about meeting Amanda, I rush to the bathroom to straighten my hair.

Satisfied with the reflection in the mirror, I leave the room and rush downstairs. I walk to the kitchen where Maggie and Mrs. Mosley are preparing lunch.

"Oh, you look lovely in that," Mrs. Mosley says with a smile. Now that I'm wearing Maggie's clothes, she seems nice. "I'm preparing a light lunch for your aunt. I thought it would be nice since she's been driving for most of the day."

"Let me help," I say as the doorbell rings. I stand frozen next to the kitchen counter, unable to move my legs. Fear takes over, as I know things are about to change.

"I'll answer the door and greet Ms. Gordon. Girls, you finish up here," Mrs. Mosley says in her commanding voice.

I look at Maggie for instructions.

"You look nice in that dress. I think it looks better on you than it looked on me," Maggie says, smiling. "Get the hot pad and take the quiches out of the oven."

I do as instructed, following Maggie's lead as we prepare the table out on the patio near the pool. We're pouring the punch into glasses when Mrs. Mosley and my aunt come out onto the patio.

"Amanda, this is my daughter, Maggie, and this is your niece, Rebecca," Mrs. Mosley says as she waits for Amanda and me to greet each other.

Amanda approaches me and gives me a stiff hug. She already seems nothing like Mother. She is shorter than Mother and has light-brown hair with blond highlights. Her hair, stylishly cut, sits at her shoulders. Her clothes look expensive; she's wearing a tan suit with a coral-colored blouse. Her voice sounds soft with a bit of an edge.

"Rebecca, I'm sorry for your loss," Amanda says. "You have grown since I last saw you. I wouldn't have recognized you—"

"I wouldn't have recognized you either, since you don't look like my mother," I reply quietly, so no one else can hear. "I'm going to try to love you, but please don't be cold like Mrs. Mosley. You're sorry for my loss, but didn't you lose a sister?"

Amanda doesn't reply. Instead, she sits down at the table, and I manage a smile as I join her, but words don't come. I choke back tears, and my stomach churns. Am I supposed to live with this person? What can I expect from her? Will she be warm and caring? Does she even want me?

We have a salad and quiche, which is new for me. Did Mother know about quiche, and did she ever make one? We could have had quiche, because we had all the eggs from the chickens. Then Mrs. Mosley served an assortment of mini cupcakes and a lemon bar. All of it was delicious.

"Margaret, it was so nice of you to prepare lunch—such a lovely gesture. It's a long drive from her home to Clark Creek, and not many places to stop along the way. I enjoyed the salad, but I'm not a quiche person. I did eat some of mine though, because I didn't have time for breakfast." Amanda rattles on, and I can see the irritation on Margaret's face.

Maggie and I clean off the table, and Mrs. Mosley and Amanda go back into the living room. I'm nervous; what will Mrs. Mosley say to Amanda?

I need to make a good impression on Amanda, since she is my only living relative—and a total stranger.

My hands shake, and I almost drop the dishes.

"What's wrong?" Maggie asks.

"Maggie, I'm scared. That woman is my only relative. I don't know her, and I'm about to leave and go live with her in a strange place. I'll leave behind the only things that I know." My voice cracks.

"Now Maggie, don't cry, you'll mess up your makeup. Remember, you can always call or write to me. I know you didn't ask for any of this. I'm amazed at how brave you've been. I would have fallen to pieces."

"Oh, and you think I haven't already fallen apart?" I manage a smile.

"Let's look at this like it's an adventure. Just pretend it's only for a little while, and you'll return home," Maggie says.

"I'll try that. Thanks for being so kind to me." I rinse the plates and place them in the dishwasher.

Mrs. Mosley enters the kitchen, interrupting our conversation. "Rebecca, your aunt is ready to go. Why don't you go and collect your things? The clothes and makeup are yours to keep, as we've said."

I rush upstairs to grab my things. What Maggie said about this being an adventure somehow makes things seem more natural. Just thinking of it being temporary takes the edge off. I grab the two bags and throw the makeup and purse on top and then head back down the stairs. Amanda is waiting for me by the front door. Mrs. Mosley and Maggie are standing near her.

"Mrs. Mosley, thank you so much for everything. Thank you for taking care of me," I say, putting down the bags and hugging her. I'm used to Mrs. Mosley and her stiff hugs.

I hug Maggie, saying, "I'll miss you too, Maggie. You've been like a sister. Thank you." I bend down and pick up the bags.

"Don't forget to call me. I'll miss you," Maggie says.

I walk out the door and follow Amanda to her car. She opens the trunk, and I place my bags inside next to her suitcases.

We get in the car, and it's quiet. I'm afraid that I might disappoint Amanda, and she won't want to keep me—and then what? She backs the car out of the driveway, and I give the Mosleys' lovely house one last look as we drive down the street.

"We're going to the funeral home. I made some of the arrangements over the phone, but this is to finalize everything. It shouldn't take long. I understand that there's a nice hotel downtown."

"Yes," I reply, "it's an older hotel they renovated last year. It seems the little town has become a tourist destination because of all the updating. They're trying to draw people here. It's the mayor's plan. You know, the mayor is Mr. Mosley. I've learned a lot about this town from Maggie." I can't believe how I'm just blabbing on about the town and the mayor.

"Oh, I didn't know that. Where is Mr. Mosley?" Amanda asks as she parks the car in the funeral home's parking lot.

"Mr. Mosley is out of town. He's in Florida, deep-sea fishing, I think."

I look down at my folded hands. Planning the funeral is one of the last things I'll be able to do for my parents. I'd somehow thought I'd see them grow old, and that I would bring my children to visit them and hold their feeble hands. I'd thought they would be old and gray when I looked at them in their coffins.

I choke back the lump that's in my throat, and my hands are shaking as I reach for the door handle.

"Are you ready?" Amanda asks.

"Yes, I think so." I open the car door and step out onto the parking lot.

I'm overwhelmed with sadness as I walk to the door. The large, carved-wood door swings open into a beautifully decorated reception area. The air is filled with the scent of flowers and sanitizer.

The funeral director greets us at the door and takes us to his office. He reads over some notes, and Amanda says the information is correct. He then shows us some pictures of caskets and asks which one we prefer.

"I like the silver one. Do you have two of them so that they match?" I ask, wanting everything to be perfect for my parents.

"Yes, we have two, and I'll make sure the casket sprays are also matching. It will look lovely. There will be a lot of flowers at the funeral, because flowers are already arriving. I have them stored in the refrigerated area." The funeral director says, shoving the bill over to Amanda. Amanda writes a check and gives it to the director.

"Everything will be ready tomorrow morning," the director replies as he escorts us to the door.

We get back into the car and leave the funeral home.

It's a short drive to the hotel. Amanda parks the car at the curb. A gentleman opens the car door and I step out and follow Amanda inside. I stand back and take in the grand lobby, looking at the wood carvings on the moldings. Amanda is short-tempered with the man behind the desk and she snaps at him before turning to walk to the elevator.

I sigh. I had hoped that we would go back to the farm instead of the hotel, but Amanda explained that the sheriff felt it wasn't safe for us to stay there. I want to scream; the farm is my home. Why can't I go there? But maybe it isn't safe.

We follow the man to our room, and he leaves our luggage. I sit on the side of the bed and my eyes scan the room. It's newly decorated, with beautiful fabric in rich tones. The furniture is also new, and the chairs look uncomfortable, but overall the room is beautiful. It's a stark contrast to the farm, and all of its worn and comfortable furnishings. I miss home.

"I need to know if you have a black dress suitable for the funeral," Amanda says as she unpacks her things.

"I don't know. I can go through the sacks and look for something," I say, getting off the bed.

"I have a better idea. We're going to buy you a new outfit for the funeral. Mrs. Mosley told me about a boutique where she shops for Maggie. I want you to look nice for the funeral. We'll leave for Dallas the day after the funeral."

"Will we be able to go to the farm before we leave?"

"Yes, briefly—you can go there and get your things. The sheriff has agreed to go to the farm with us. I've made arrangements for someone to feed the animals."

Who did she get to feed the animals? I wonder. *Does she even know if they're knowledgeable about animals?*

"Thank you," I reply, forcing a smile. "I've been worried about the animals. What about Bruiser?" I'm longing to see my dog.

"We can't take him with us. Sheriff Webster wants to keep him. Are you satisfied with that arrangement?"

"No—Bruiser is mine. He's all I have left. Who will brush him and love him?"

"We can't take him with us," Amanda firmly states.

I drop my head. I can feel my life changing.

Chapter 6

Amanda unpacks her clothes. I appreciate the clothes Maggie gave me, but I doubt with all the clothes Amanda has that there will be any room for me to hang anything in the hotel room's small closet. I dangle my feet off the bed.

"We should go to that little boutique. I don't know what we'll do if they don't have a little black dress. Do you have black shoes?" Amanda looks down at my pink flats.

"No, I don't have any black shoes with me, but I do have them at home," I respond, knowing the shoes I have at home wouldn't meet her approval. Those shoes have scuff marks and came from a discount store. I'm not sure Amanda approves of anything I have.

"Are you ready to go?" Amanda stands, holding her purse, and walks to the door.

After having breakfast in the hotel restaurant, Aunt Amanda says that we're going to the funeral home to see my parents this morning before the ceremony this afternoon. Sitting at the table, my hands begin to tremble, and I slide them under the edge of the tablecloth to hide how nervous I am. I haven't seen my parents since I found them in the barn. How will they look? I straighten my pale-blue V-neck dress and look down at my new navy shoes. Aunt Amanda bought the outfit and insisted I wear it this morning. At some point I will change into the black dress and shoes she also bought for me.

What'll life be like with Aunt Amanda? I wonder. *So far she has bought me clothes and food, but after today, will she take care of me? Where will we live? Will I ever get to call the farm home again? Will I ever get to sit in that kitchen and have a meal at the table? Will I get to say goodbye to the animals and Bruiser?*

"I called for the car. It will take a few minutes." Aunt Amanda smoothes her gray dress and picks at an invisible piece of lint; as Mother would say to me, "She is dressed to the nines." I smile at the thought, but there's an awkward silence between us. I don't know what to say. I resent Amanda, and at the same time, I'm thankful that she's here and taking care of me.

"There's the car." Aunt Amanda leads the way to the door, and I follow along behind her. I'm lost and dependent on this stranger. She has Mother's eyes and nose. Yesterday there were moments when we were shopping that she smiled, and once she even laughed.

We get in the car and drive the few blocks to the funeral home.

"Are you nervous about seeing your parents?" she asks. I hold my hands in my lap so she can't see that I'm shaking.

"I haven't seen them since that morning in the barn." I choke back the tears. My breakfast swirls in my stomach. "I thought my parents would be old when I went to see them at the funeral home."

"Have you been to a funeral before? Do you know what to expect?"

"Yes, I've been to a funeral, but it was for people I hardly knew. But we're going to see my *parents*." Tears flood my eyes. I pinch my arm hard to stop myself from crying. I'm thankful her eyes are averted and not looking at me.

"This could be hard for you." She pulls into the parking lot.

Amanda stares out the windshield in a daze. I'm ready to speak, but she breaks the silence.

"Are you ready?" Amanda frowns, and her voice cracks.

"I'm as ready as I'll ever be." I reach for the door handle.

"We can do this together." She smiles.

What does she mean that "we can do this?" I think bitterly. *She hasn't shown any emotion. Is this hard for her too? Did she love Mother? She spent very little time with her . . .*

We walk into the funeral home, and a man in a suit greets us at the door.

"I have everything ready. Follow me." He turns, and we follow behind him.

We walk through the beautiful reception area and down a hallway. My stomach is doing flips again, and my knees are shaking. I blink to hold back tears. Just the anticipation of seeing my parents is overwhelming. Amanda is following along and looking straight ahead.

We reach the door to the room where my parents are. It's a large living room with two matching gray caskets. On each coffin is a beautiful bouquet of white flowers. Aunt Amanda enters the room ahead of me. She approaches the first casket, and I wait. She has her back to me, so if she has any reaction, I can't tell.

I take one step just inside the room, but I hesitate to go any further. I still have the picture of my parents lying in the barn in their pajamas swirling in my head. Do I dare look at them again? I remember their lifeless bodies and that horrible expression on their faces and the big hole in their chests. I take another step closer but pause, afraid to look.

"Come on. It's time to see your parents," Amanda says with a harsh tone.

I know that seeing Mom and Dad in the caskets will make everything so final. It will mean that this is truly the end; I know this in my mind, but it isn't a reality in my heart. As long as I can visualize them in the barn, there is a chance they're still alive somehow. If they're in the caskets, it will mean it's the end.

I step up to the first casket. There's my dad dressed in a nice suit and tie. I only saw him in a suit on Sundays, but he looks natural, almost as though he could be asleep. I choke back my tears and walk to the next casket. Here's Mother and her long hair, and she's wearing makeup. She's beautiful, and I notice that she and Amanda look a lot alike.

Sheriff Webster enters the room with a nod and smile. He holds his hat in his hands in front of him. My breakfast swirls in my stomach, and I can taste the bile in the back of my throat. The room spins, sweat beads on my forehead, my knees buckle, and I fall backward. Just before everything goes dark, someone catches me. When my eyes flutter open, Amanda and the sheriff are seated on the floor next to me. Amanda is putting something smelly under my nose.

I cough and say, "I'm going to be sick." But it's too late, and I spill my breakfast on the carpet. When I finish, Sheriff Webster picks me up and lays me on the sofa.

"I guess that was a little too much for you," Sheriff Webster says, standing next to the sofa. He smiles at me and pats my hand. Amanda is on her hands and knees with tissues, trying to clean up my mess. I lie here, not wanting to move. I wish I could die. If I died, they could bury me with my parents. I'm sure one of them would slide over and let me get in the casket with them. My life is worthless now. Nothing will ever be the same.

I must have fallen asleep because Amanda nudges me, and I wake up.

"Rebecca, we're going back to the hotel. I think you should rest before the service this afternoon. Do you think you can stand up and walk?" She looks concerned.

I nod my head yes and sit up. Taking a deep breath, I stand up. I want to take one last look at Mom and Dad, but I'm afraid that I'll get sick again. So I turn and walk out of the room. Amanda follows.

Sheriff Webster walks with us back to the car and says, "Deputy Rogers is with me, and he has Bruiser if you want to see him."

I feel a surge of energy. I ask Amanda, "Please, may I?"

Amanda frowns and places her hands on her hips before nodding her head "yes." I run to the lawn on the side of the funeral home, and Bruiser runs to meet me. I fall to my knees, and he licks my face. I hug him tightly, saying, "Bruiser, I've missed you. Is Mr. Webster taking good care of you? Are you a police dog now?" Bruiser barks.

"Rebecca, we should go now," Amanda says, and I walk to Amanda's car with Bruiser following.

Sheriff Webster stands by the car and leans in. "I'm bringing Bruiser to the funeral. I'll have him walk among the guests to see if he has an adverse response to anyone. Maybe he was there when it happened and knows the killer." He puts his hand on my shoulder. "We'll find out who did this."

We drive silently back to the hotel.

I nap until the afternoon and sip on tea to settle my stomach. Amanda begins to change and tells me to put on the black dress. I reapply my makeup and fix my hair before putting on the dress. I take great care in looking nice for my parents. If the dress were purchased for any other reason, I would think it was beautiful, but knowing it's for my parents' funeral makes it not so impressive. Amanda puts on a black dress, and we are ready to leave.

"Before we go, I think you should eat a few of these crackers. It's best not to have an empty stomach. We'll eat after the funeral," Amanda says, giving me the crackers. I chew on them slowly and then drink the remainder of my tea.

We pull in at the church and park behind the hearse: a spot reserved for us. Amanda frowns and puts her hands in her lap.

"Do you think you can make it through the service?" she asks.

"I hope so—I need to do this for my parents," I say, wringing my hands in my lap.

"They will tell us when to enter. We'll wait here for the signal and walk up the aisle and sit in the pew at the front. We'll sit there together," she says, looking worried.

She seems so sure that we can do this. I'll do this for my parents. The last time I'll ever get to see them.

We receive the signal from the man at the funeral home to come inside for the service.

"Are you ready?" Amanda asks, reaching for her door handle.

"I think so," I open the car door. I look at Amanda for direction. How can she be so calm? She's showing no emotion. I'm relaxed on the outside, but I'm screaming on the inside.

We enter the chapel, and side by side, we walk down the aisle. The church is full. I see Erica and wonder if she thinks I killed my parents. We proceed down the aisle. Amanda motions for me to slide into the pew, and she sits down next to me. Mrs. Mosley and Maggie are sitting right behind us. Maggie taps me on the shoulder, and I place my hand on hers. Just knowing she is behind me gives me courage.

The minister from our church, a tall handsome man, stands and reads the obituary. I try to listen, but my mind takes me to other places. I remember times when Dad would carry me on his shoulders, and we would run through the house. I would laugh, and Mother would say, "Duck your head, or you will hit the doorframe." I remember when Mother taught me how to make cookies, and then we decorated them. And Christmas was always special; one year, Dad made me a little dollhouse and even made the furniture. Mother put tiny curtains on the windows and tiny rugs on the floors. I'd been so proud of that dollhouse. Then there was the night that Mother woke me when Farrow was giving birth to a new colt—a colt that would be mine. We dressed and went into the barn. Dad was with Farrow, and I watched in awe as the foal was born, the colt that I named Velvet.

What will happen to Velvet now?

"There are times when people are taken away too soon. That is the case for Carol and Bruce. But you can have comfort in knowing that you'll see them again in Heaven." The preacher's comments bring me back to the present. Amanda has tears rolling down her cheeks. I reach over and take her hand in mine.

"We have each other," I whisper. But *do* we have each other? Does she care about me? I still can't tell for certain.

The people come up the aisle and look at my parents in their caskets. I begin to sob. I grab a tissue and try to keep the tears wiped away. Amanda is crying. *So,* I think, *she* does *have a heart—she isn't so cold. I need to get to know her.*

Everyone has left the church, and it's just Amanda and me. We approach the caskets. The minister stands next to the casket to comfort us.

I take one last look at my parents and my insides tighten; my heart is breaking. The tears flow as I stand and have one last look at the two people who mean the world to me. Amanda sobs, and that only brings more tears. Together we stand and hold each other as we both cry.

They close the caskets and motion for us to walk out of the church. We're still holding each other as we walk out. People are standing outside the church, talking and waiting for us to leave. We get into the car, and they load the caskets into two hearses. There's a tap on the window, and I roll the window down. It's Erica Ward, my best friend—at least, I thought she was.

"Rebecca, I'm so sorry about your parents," Erica says.

"Thank you, Erica. I don't feel like talking right now." I say, rolling up the window. I wipe the tears from my eyes and look over at Aunt Amanda.

"So you did love Mother," I say.

"Carol was my sister. We grew up together. She was all that I have in terms of a family—except for you." Amanda chokes back her sobs.

"I'm sorry for your loss," I say, wiping my eyes.

"I'm sorry for your loss, too. As you said, we do have each other." She reaches over and squeezes my hand.

Maybe she isn't as bad as I thought. Perhaps we'll grow to like each other, and we can be happy together. But how will I ever live away from the farm? How can I survive without the horses and my dog? How long will my heart feel like there is a big hole in it?

Chapter 7

The two hearses move forward, and Amanda and I follow. It's only a few blocks to the cemetery. I glance behind us, and there are cars following us. It seems like the whole town is going.

"There are a lot of people. I thought we would be there alone," I say, almost in a whisper.

"Maybe they're friends of your parents, or curious because it was a murder," Amanda says without looking at me.

"Whatever the reason, I'm thankful they'll be there with us." I choke back tears. The hearse turns in at the cemetery, and we follow. We turn and stop near a tent. The pallbearers remove one casket, and then the other. Tears pour down my cheeks, and I just let them go; I don't wipe them away, because they feel cleansing. I'll be leaving my parents here and never again see them.

When the caskets are in place, we get out of the car. We're ushered to our area under the tent and seated in folding chairs. People enter the tent and stand behind us. Maggie's hands rest on my shoulders, and I turn around.

Maggie leans forward and says, "I'm here, Rebecca. Be strong. You're not alone."

"Thank you, Maggie." I pat Maggie's hand, and she keeps them on my shoulders.

The minister stands and reads from his Bible. "Then shall the dust return to the earth as it was, and the spirit shall return unto God who gave it," he says. "Now let us pray.

Our Father, who art in heaven, hallowed be thy name. Thy kingdom come,

thy will be done, on earth as it is in heaven. Give us this day our daily bread, and forgive us our trespasses as we forgive those who trespass against us. And lead us not into temptation, but deliver us from evil. For thine is the kingdom, and the power and the glory, forever and ever.

Amen."

The minister comes and shakes my hand and then walks out of the tent. The pallbearers follow behind him; they're high school boys who were in Dad's Sunday school class. Dad always told me he had to teach those high school boys how to be good Christians so that they would be kind to me if I dated them. But now I won't be here to date them.

Instead of the pallbearers placing their boutonnieres on the casket, each boy bends down and hands me his boutonniere, and as they do, they whisper to me.

"Your dad loved you. This flower is from him." After the last boy gives me his flower, I'm ready to leave, but all the people come to shake my hand and wish me well.

After the people finish, Maggie removes her hands from my shoulders and takes me in her arms. She is sobbing too.

"You and I are sisters now. I'm always here for you. Please let me see you before you leave," Maggie whispers.

"You're the best, Maggie. I'll keep in touch, I promise, and I'll make Amanda bring me by to see you before we leave," I say, crying.

"You've been crying, but your mascara hasn't run at all," Maggie whispers.

"That's because I didn't wear any," I laugh.

"Good job, girl," she chuckles, and we both smile.

The men from the funeral home escort Amanda and I back to the car, and we get in. Sheriff Webster has Bruiser walking around among the people. Bruiser has a new life now. *How long he will remember me?* I wonder. Bruiser and I are the real victims; the life we had and loved had been ripped from us that one terrible morning.

We drive back to the hotel. I have my head resting on the back of the seat, and I close my eyes because they're burning. My stomach churns because I haven't eaten.

"You look tired. I think we'll go back to the hotel and freshen up before we go to dinner." Amanda is looking over at me.

"I've cried so much that my face feels swollen," I say.

"Your eyes are a bit puffy, but you look fine. How are you feeling?"

"I feel tired, and like I don't have any tears left to shed," I say as we drive through town most of the stores are closed.

"It looks like the whole town went to the funeral." Amanda parks the car in front of the hotel and the attendant opens the car doors. I follow Amanda into the hotel and onto the elevator. We don't speak but watch as the elevator climbs to the sixth floor, and then we get off. Silently we walk to our room, and Amanda opens the door. I walk inside and fall onto the bed, kicking my new black shoes to the floor.

"You must be as exhausted as I am?" Amanda says.

"I think so." I'm hungry, but too tired to move.

"I made reservations for us to have dinner at a nice restaurant tonight. Remember, we're leaving tomorrow."

"Where are we going?" I'm stunned that we're leaving so soon, but she had said at the Mosleys that we were leaving the day after the funeral.

"We're going to my home. Where I live and have a job," Amanda says, taking off her shoes and sitting on the side of her bed facing me.

"We're going all the way to California?"

"No. I was in the process of moving when your parents died. That's why I was delayed getting here. I accepted a job and moved to Dallas. We can drive to the farm occasionally. It's only an hour and a half from here to Dallas."

"I didn't know you were moving. I was just told you'd be delayed."

Amanda rolls her eyes, saying, "That doesn't surprise me."

"Did you move to Dallas so you could see Mother more?" I'm excited; perhaps this is more proof that Amanda did care for Mother.

"That's only a small part of it. I'm an attorney and work for a large law firm. I was promoted, and I moved to Dallas. I was glad about the extra money. In the back of my mind, it did occur to me that I would be close and could visit Carol more. I was thinking more about the holidays."

"So, you would have spent Thanksgiving and Christmas with us?" I ask, turning on my side to face her.

"That's what I had hoped."

"Tell me more," I say. "Are you settled in your new office? I want to hear about your life,"

"Not unpacked; I was there only two days when I got the news of your parents' deaths. I couldn't leave because the moving truck was scheduled to arrive the next morning. So I waited."

"What kind of attorney are you?"

"I'm a business attorney. I handle mostly mergers and acquisitions. I often have to travel, so I don't know what I'll do with you when I'm away."

"We'll work something out. I've never stayed alone before," I respond fearfully.

"Let's freshen up and go to dinner. A nice dinner will give us the extra energy we need for tomorrow." Amanda stands and walks to the bathroom.

I jump off the bed and pause in front of the mirror. A thin girl with messy long red hair stares back at me. The black dress with the scalloped neckline and short sleeves is beautiful, but it makes me look pale. I wait for Amanda to finish in the bathroom before I enter.

I have so many questions. Where will we live? Dallas is a big city. And where will I go to school? Will I be alone when Amanda travels? Will she be kind to me? So far, she's been nice—maybe a little cold, but then again, I'm an interruption to her life.

I apply makeup and fix my hair. I'm thankful that my dress is a soft creped because it hasn't wrinkled. I smooth it down as I leave the bathroom and reach for my shoes.

"We have just enough time to get to the restaurant for our reservation," Amanda says, and I follow her out the door.

We drive almost an hour to a small town called Benders Corner, which I've never been to. Amanda pulls up in front of the restaurant. A valet opens the car doors, and we get out. The city is small, but here in the middle of town is this unusual place. The stone facade has ivy; enhancing its charm and making it look quaint and beautiful.

We're seated at a table in the center of the room. The waiter pours our water and asks for our drink order. Scanning over the menu, I feel out of place. I've never been anywhere to eat except a chicken place or a hamburger place, and both are fast food. I'm nervous and unsure of what to order. I put down the menu and look over at Amanda.

"Will you please order for me? I've never been to a nice restaurant."

"I'll be happy to order for you. Would you like chicken or steak?"

"I think steak, because I'm starving," I say, taking a sip of my water. The waiter returns with a glass of wine for Amanda and a glass of iced tea for me. Amanda places our order; she's confident and comfortable in this expensive place. This must be the norm for her. Mother would not know what to do here. How can they be sisters and have such different lives?

My hand rubs the edge of the table and the texture and crispness of the tablecloth. It's white, but my napkin is black. The waiter switched our napkins because we were wearing black; I find that oddly funny.

The waiter brings bread and butter to the table with a small plate. Amanda takes a piece of the bread and places it on her small plate. I do the same.

The food is good—probably the best meal I've ever had. The steak melts in my mouth, and the salad is cold and crisp. The potatoes are creamy, and the asparagus is lemony.

"I want to start our life together with something nice. Some people live differently than you did. I want you to experience some of the nicer things in life. That way, whatever you chose for yourself in the future will be an educated decision," Amanda says. I listen intently.

After dinner, we drive back to the hotel. I'm tired and sleepy. I lean back in the seat, and my mind wanders. I'm ashamed that while my parents lie in the ground at the cemetery, I'm enjoying life. I'm embarrassed that the meal was so good, and I'm happy. Should I remain sad and live my life in mourning, or is it okay for me to move on? Should I be pleased with Amanda? What about Bruiser? Is he happy in his new life? If it's okay for him to move on, then is it all right for me?

I'm startled when the car stops in front of the old red-brick hotel. The six-story building stands out because it towers over everything else. The attendant opens my car door and I step out. I must have fallen asleep.

"Rebecca, we're back at the hotel. Come, let's go to our room," Amanda says, and together we go back to the room and prepare for bed.

After breakfast, Amanda and I drive to the farm. I place my hands in my lap and twiddle my thumbs to hide my excitement. I look out the window to see every mile as we pass, memorizing each landscape, the barns of weathered wood and cows grazing in the fields. My heart leaps when she turns on the lane that leads to the house.

"I've missed home," I say, staring at the house as we approach.

"It won't be the same here without your parents." Amanda frowns at me.

"Do you mind if I run and check on the animals?" I ask when she stops the car.

"Go ahead, but don't get dirty. We have a long drive ahead of us and other places to stop."

I rush to the barn and check on the two horses. I stroke Velvet's nose.

"Velvet, I can't come and see you every day or bring you a carrot. I have to move away. Someone else will be feeding you. I'll be back, and I love you bunches." I wipe the tears from my eyes with the back of my hand. Leaning my forehead against Velvet's nose I linger there, taking in her scent. Then I rush over to the chicken coop, and then to the fence to see the cows. The goats are playing, and I can't get them to come near. Not wanting to keep Amanda waiting too long, I rush back to the car.

"We might have to leave because the sheriff isn't here. He said he would meet us because it might not be safe," Amanda says. I drop my head and walk to the other side of the car, but before I get in, Sheriff Webster drives up.

"I'm sorry to be late—something came up," the sheriff says, getting out of the car with Bruiser.

Bruiser runs up to me, and I drop down in front of him.

"Bruiser boy, I think this is it for us. I'm going away. You have been my best friend, and I know you tried to save Mom and Dad. You're such a good boy," I tell him. Bruiser places his paw on my arm as I pet him. He understands.

I pet his head and remember the sweet pup with his small body and long legs. I would sneak him my bacon. He walked me to the end of the lane and waited with me for the school bus every day. It always brought great joy seeing him waiting there for me in the afternoon. A few times, I brought him into the house, but my parents wouldn't allow him to stay. A tear rolls down my cheek. "Goodbye, Bruiser," I say. "Remember that I'll come back to see you. I love you, Bruiser." I get up, and Bruiser lets out a whimper.

We follow Sheriff Webster into the house. Everything is the same as it was the morning I found them. The cleaned popcorn bowl sits by the sink. Mother's cookie jar is nestled securely on the counter in the far corner.

"Come into the den. I want to talk to you before you pack," the sheriff says.

Amanda and I walk into the den and sit down. I sit on the comfy overstuffed sofa and rub the cushion next to me, remembering Mother sitting there that final night. Glancing at the television, I can still remember scenes from the movie.

"I have some of the DNA tests back. The blood they found on Bruiser belongs to your parents, and the third sample belongs to a male, unrelated to your parents. Bruiser took a chunk out of that person. The lab discovered a little skin hanging from a tooth. I found a button lying in the barn next to your parents. It's off of a shirt. None were missing from the top your dad was wearing. I checked in your dad's closet, and he doesn't have any buttons missing from anything. I think it's from the shirt of the killer. I also found a piece of material lying at the edge of the yard where we found Bruiser. The fabric was covered in blood, and it looks like it came from a dress shirt—I would say a costly dress shirt. The material is pale blue. The lab is also testing that."

"Did Bruiser pick out anyone at the funeral yesterday?" I ask, hoping they'll find the person.

"No, but we aren't giving up. With Bruiser's help, we'll find out who did this," the sheriff says and stands. "I'll give you some privacy. I'll be outside looking around."

The sheriff leaves, and I get up.

"Let's go through your things. We're only taking the best clothes, but you may take any books or personal items you want." Amanda says.

We walk to my neatly kept room; there's a soft glow of the sun peeking through the curtains. I begin to place my books, hairbrush, powder, and cologne on the bed that I want to take with me. I go through each drawer, taking out shirts and jeans, and the pile grows.

Amanda brings me a few trash bags to fill since we didn't think to get boxes. I rush to the bathroom for toiletries and then head for my parent's room. I grab Dad's work shirt and Mother's blouse and then pick up her jewelry box.

"Are you almost finished?" Amanda asks, lugging one of the bags down the hall.

"I think so. Oh, wait for the pictures and Bibles. I must get those." I rush to the den.

"Where are we going to put all this stuff?" Amanda says, shaking her head.

In the den I go to the chest that holds the television. I open a drawer and pull out two boxes of pictures and then I grab the Bibles from the bookcase.

"Okay, I think this is all for now. I wish I had a picture of every room because I'm going to get homesick."

"I can take care of that. I'll take pictures of every room with my phone. Do you have a phone?" Amanda asks.

"No, I don't."

"I'll take care of that when we get to Dallas. You'll need a phone so that we can keep tabs on each other," Amanda says as she snaps pictures in each room.

I want to take more, but we can't fit everything in the car.

We stuff the bags in the back seat and load the rest in the trunk. We wave to Sheriff Webster that we're leaving, and we drive out onto the road. I turn and take one last look, and the sheriff drives out behind us.

I sink back into the seat and close my eyes, visualizing the den in my mind—the coziness of the room and the sweet times we spent there together. A sick feeling comes over me. Nothing will ever be the same.

We stop by Maggie's and I rush to the door to say goodbye. We give each other a hug and she walks out to car with me. She hands me a beautifully wrapped gift and we back out of the driveway.

We are on our way out of town and away from the only home I've ever known.

Who in our town wears dress shirts during the week? I wonder.

Chapter 8

I sit in the car and all things familiar fade into the distance. With each mile, I feel myself sinking into a deeper level of sadness.

I glance down at my feet and the beautiful present Maggie gave me. I wish I had thought to get Maggie a gift. Maggie took me under her wing and guided me through a horrible time. I smile, remembering how Maggie had suggested that I view this as just temporary.

"Rebecca, you've been quiet for over an hour, and I can see you're not sleeping."

I glance at Amanda, but her eyes are focused on the road. "I'm just watching my life change with every mile," I reply.

"You're too dramatic. Most kids have moved many times before they're your age."

"I feel bad for them," I respond, but I don't turn to look at her. I bite my lip; I should be more considerate of her. She has agreed to take care of me, and if this doesn't work out, my only option is foster care. I've heard foster homes aren't always good.

I've lost everything in life that's familiar, I silently mourn. *How will I adjust? How will I meet anyone?*

"I think you'll like your new school. It's a Christian high school just four blocks from our apartment."

"I'm sure it'll be fine. I won't know anyone." I swallow the lump in my throat.

"You see the skyline off in the distance? That's where we're going. We will be right in the middle of downtown. You'll get to experience city life. The apartment building is right across the street from the building where I work."

"I can hardly wait," I say with no enthusiasm.

"I think you'll learn to like it. It might be hard at first, but you'll get used to it." Amanda gives me a stern look.

I sink deeper into the seat as the heavy traffic inches along.

A horn honks. I sit up and see that we're turning into a parking garage. As we enter and drive around in ascending circles, moving higher and higher, large numbers appear on the walls in front of us. She parks in a space after seeing the number eight.

"We're here," she tells me. "Grab a load of your things and follow me."

"Does that eight mean we're on the eighth floor?" I ask, grabbing the door handle and feeling naive that I know nothing about city life.

"That's what it means. Now grab your things and follow me," Amanda says with a harsh voice.

I step out of the car and gasp for air, not expecting it to be this hot. There must not be any ventilation in the garage. I reach into the back seat, grab some of the bags, and follow behind Amanda.

I feel lost and alone as I walk with her into the unknown.

We walk down a long corridor, and every door is the same. *How do people live so close to each other?* I wonder. Amanda stops outside a door. She places her suitcases on the floor in front of a door marked "832" and takes out her key. She opens the door and switches on the light. I follow her inside an entry hall.

"Your bedroom is at the far end of the hall. Take your things in there and come back, because we're going to unload the car," Aunt Amanda says, pointing down the hallway. I walk to the end of the hall and open the door to a small room. There is a bed in the center of the room and the far wall is covered in drapery. I place the bags on the floor next to the bed and head back to where Amanda waits.

After unloading the car, I open the closet door and find no hangers. Some of my clothes in the bags have hangers, so I grab them and hang them in the closet. I guess the rest will have to wait.

I sit on the edge of the bed. I remember what Sheriff Webster had told me when we were leaving the farm: "You're still young. You can create a whole new life. You'll see." *If I were going to create a new life for myself, this wouldn't be what I would choose,* I think. *I feel like I'm in a box. Prisoners must think like me, trapped in a confined space. The door to this apartment looks no different than any other entry except for the number. When God looks down, will He find me in this building?*

"Hey, Rebecca," Amanda calls, "I ordered pizza for dinner. Come into the kitchen, and we'll eat. I realize you don't have hangers. I ordered some online. They should be here by tomorrow afternoon. I order most stuff because it's just easier."

I follow her into the kitchen. It's very modern with beautiful wood cabinets and granite countertops. There is a round dining table next to a wall of windows. There are salad plates and water glasses on the table.

"Go ahead and sit down. The pizza will be here any minute. We'll start with our salad." Amanda says, sitting down first. I sit down across from her. We never ate pizza like this at home. We had to go and pick it up, and we would sit in the den and watch television while we ate. We would also have sodas and popcorn, but there's none of that here.

Does she even know how to have fun?

I take a few bites of the salad, and the doorbell rings. Amanda gets up and goes to the door. She comes back with the pizza and places it in the center of the table. I eat my salad and then take a piece of pizza.

We hardly talk during the meal. Amanda has her phone at the table and keeps looking at it. She must be sending and receiving messages.

"I forgot to tell you that I ordered you a phone. It will come tomorrow. So when the packages arrive tomorrow, you can open them because they're all for you. I ordered your school uniforms, and I'll take you to enroll tomorrow morning. So plan to be up and dressed by eight. I'll bring you back and then I'll be going to work."

"What will I do?" I ask. I'm afraid to be here alone in this strange place.

"When the hangers arrive, you can put away your things and get yourself organized. We'll get your school supplies this weekend. I thought you might want to pick them out yourself," Aunt Amanda says, finishing her pizza. She gets up and takes her dishes to the kitchen. I watch as she rinses the plate and glass and places them in the dishwasher. I get up and do the same.

"I have work to do for tomorrow. You have a clock radio—set it so that you can get up in time," Amanda says as she leaves the room. The clock on the microwave shows 8:30.

What will I do with myself until bedtime? I ask myself. *I certainly prefer my old life. I miss my parents, and hugs before I go to bed, but there are no hugs here.*

I walk to my room and take a look around. Going over to the wall of draperies, I pull them apart to find no window; it's all wall. I take my toiletries out of the bags and carry them into my bathroom. I take all the clothes out of the bags and stretch them out in a stack on the floor. I'm now ready when the hangers arrive. I place my shoes in the bottom of the closet and then go into the bathroom to wash my face and prepare for bed. I switch off the bathroom light and set the clock radio before climbing into bed. I reach to turn off the light, and see the gift Maggie gave me, with its pretty pink floral paper and the giant pink ribbon tied in a pretty bow. I have never had a present that looked so pretty. I touch the paper and smile; sweet Maggie. I want to open it, but maybe tomorrow while I'm alone will be a better time.

Just because I crawl into bed, however, doesn't mean I'm able to fall to sleep. *I can't believe the hustle and bustle outside of my window, with those sirens and car horns blasting. How do people sleep in the big city?*

This evening Amanda had kept her head in her phone. There were no kind words or tenderness. I miss the hugs and the laughter. Tears flow down my cheeks, and I cry myself to sleep.

I dress with care, wanting to make a good impression at school. I chose a navy-blue sleeveless dress and navy shoes. I put on my makeup and style my hair, and then continue to adjust until I've reached perfection. I head to the kitchen anticipating an excellent hot breakfast. Amanda is standing in the kitchen sipping on a cup of coffee and hands me a glass.

"What's this?" I ask, looking inside.

"Your breakfast. It's a protein shake. Don't worry—it's very filling and healthy. Now hurry up. We have to get going," Amanda says, taking another sip.

I drink the shake, then rinse out the glass and place it in the dishwasher.

"Let's go. We're walking to school," Amanda says, and I follow her out the door.

We walk the four blocks in silence. Approaching a large two-story building, I take in a deep breath but hope that Amanda doesn't sense my panic. We enter the main office and approach an older woman who sits at the desk. Her hair is silver and neatly pulled into a bun on top of her head. My knees are shaking, and I wring my hands in front of me.

"May I help you?" she asks, looking at me with a sweet smile.

"We're here to finalize the paperwork. I called and pre-registered two days ago," Amanda says.

"Let me get the principal. She'll handle the registering and class schedule. Why don't you have a seat over there?" the lady says, pointing at a row of chairs. I can tell Amanda is impatient, because she keeps tapping her foot and looking at her phone.

A tall, attractive woman comes out of an office and walks over to us. She has dark hair and pink lipstick. She extends her hand to Amanda and then glances at me with a quick smile.

"Good morning, I'm Mrs. Scott, the principal. I hear you're here to enroll. Please follow me."

I wish Mrs. Scott would look at me more. Who is the student anyway, me or Amanda?

Amanda and I follow her into her office. She closes the door, walks to her desk, and sits down.

"Who is it that we're enrolling?" Mrs. Scott asks.

"My niece, Rebecca Wild. I called two days ago, and we did the pre-registering over the phone. You said it wouldn't take long. I'm on my way to work," Amanda says, still tapping her foot.

"Hello, Rebecca, it's nice to meet you. Let me get your file," Mrs. Scott says as she shuffles some folders on her desk. "Yes, here it is. I think all I need is the tuition and a signature. I've already prepared your class schedule." Mrs. Scott hands me the class schedule and Amanda the papers to sign.

I gasp as I scan over the schedule.

"Is there something wrong?" Mrs. Scott asks, looking at me.

"Choir, you didn't put me in the choir," I say, shaking my head.

"Rebecca, stop it. You know I'm in a hurry. Stop making this difficult," Amanda scolds.

"Well, you see, the choir at our school is not an elective," Mrs. Scott tells me. "You'll have to try out for the choir. I can put you on the schedule to try out. I think we have tryouts tomorrow at ten. Can you make the tryouts?"

"Yes, that's fine. Where do I go?" I ask.

"Why don't you come by my office about nine thirty, and I'll take you on a tour of the building. I understand your aunt is in a hurry this morning. I look forward to seeing you tomorrow," Mrs. Scott says as she stands to walk us out.

"Thank you, Mrs. Scott. I'll see you tomorrow," I say, walking out of the office.

Amanda is on edge. Is she worried about work, or does she not like something about the school? We leave the building and start walking the four blocks.

"So, are you going to cry if you don't make choir?" Amanda asks, glaring at me.

"No, I won't cry, but I'll make it," I say, making it a point of looking ahead and not at her.

"Your mother didn't sing, and I don't either, so I'm sure you don't have much of a voice," Amanda says.

"I guess we'll find out tomorrow," I say, not wanting to argue with her.

I need this to work out.

"Here's a key to the apartment. You go on up, and I'll see you after work. There's food in the pantry. Fix you something," Amanda says, and then she leaves me standing at the corner.

I shudder when the door closes. I'm left alone in the apartment with my thoughts.

I don't know how I feel about school. It did seem larger than my high school, but it's the city. Amanda said this private Christian school would be smaller, so how big are the public schools here? I walk to my room and sit on the side of the bed. I'm angry about everything. *I planned for Amanda and I to have breakfast together, but she just handed me a protein shake and told me to drink it. She hasn't learned to be with others. Amanda is just selfish, and I want to go home.*

I lay on the bed in misery until I fall asleep. I'm startled when the doorbell rings. I jump up and rush to the door. Looking out the peephole, I see the doorman is standing there holding packages.

I open the door, and he enters the apartment.

"Don't close the door. I have more packages outside. Where would you like for me to put these?" he asks, out of breath and looking at me. The doorman is a big muscular guy with rosy cheeks and a great smile.

"Here beside the table is fine. Thank you for bringing these up," I say, and he nods as he continues to go out to the hall and bring in more packages. When he finishes, he leaves, and I lock the door. I walk into the kitchen, and the clock on the microwave shows it to be three o'clock; I'd slept for most of the day.

Turning to look at the boxes, it seems like Christmas. Grabbing a knife from the kitchen, I begin to open them. There are hangers, uniforms, and sweaters. *If I stay busy,* I figure, *it will take my mind off of things.*

My thoughts keep swirling. *I never imagined my life would be so confining. When will she return home? How long will I be left here alone? I should go and hang up the clothes, but I'm not sure I want to stay. I have money in the bank at home and a little in my purse. Maybe I should find the bus station and take a bus home. Do I have enough money with me for a bus ride?*

I prepare a sandwich and sit at the table among the boxes. Forcing myself to eat, I choke down the sandwich. Then I walk to my room and sit on the side of the bed. Looking around at the mess, I reach for the hangers.

Should I hang up these things, or throw them in a bag and leave?

Chapter 9

I pace back and forth wring my hands. Horns are honking and police sirens blaring from the streets below. I occasionally stop to gaze out the living room window. Amanda hasn't come home, and it's almost ten. *She told me she works in the tall building across the street. Should I go over there and check on her?* I wonder. *What if something happened to her? Earlier I was mad and just wanted to leave, but now I'm worried sick about her. She did tell me that sometimes she works late—but how late?*

Exhausted from pacing, I go to my room. I've never felt more alone.

In the bathroom, I splash water on my face and use the soap with a floral scent. It smells just like the jasmine growing near my bedroom window at home. Putting on my pajamas, I climb into a soft bed with silky pink-colored sheets. It's heavenly. Grabbing a book off the nightstand, I see it's the romance novel Mother gave me that I've never read. *Mother and I like innocent stories that have happy endings. Maybe reading will lull me to sleep.* I open the book and before I start to read, I see the beautiful package from Maggie. A thrill comes over me every time I look at the box. I decide to enjoy looking at it for a while longer. I feel as though what's inside couldn't possibly bring me any more pleasure than the beauty of the wrapping. I turn my attention back to the book.

I'm into the third chapter when there is a noise that startles me; it's a loud thud. I leap out of bed, rush to the closet, and pull the door closed behind me. At first there is silence, and then a door closes. I hunch down in the bottom of the closet, surrounded by darkness and new-carpet smell. *Someone is here in the apartment. Is it . . . Amanda?* Footsteps walk towards me.

"Rebecca, where are you?" It's Amanda's voice.

"I'm here. I heard someone at the door and got scared. It's late," I say, stepping out of the closet.

Standing in the doorway to my room, Amanda speaks with her arms folded in front of her. "I often work late. It's Friday, and after missing most of the week, I had to get caught up. How was your day?"

She seems to be more open and talkative now than she was earlier.

"I was bored, maybe even scared, but I did enjoy opening the packages. The phone came, but I'm not sure how to set it up. I need your help. I would love to call Maggie and Erica," I say, following her down the hall.

"I'm going to have a glass of wine and some cheese. Would you like anything?" she asks, turning on the kitchen light.

"Do you have hot chocolate?" I ask. At home we would sit around the table in the evening and have hot chocolate.

"Of course I have hot chocolate. I'll get it. Sit down at the table," she says. I sit down, and she pours her wine. I look at her. *She's professional looking in her black suit and cream-colored blouse*, I note. *She's a beautiful woman. Why isn't there a man in her life? What if there is a man in her life and I'm in the way?*

"Do you have a boyfriend?" I ask.

"No, do you? And what did you think of the school uniforms?" she asks, still working in the kitchen.

"No, I don't have a boyfriend. And the uniform is a skirt and blouse. The blouse is plain white, and the pleated skirt is a tartan black watch pattern."

"How do you know that it's a black watch pattern?" Amanda asks, stirring the hot chocolate in the cup.

"It says it on the package. I like the pleated skirt. There were some navy sweaters in the box too. I guess they are for cooler weather."

"Yes, they are." She sits down at the table and hands me the cup of hot chocolate.

"How's the new job?" I ask, and she looks up at me as she takes a sip of wine.

"It's difficult. I had just gotten to Dallas when I got the news about your parents. I had to leave, and now I'm trying to get caught up. I worry about you. I feel like it's a little too much."

"I'm fine. I was just scared because this is a strange place. I haven't gotten used to all the city noises and not being able to go outside."

"So we're both trying to adjust. How's the hot chocolate?"

"It's soothing. And I'm so glad you're home. I was worried that something had happened to you," I say, sipping the chocolate.

The smell of the sweet chocolate transports me back to the kitchen table at the farm. I remembered all the marshmallows, and getting chocolate stuck in the corners of my mouth. Dad would tease me and say, "Rebecca, you always seem to wear your chocolate, but you wear it well."

"I told you, I work late. You've had Maggie's company since your parents died, and now, with me working, you have no one." Amanda takes a bite of cheese.

"I just never thought you would work this late. Maybe I shouldn't tell you, but I was thinking about leaving today."

I'm taking a significant risk telling her this, I fret. *She could send me away.*

"Leaving? Where would you go?" Amanda looks startled.

"I wanted to go home. I was bored and lonely, and I feel like this apartment is a prison," I say, wishing I hadn't told her.

I must sound so ungrateful and selfish.

"I know this is hard for you. Your world has been turned upside down, and I'm buried in work and not helping you. It's an adjustment."

I reach over and touch her hand. *I sound so selfish, only thinking about myself and everything I have lost—my parents, my home, and my friends*, I think with guilt. *If Amanda and I could talk more, it would help.*

Amanda takes my hand in hers, and I feel the coldness of her fingers. Her hands are thin and delicate like Mother's.

"I need you to talk to me more," I say, looking into her eyes. "Can we eat our meals together and sit around the table? It would give me a feeling of being home. A hug at bedtime would be nice."

She stares back at me.

"Rebecca," she begins with a sigh, "I have been selfish. I like doing what I want when I want. Now I have you with me, and a little bit of me didn't want to bring you here." She drops my hand and takes a sip of wine.

"You mean you wanted to put me away? You wanted me to go to a foster home?" I'm startled by her comment. My body gets rigid, and I feel every muscle tighten. I choke as I swallow the chocolate. It's possible I could still end up in a foster home.

"Please don't misunderstand. I wouldn't send you away, but I didn't want my life to be interrupted. I'm on track to a full-blown partnership, and you're a distraction. Perhaps I need a life outside of work, but I certainly didn't ask for this." I'm stunned that not only did I not want to come here, but she also doesn't want me in her way. I'm not the only one who has had their life turned upside down.

"I'm sorry—I didn't know. I thought I was the only one making a sacrifice. Can we please try and make this work?" I ask, getting up and putting my arms around her.

She hugs me back, and we hold the embrace.

I get up late on Saturday morning and dress before entering the living room. Amanda is sitting in the living room, reading the paper and drinking coffee. I walk over and sit down beside her on the sofa. "Are you ready for breakfast?" she asks, smiling at me.

"Whenever you're ready, I can wait," I say, leaning back on the sofa.

"Did you sleep better last night?" she asks, looking over at me.

"Yes, a little better. The noise outside still bothers me, but I'll get used to it."

"Let me finish my coffee, and we can cook breakfast together." Amanda reaches for her cup from the coffee table.

"Did you sleep well?" I ask, wanting to keep the conversation going. The way she leaned over and picked up her cup, and the way she tilts her head and smiles, are familiar—mannerisms like my mother's.

"I slept fine," she says, sipping her coffee.

"Do I start school on Monday?"

"Not until Tuesday. We'll get your school supplies today and groceries. Bring me your phone, and I'll set it up for you."

I hand her the box. She pulls out the phone and reads the instruction sheet.

I never had a phone. My parents didn't have one either. I guess we couldn't afford them. Does that mean that Amanda has a lot of money? I wonder.

"Here you go, it's all set up and ready to use. I entered my work number and cell number into your phone. Now I'll enter your number into my phone," she says, handing it back to me and grabbing her phone to add my number.

Our talk last night must have helped, I conclude. *She seems more open and more relaxed around me. Maybe this will work out.*

"Are you ready to help with breakfast?" she says, getting up with her cup in hand.

"I'm ready. What are we having?"

"I thought we could have bacon and pancakes. Is that something you would normally eat?" she asks as I follow her to the kitchen.

"Yes! How can I help?"

"Get out the small glasses in that cabinet and fill them with orange juice," she says, pointing at the cabinet.

I place the glasses on the table after filling them, and she hands me napkins. I put the napkins on the table and go back to the kitchen for silverware. The smell of the bacon makes it seem more like home. We didn't have pancakes very often, but I do like them. For a brief moment, out of the corner of my eye, I think I see Mother.

Amanda stirs up the pancake mix and pours it into the pan. I grab a piece of bacon off the plate and eat it while I watch her. The pancake begins to bubble and she flips it over.

"Sit down. I'm bringing our plates," Amanda says, and she walks to the table with two plates. The butter was melting and running all over the plate, and the syrup is racing behind it. The two strips of bacon are placed neatly to one side.

"This looks great." I smile at Amanda. "Do you mind if I say grace?" I ask, placing the napkin in my lap.

"Go right ahead," she says, bowing her head.

"Lord, we are thankful for your love, protection, and this food. Amen." I reach for my fork.

"So, did you always say grace at the table?" Amanda asks.

"Yes, we also went to church every Sunday. I was in the youth choir. I often would sing a solo at church, but our church was small."

"So you are a singer. Is that why you said one of your classes has to be choir?" Amanda takes a bite of her bacon.

"Yes, and when I try out, I will be placed in the choir. I also love volleyball, and I'm hoping that they have a team," I answer, eating my pancakes.

"Your dad was a famous singer."

"What? I didn't know that," I say. "Dad didn't sing at all—or at least I never heard him."

"It was before he married Carol. He was touring all over the country and had sold thousands of albums. But he got into drugs. Carol told him if he loved her, he would have to leave music behind. It seems the music and drugs went hand in hand," Amanda says, taking a bite of her pancakes. "He left the music industry and took his money and bought the farm. To help pay the bills, he wrote songs off and on."

"Wow! I never heard that. I never heard him sing, but he did write a lot of poems. I wonder if his death had anything to do with him leaving the music industry." I'm stunned at what little I knew about my parents.

"I don't know. That was seventeen years ago, but maybe we should mention that to the sheriff."

"That's a good idea," I say, drinking my orange juice. "So what do you know about the school?"

"I don't know anything about the school other than it is a church school. They have a church service every morning to start the day."

"I like that!" I respond, finishing my food.

"You'll be walking to and from school every day, so be sure you have your cell phone with you." Amanda gets up and takes her plate to the kitchen.

I follow behind her, picking up the glasses and my plate. I help her clean the kitchen, and then she goes to her room.

I'm in the bathroom applying my lipstick when Amanda calls, "Rebecca, are you ready? We're going shopping now."

"I'll be right there," I say, grabbing my purse and phone. I walk down the hall and out the door.

It's quiet on the drive, and so my thoughts of Dad being a singer rush through my mind. *Did he love Mother so much that he gave up singing for her?* I wonder. *Dad made enough money to buy the farm and the animals. Our farm was big—a lot for us to manage. Could it be that someone in the music industry tried to get him to sing again? Could it be that they killed him? Would they be wearing a dress shirt?*

Chapter 10

We jump in the car after a full day of shopping. We started at the mall, the office supply store, and finally the grocery store. With our groceries loaded, we head back to the apartment. My head is still spinning from all the large stores and the selections that are available.

"Are you tired?" Amanda asks as she navigates the car onto the freeway.

"No, just overwhelmed. I've never been to a mall or seen so many large stores," I respond, watching all the traffic.

"I hope you like your new computer and printer. I think it'll be useful for your homework."

I don't reply. My head is spinning. Everything around me seems to be turning, and life is moving so fast. There are too many new things coming too quickly.

Then a song comes on the radio. It's an oldie, and I reach to turn up the volume and start to sing along.

"I see you like that song," Amanda says, turning the radio down a bit.

"Yes, it's one of my favs!" I respond, still singing.

"You know that's your dad singing, right?"

"No way—this is Jackson Nash, my favorite singer. At least he was my favorite; I hear that he's no longer in the business," I say, still trying to listen to the song.

"Yes, it's Jackson Nash. Your dad was Jackson Nash," Amanda says, glancing over at me.

"My dad was Jackson Nash?"

"He had a stage name. I guess the producer thought that no one would listen to someone named Bruce. So he chose Jackson, and that is his mother's maiden name. I don't know where he got the Nash."

"So Jackson Nash is my dad?" I say, still unable to comprehend. Jackson has always been my favorite singer. How could dad walk away from music? But I'm still so proud of him. I want to scream from the rooftops that Dad is Jackson Nash!

"Yes, it's true. When Bruce left the music industry, there were a lot of outraged people. His agent, the producer, and the music company all threatened to sue him. Even the guys in the band were angry. All of them were calling your dad nonstop. He got tired of the calls and threw away his cell phone, then moved to the farm in Texas. I guess you could say he was hiding out."

"What about royalties?" I ask. "Musicians get royalties for their music years after they record the song. Did he get his royalties?"

"Bruce had bank accounts in California and Texas. The record company is in California. The funds get transferred between banks," Amanda says, moving into the right lane.

"Can that be traced?" I ask. Did someone trace it and find Dad?

"I'm sure anything is possible. It could be that someone from Bruce's past found him. Someone upset he gave up his career. I'll talk to the sheriff on Monday," Amanda says, taking the exit off the freeway.

"Thank you for telling me that it was Dad on the radio. I would have never known."

"You must keep that a secret. If Bruce died because he gave up being Jackson Nash, you could be in danger. So keep quiet," Amanda says, turning into the apartment garage.

That last night before the movie we were listening to music, I remember. *A Jackson Nash song came on the radio, and I sang along. Dad looked at me and smiled. Oh, I wish he had sung along with me. What other secrets are there that my parents took to their grave?*

We drive up to the eighth-floor parking area that leaves us just several feet from the apartment.

"How can I be in danger?" I ask.

"I thought if someone is after his royalties, it could put you in danger."

Scared, I change the subject. "It must have been hard for Dad to walk away from a singing career," I say, looking over at Amanda.

"I'm sure it was. I caught Bruce singing a few times in the barn," Amanda says. "I'm sure it was hard for him. I told Carol that someday he might decide to leave her and go back to singing.

"And what did Mom have to say about that?" I ask.

"She didn't believe me. She thought Bruce loved her so much that he would stick with his choice. I think it's strange he didn't even sing at church."

"Why do you think he didn't?" I ask. He could have helped the choir.

"Maybe he was afraid someone would recognize his voice or figure out who he was," Amanda says, turning off the engine and reaching for the door.

"That makes sense. So you were around when Dad left the business?" I ask, more curious than ever. Had she been close to my parents? What kind of relationship did they have?

"Yes, I was. I could tell it was hard for Bruce in the beginning," Amanda replies, opening the car door. "Well, we have a car full of stuff to unload. Wait here; I'm going to get the cart," she says and disappears.

I get out of the car and stand beside it, waiting for her to return. Could I be in danger if someone discovered that I'm Jackson Nash's child?

"Here's the cart. We can load it and only make one trip. I think it's nice that the apartment building provides one for every floor," Amanda says, opening the trunk.

We load the groceries, the computer, and the school supplies onto the cart and push it to the apartment.

After unloading the cart, Amanda leaves to return the cart to the garage. We put away the groceries.

"So, were you around when my parents got married?" I put away the groceries.

"Yes, I was. I was still young when your parents married, and I lived with them for a while. I lived on the farm when they first moved there. Your mother got pregnant with you, and about that time is when I left for college. It's a good thing, because the house only had two bedrooms."

"So, it was school and your job that kept you away?" I ask.

"Yes, but your mother and I talked on the phone several times a week," Amanda says, stowing the meat in the freezer.

Is that true? Mother told me they never talk . . . I brush away this thought.

I watch Amanda. I'm beginning to like her and admire her patience with me. For a woman who hasn't had any children, she seems to know how to handle me and my needs. I could even be Amanda's child.

"What are your plans for the evening?" I ask, walking into her bedroom later that evening. She's sitting at her computer.

"We had a late breakfast and a late lunch, so I thought we wouldn't be hungry. Maybe we can make some nachos and then eat popcorn and watch a movie."

"That's a great idea!" I say.

I enjoyed the weekend with Amanda. On Sunday, we didn't go to church, and Amanda hooked up my new computer.

Now it's Monday, and Amanda has left for work. I go into my room and pick up the gift from Maggie and hold it in my lap, admiring the pretty pink paper and large bow. I'm curious and want to open it. My fingers delicately trace the ribbon. I reach for my phone, wanting to capture this beautiful package and hold on to the memory. I take a few pictures of the package, then put the phone down and begin to rip the paper. My fingers are shaking as I lift the lid off of the box.

Under the lid, there's a mound of white tissue paper and an envelope lying on top with my name on it. I place the card on the bed beside me. I peel back the tissue paper and find a large, soft, leather-bound book. I pick it up and the pages are empty. Underneath the journal is a beautiful pale-blue wool dress with a white satin collar. The material is so soft; it must be cashmere. Under the dress is a pretty black velvet box. I open the box to find a beautiful necklace with a heart-shaped pendant covered in diamonds.

I reach for the card, open it, and begin reading.

Hey, Becca . . . I'm sad that you're leaving. I'm giving you the journal to document all of your new adventures. You're in the big city, and I'm stuck in this little town. I gave you the heart necklace because you'll forever be in my heart. The dress, well, I couldn't resist. Every girl needs one perfect dress. I hope that you'll call me real soon. We will forever be sisters! Love, Maggie

I hold the card next to my heart. Maggie and I had shared beautiful moments together during those first few days without my parents. I learned so much about life and how to be a teenager. I reach for the journal and grab a pen and begin to write:

I wish I had this journal from the beginning. It all started when I found my parents dead. I felt lost knowing I'm now alone in this world or at least I thought I was. Spending time with Maggie helped me to see life so differently. She showed me how to be a teenager, and that I have and will always have this friend who I can call my sister.

I close the journal and put it on the nightstand. I reach for the necklace and put it on. I touch the heart and smile. Then I grab my cell phone and dial Maggie's number.

The phone rings several times, and just as I'm about to give up, Maggie answers.

"Hello?"

"Maggie, it's me, Becca."

"Rebecca, I've been so worried about you. I know it's only been a few days, but I was going crazy with worry," Maggie says.

"I'm fine, and the ice princess has turned out to be great."

"That's good to hear. I was worried that Amanda would stay in her shell."

"Tell me," I ask, "what's going on with you? Have you hung out with anyone?"

"I haven't been doing much. The choir performed on Sunday, and I can say that without your amazing voice, we were just average. School starts tomorrow. My dad came home from his fishing trip the same day you left. And I went on a date with Lance Richards."

"You went out with Lance?" I say. He's the football captain, and with Maggie being a cheerleader, it just makes sense.

"He's great! We went to dinner and bowling. Not a real romantic date, but it gave us a chance to talk."

"I'm so glad you got to go out with him. Thank you for the gift. I love the journal, dress, and necklace. Most of all, I'm just glad you're my sister."

"When are you coming for a visit?" Maggie asks.

"I don't know; I start school tomorrow. I'm going to a Christian school and have to wear a uniform."

"It sounds like it could be boring—at least the uniform part." Maggie laughs.

"I'm just scared because I don't know anyone. It's bigger than our school," I say.

"Anything is bigger than our school. You'll do great. Just think of all the guys you'll meet." Maggie giggles.

"You always have a way of making me look at things differently," I laugh.

"I have to run. It's time for cheerleader practice. See ya." Maggie says, hurriedly.

We hang up. I put my phone down on the nightstand and pick up the bow and wrapping paper.

Maggie now seems so far away. Will I ever get to see her again? Will I ever go back to the farm? I stand up and walk out of the room when there is a loud thud. Amanda is at work, so what is it I'm hearing? I walk into the living room and again hear another thud. Someone is at the front door.

Chapter 11

I stand in the living room, gazing at the entry hall and the front door. I hear a shuffling sound, and something scratching. Then it sounds like someone hits the door—hard. I reach for my phone.

Is the killer now coming for me?

My hands shake as I dial 9-1-1.

"Hello, 9-1-1, what's your emergency?" a woman answers.

"Someone is trying to break into my apartment. My address is—" I give her the address and the apartment number. "Will you please hurry? I'm here alone."

"I'll stay on the line with you until the police arrive."

I rush down the hall to my bedroom, slamming the bedroom door and locking it. Glancing at the clock, I see that it's two in the afternoon. Tomorrow I will be at school, but today I'm here, and I'm alone.

I sit down on the floor next to the bed, staring at the door.

"My aunt works in the building across the street. I tried to call her, but she didn't answer," I say to the operator, just rambling. My whole body is shaking, and I wonder if I should hide in the closet.

"Do you hear any noises?" the operator asks.

"I don't hear anything. I'm back in my room with the door closed," I say.

"Stay in your room. The officers are on their way. Stay on the line with me until they get there. You are on the eighth floor, is that correct?"

"Yes, that's correct," I reply to the operator.

"It's probably for the best that you didn't reach your aunt. You don't want her walking into danger. The officers should arrive first."

Will the police get here in time? I wonder with panic. *Will someone bust down the door? Will I survive? Why did Amanda not answer the phone?*

"Do you hear anything?" the operator asks. "The police are in the building and on their way to the eighth floor. Stay calm. They will be there at any time."

My thoughts continue to race. *Amanda said she is just across the street. I thought if I needed her, she would be right there, but that isn't the case. Amanda gave me false security. I felt safe because she was near, but if she doesn't answer, she might as well be miles away.*

"I don't hear anything. Maybe they couldn't get in, or someone scared them away. Or maybe they're in the apartment waiting for me to come out," I say, sitting frozen on the floor. *Is this the person who killed my parents? Are they ready to kill me now? Will I survive this?* My whole body shakes as I try to hold on to the phone.

The phone is my lifeline. The operator has a calming voice and helps to ease my worries.

"The officers are on the eighth floor and making their way to Apartment 832. I will let you know when they're in the apartment," the operator continues in her calm voice.

There's a loud noise like a banging or pounding sound, and then all is quiet. Then I hear voices. There is silence, and it seems like an eternity before the operator says anything.

"The officers are in the apartment. Wait where you are until an officer knocks on your bedroom door. Do you understand? Do not open the door until the officer knocks. Ask to see his badge," the operator instructs.

I wait, and it seems like an hour before there is a knock on the door.

"Who is it?" I ask, standing up and still holding the phone.

"That's good—make sure it's the officer, and not the intruder," the operator reassures me.

"I'm Officer Lawson," the officer says.

"He says he is Officer Lawson," I tell the operator.

"Let me verify," the operator replies.

I wait. There's a buzz, and I look at my phone and see that Amanda is calling.

I don't answer because I'm still on the line with the operator.

"Officer Lawson is the officer in the apartment. It's safe to open the door," the operator says. "I will hold on to the line until the door is open and I know that you're safe."

I unlock the door and open it. Standing outside the door staring down at me are two police officers in uniforms.

"The officers are here," I say to the operator.

"Thank you. I will hang up," the operator replies.

"What was the noise I heard?" I ask the officers as I walk out the door and into the hallway.

"Someone busted down the door and entered the apartment. You don't have to worry. We caught the guy," Officer Lawson says, and we walk down the hall and back into the living room. I sit down on the sofa.

I glance at my phone, and Amanda has left me a text: *Call me immediately. What's wrong?*

"I need to call my aunt," I say. Then I call her.

"Rebecca, what's going on? Are you okay?" Amanda asks.

"Someone broke into the apartment." My voice trembles as I attempt to talk. "The police are here now. He busted down the door and got in."

"Let me talk to the officers," Amanda says.

"My aunt wants to talk to you." I hand the phone to Officer Lawson.

"Hello, this is Officer Lawson. Someone broke into the apartment. We arrived just as they entered the premises. The burglar has been arrested and your niece is safe."

They chat briefly before he hands my phone back.

"She's on her way here now. She thinks the person that killed your parents might be looking for you," the officer says, sitting next to me on the sofa.

"Why now? Why would he come for me? Who is he? Can I see the man? I want to see if I know him. Where is he?" I say, starting to cry. I reach to wipe away my tears and see that my hands are shaking.

"The other officers took him to the station. There were four of us that answered the call. You and your aunt will need to come to the station and file a report. You'll be able to see him and see if you can identify him. Someone killed your parents?" Officer Lawson responds.

"Yes, just about two weeks ago. Or maybe a week, I don't know—I've lost track of time. Was the intruder in the apartment when you got here?" I ask.

"Yes, he was inside when we arrived. He had just busted in the door and stepped over the threshold when we caught him," Officer Lawson says.

"What was he doing?" I ask.

"Fortunately, we arrived just as he entered the apartment. He didn't have time to do anything. It's good that you called 9-1-1 when you heard the noise."

I nod, but I still don't feel right. *Why didn't Amanda answer when I called her? What if the police hadn't arrived when they did? Would the intruder have killed me? Isn't there security in this building? How did the intruder get to the eighth floor without being seen?*

Soon Amanda comes running into the apartment. She's nervous and shocked.

"I can't believe this. Are you hurt?" Amanda asks, wide-eyed and shaking.

"I'm fine, thanks to the officers. I can't say much for the door. How did he get into a secure building?" I ask.

"That's a question for building security. You'll need to call someone about the door," Officer Lawson says, looking at Amanda.

The doorframe is lying on the floor, and the door is still in one piece, but the doorknob is broken and in pieces.

"Yes, I'll do that right now," Amanda says and dials a number on her cell phone.

"Maintenance is on their way to fix the door. Have you talked to security?" Amanda asks the officer.

"No, we haven't talked to anyone. Our main concern was to get here before someone reached your niece."

"So, you caught the person, and they had entered the apartment?" Amanda asks.

"That's correct," Officer Lawson says.

Amanda bursts into tears. She stands next to Officer Lawson sobbing.

"Maybe you should sit down. I guess all of this is just a bit too much," Officer Lawson says.

"I thought this building was safe. We have security. How could something like this happen? So you caught the person? Did they say anything? Did they know it was our apartment?" Amanda chokes back her tears.

"After the door is taken care of, you'll both need to come down to the station and give a report. At that time, we will let you see the person and hopefully be able to identify him."

"Yes, of course. Thank you for getting here so quickly." Amanda sits down next to me.

Why didn't Amanda answer her phone? I wonder again. *Why didn't she come? She seems concerned, but is it too little too late?*

Chapter 12

The officers leave, and I escape to my room. I'm angry at Amanda. She told me she was just across the street, but she hadn't been here to keep me safe.

I reach for the journal, grab a pen, and write:

> *Something terrifying happened today. Someone broke into the apartment. Thankfully the police got here in time. Amanda acted strange afterward. Am I angry she didn't answer my call? I thought we were getting along well. Will I ever be safe? Someone could grab me right off the street tomorrow when I'm walking to school. Can I trust Amanda? Am I safe? I don't know what to do. I feel so lost and so helpless.*

I put the journal back into the drawer and pick up my cell phone.

I quickly call Maggie and then remember she has cheerleader practice today, and I start to hang up when she answers.

"Hey, great timing, I just got in my car to drive home," Maggie says, sounding out of breath.

I'm relieved that she answered. "So cheerleader practice is over?"

"Yes, it's over. We had a short one today, since school starts tomorrow. Are you ready for your new school?"

"I guess." I change the subject. "Maggie, I'm scared. I wish I were back there with you."

"What's going on, Rebecca? I thought things were going well. You and Amanda seemed to be getting along," Maggie replies.

"Someone broke in the apartment. I heard a noise and called the police; the officers got here just in time."

"Geez, so they caught the guy?

"Yes, but I didn't see him."

"Who was it?" Maggie questions.

"I don't know—they took him to the station. I didn't get to see him. I wanted to know if I knew him. I tried calling Amanda, and she never picked up the phone. She shows up after the police arrive. Then she breaks down into this offensive outburst."

I stop myself. *Was it really offensive, or was I just angry that she wasn't with me when I needed her? No one can be with me at all times . . .*

"Rebecca, give the poor woman a break. She's been good to you. I know she started as the ice princess, but isn't she better now? Maybe her crying was genuine. Maybe she's afraid for you."

"Maybe you're right—but why didn't she answer when I called her? She told me she works right across the street. Knowing she's across the street made me feel like I'm not alone, but then she didn't answer! I just think I'm the one who should have been breaking down into tears."

"Listen to yourself. No one will be available at all times. You're scared, and that's fear talking. Talk to Amanda and ask her what happened. You have to communicate."

"Maggie, I want to go home."

"No, you don't, because you won't be safe there either. Please calm down and think."

"You're right—I'll talk to her. I'm so scared," I say, holding back the tears. A lump is building way down deep and working its way up to my throat.

"I love you, girl," Maggie says.

"I love you too. Bye, Maggie," I say, ending the call.

I'm not safe here, but I'm not safe at home either, I think to myself. *Whoever it is that wants to kill me will find me no matter where I go. Amanda can't be with me every minute, so she can't protect me. Why does someone want to kill me? Do they think I know something?*

I walk back into the living room, and Amanda is pacing the floor, wringing her hands. I can see the puzzled look on her face.

"Amanda, what's wrong?" I ask, stunned that she's so upset.

"Rebecca, what if you hadn't called the police? How will I get you to school tomorrow? The building is secure, and you still weren't safe." Amanda sits down on the sofa, and I sit down beside her.

"I tried to call you." I look into her eyes for a reaction.

"I was in the conference room, in a meeting. I left my phone in my office on the desk. I'll never let that happen again. I never dreamed anything like this could or would happen. I thought because of security, you were well protected."

"It isn't your fault." Glancing over my shoulder, I see the men working on the door. The door looked fine, but all the trim around it had come off and allowed the door to come crashing inside. "Will it take long to fix the door?"

"The door is steel—its fine—but it now requires new trim and new hinges."

"How long will that take?" I ask, watching the men. It's uncomfortable to have this conversation with strangers in the apartment.

"It should be finished within the hour. I need to call the office. I hope all of this missing work isn't going to cause me to lose my job," Amanda says, grabbing her cell phone.

I get up and walk over to the windows. The sky is blue, and it's sunny. In the tall building across the street, there are people walking around in their offices and people sitting at desks. *What if someone across the street was watching this apartment? What if someone knew that I was alone? What if someone is watching us now?* I reach for the cord and close the draperies, leaving us in a dark room.

"Rebecca, it's dark," Amanda scolds.

I walk to the switch, turn on the light, and then walk down the hall. *Maybe the break in had nothing to do with my parents, but our being exposed.*

I walk into my room and sit on the bed. My nerves are on edge, and my hands are shaking. The lump that rose to the back of my throat is now residing there. I lay my head on the pillow and look up at the ceiling.

"Are you okay?" Amanda says from the hallway, looking into my room.

"You know, someone could have been watching us from across the street. Someone may have known that I was alone. We should keep the drapes closed at all times." I sit up and look at her.

"You may be right. We can keep the drapes closed. I was enjoying the view, but maybe we should think about finding us another place." Amanda turns to go back down the hall.

I jump up and follow her. "What did they say at work?"

"They said to do what I need to do to get settled."

How long will it be before the men finish and we go to the police station? Who broke in, and do I know the person? Will I recognize him?

Amanda goes into the kitchen and starts making sandwiches. I watch her without saying a word. I'm not hungry, and I doubt that food will pass the knot in my throat. I reach for glasses and fill them with ice and then open the soda container and fill the glasses. We both work in silence. I'm deep in thought about what happened, what could have happened, and what the future holds.

Amanda carries the sandwiches to the table, and I follow her with the glasses. We sit down across from each other, but we don't say a word, and we don't even look at each other. I pick up my sandwich and take a tiny bite. I sit back and chew. *Will this go down?* I reach for the soda and take a sip just as I swallow. The sandwich must have pushed the lump down a bit, because I now have heaviness in my chest.

"Ma'am, we finished," one of the men working says. "I checked the lock, and everything seems to be working fine."

"Thank you for working so quickly. I will see you out," Amanda replies, following the man to the door. The men leave, and Amanda closes and locks the door.

"At least that's taken care of," she says, sitting back down at the table.

"Are we sure the lock works?" I ask.

"It's working fine," Amanda responds.

We finish our sandwiches in silence.

"Are you ready to go to the police station?" Amanda asks when we're finished. "It's only five blocks. We can walk." She stands and takes her plate and glass to the kitchen.

I follow her into the kitchen and wash off the dishes and place them in the dishwasher. I reach into the freezer, pull out a package of cube steak, lay the container on a plate, and then put it in the refrigerator to thaw. I turn around; Amanda has her purse and is waiting for me. I turn to go to my room.

"Where are you going?" she asks.

"I'm going to get my purse and phone."

"Hurry—let's go and get this over with," Amanda says, opening the door. I follow her out into the hall, and we walk to the elevator. Her impatience makes me nervous. Is it that she doesn't want to go to the station, or that she wants to get back to work?

We exit the elevator and then walk through the lobby, out the glass front doors, and onto the street. I take in a deep breath, thankful for some fresh air—if you can call all of this polluted air "fresh." We walk in silence. Amanda has a worried look on her face. *Is it what happened that's causing the concerned look, or is it all about her fear of losing her job? What is most important to her—me, or the job?* I stop myself. *I guess I'm selfish—she needs the job to survive. I need to be less of a bother.*

"I'm sorry that I'm a problem, and this is taking time away from work. I know your job is important," I say.

"Whatever made you say that? I never said anything to you about being a problem. Let's not get ugly over this," Amanda replies, and we cross the street. The sign on the building ahead lets me know we'll be there in minutes, and there'll be no time to talk about anything too serious. "We're almost there. I trust that you will let me take the lead."

What does she mean to let her "take the lead?" She wasn't even at home. I was the one that was alone and heard someone breaking in. I was the one who called the police. So now she knows nothing, and she wants to take the lead. I try to rein in my angry thoughts. *Well, I'll keep quiet. I want to see the person. I think I will recognize them.*

We step inside the large cream-colored brick building and take the elevator to the third floor. I follow Amanda to an office and watch her every move. *She sort of scolded me after the break-in,* I think. *Maybe she blames me for the break-in.*

An officer greets us and shows us where we need to go. Officer Lawson is sitting behind a desk, and he pulls out some papers as he motions for us to sit down. He starts talking, but I have zoned out. I'm looking around the station at all the officers and the desks divided by cubicles. There are several women. *Are they officers too?*

I turn and look at Officer Lawson, and he is writing stuff down on paper. Amanda is on the edge of her chair, watching as he writes. *Did she give him information?* I wonder. *Why wasn't I listening? What did she tell him? You weren't even there! What are you doing here?*

"Please follow me. We'll see if you can identify the perpetrator," Officer Lawson says, leading us down a hallway.

"Do you have his name?" Amanda asks, getting up to follow Officer Lawson.

I follow along, wanting to hear the name.

"Gene Maxwell. His name is Gene Maxwell. He has quite a rap sheet," Lawson replies.

Have I ever heard that name? I ask myself. *The name means nothing to me.*

"Stand here. A light will come on in the other room, and you'll be able to see the man. He won't be able to see you. I need both of you to look and see if you can identify him," Lawson says.

The light comes on in the other room, and there he stands. He is a big man, much bigger than my dad, and heavier. He has tanned skin, dark hair that he wears long, and hasn't shaved in several days. There's a tattoo on his arm: a heart with a snake wrapped around it.

"I don't recognize the man. I have seen the tattoo before, but I don't know where," I say to Officer Lawson.

"I don't know him," Amanda says, and Lawson turns off the light.

"Did he say why he was breaking into the apartment, and why he chose our apartment?" Amanda asks.

"He knows both of you. He didn't make any mistakes; he was right where he wanted to be. He intended to harm both of you. He just hasn't given us any other information. We don't know why he was looking for you. Are you sure you don't recognize him?" Lawson asks.

"I've never seen him before," Amanda says, crossing her arms in front of her.

"I don't know him, but there's something familiar about his tattoo," I say, shaking my head.

"What happens now?" Amanda asks. "Will he be coming back for us?"

"I talked to your building security. The security guy got sick and went home today before his replacement showed up. Something tells me he was made to leave by our perpetrator. I have a feeling that the building will not let anything like that happen again."

"So, we're safe?" I ask, but he can't guarantee our safety.

"I didn't say that, but Gene isn't going anywhere anytime soon. He has multiple warrants out."

"Is there anything else you need from us?" Amanda asks.

"No, I don't need anything else. Rebecca, if you happen to remember where you saw the tattoo, please let me know," Lawson says, walking out into the hallway with us.

"I'll let you know. Do you think it's safe for me to walk to school alone?" I ask.

"I would take extra precautions in the next few days. Here are some numbers of officers who might be willing to walk you to and from school on their day off—for a fee, of course." Lawson hands the card to Amanda.

"Thank you," Amanda says.

Amanda and I leave the station and start walking back to the apartment.

"Rebecca, why did you say you recognized the tattoo? That seems strange if you don't recognize the person."

"Amanda, I have seen the tattoo. His arm—something about his arm—looks very familiar, but I don't recognize him. I have even tried to remember if my parents ever mentioned him, but I can't remember anything. That tattoo of a snake wrapped around a heart, though . . . I have seen it before."

"You should try to remember where you've seen the tattoo. I'll walk you up to the apartment, and then I'm going to work. Don't wait up for me. I have a lot of work to catch up on," Amanda says, and we get onto the elevator.

I dread the long evening alone in the apartment. I fear walking to school alone tomorrow. But most of all, I fear that the memory of where I saw the tattoo would come back to me.

Chapter 13

Slamming the door behind me, I enter the apartment. Deserted: that's how I feel. A part of me understands that Amanda has to go back to work. But after all that has happened today, who would want to be alone? When my parents were alive, I seldom had alone time. Someone was usually with me. Oh, how I miss them.

I switch on the television just for the noise.

My bedroom is down the hall. Should someone break in, maybe they'll not ever make it that far. I close and lock the bedroom door, then fall onto the bed.

My mind transports me to a better time. Mother stands at the stove, stirring her chicken and dumplings while I sit at the table. Mother and I talk about the cute things that Bruiser does, like hiding his bone in plain view and thinking we can't see it. Dad comes through the back door, smiles, and with a quick whistle he says, "Something in here smiles really delicious." He leaves to wash up, and I help Mother finish making dinner. We sit at the table together and eat and talk about the horses and how many eggs were collected that day. Mother and I talk about picking blackberries and making jelly.

Thinking about home lulls me to sleep.

It's dark when I wake; the clock on the nightstand shows that it's a little past nine. I storm through the apartment, my fists clenched; Amanda's so into her work that she's forgotten all about me. I grab a soda out of the fridge and return to my room. Sitting on the bed, I take a few sips. Why hasn't she even bothered to check on me? I jump at the sound of my phone; it's a text from Maggie. How does Maggie know when I need her most?

Hey girl, her message reads, *good luck at school tomorrow. I'll call you tomorrow afternoon and see how it goes.*

I start to text her back, but then I remember in our previous conversation, she had taken Amanda's side. She doesn't need to know that I'm still upset with Amanda. If I don't respond, she'll think I'm busy or asleep. Laying the phone on the nightstand and connecting it to the charger, I put on my pajamas and crawl back into bed.

I lay my head on the pillow and pretend I'm back at the farm, lying in my bed. There's a slight breeze blowing the curtain, the wolves are howling off in the distance, and I fall off to sleep.

"Rebecca, it's time to get up. Get ready for school, and be quick about it." Amanda says from the doorway.

Opening one eye, I see she's in her robe and has already applied her makeup. I slowly push back the cover and slide one leg off the bed. Amanda turns and leaves. I rush to the shower.

Taking pride in my appearance, I style my hair in long loose curls and apply makeup. I'm hoping to make a good impression. Putting on the new uniform, I glance at myself in the mirror and walk to the kitchen. Amanda has made a lovely breakfast. The smell of the bacon and pancakes makes my stomach growl. I sit at the table, and Amanda brings her coffee and a glass of juice for me.

"I thought you should start the day with a good breakfast," Amanda says, now acting like a caring parent.

She sits at the table, and we eat quietly. Breakfast was just what I needed. I didn't realize how hungry I was, but skipping dinner had left me famished. I finish eating and take my plate to the sink. I'm still not talking to her because I'm angry.

"Leave the plate in the sink. I'll load the dishwasher," Amanda says.

I rush back to my room to brush my teeth and grab my things. The thought of walking a few blocks alone scares me. When I reach the living room, Amanda is coming out of the kitchen.

"Hold on—I'm walking with you this morning. Let me change clothes and get my purse." Amanda rushes to her room.

Where was this "parent" last night? It was kind of her to fix breakfast this morning, but I needed her last night, too.

"Okay, I'm ready. Let's go. Here's some money for lunch." Amanda hands me a five-dollar bill. I stuff it into my purse. We leave the apartment together and wait in the hallway for the elevator.

"Are you nervous?" Amanda asks.

"Of course I'm nervous. I don't know anyone, and most of the kids will have gone to this school together for years. I'll be an outsider. I hope that someone will accept me and allow me into their circle." We get on the elevator, and Amanda pushes the button for the lobby. Feeling the tightness of my shoes, I'm thankful for my new black flats. I like them, and I'm happy Amanda bought them for me. I need to give her a chance and stop being angry at her.

We step off the elevator and walk through the lobby and onto the street. We gaze in all directions as we walk.

"Stop being paranoid," Amanda tells me. "I'm walking you to school, but you'll have to walk home alone. I've arranged for someone to walk you to and from school for the rest of the week, but I'm afraid this afternoon you'll be on your own. I have an important meeting and can't miss it."

"I'm not paranoid, only cautious."

"I'm worried about you being alone this afternoon. Stay in a group and don't walk alone. There is safety in numbers. Text me when you get home."

How am I supposed to walk in a group when I don't know anyone? "I'll text you," I say. "Please don't walk me the rest of the way. I don't want the kids to think I'm a baby. You can stand here until I'm inside the door." I turn to walk away.

"Before you go, I'd like a hug," Amanda says, smiling at me.

I reach over and give her a pat on the back. At this moment, I'm thankful for her—and that she cares enough to walk me to school—but I'm angry that I'll be alone this afternoon.

"I'll text you. Good luck with your meeting." I walk away.

"Rebecca, smile a lot; it will help you to make friends."

"Thanks." I walk the rest of the way to school and turn to wave goodbye when I reach the front door.

Inside the school, the floors are polished and shining. The building has a clean smell, and the halls are wide and spacious; it's so unlike the small older school I'm used to attending. Feeling thankful that Mrs. Scott had taken me on a tour, I know where to go. I can't tell if I'm early or late, but there aren't many kids in the hallway.

My first class is history: the fourth door on the right-hand side. I enter the classroom and show my schedule to the teacher, a kind older man.

"Good morning, Rebecca. It's nice to have you. Please sit anywhere you like," the teacher says, handing me back my schedule.

There's an empty seat right in the front of the center aisle. I sit down.

A few giggles behind me cause me to tense up, thinking they're laughing at me. I feel a tap on my shoulder and I turn around. It's a nice-looking boy sitting in the seat behind me.

"I like your red hair," he says with a smile.

"Thank you," I reply, smiling back.

"I'm Blake."

"I'm Rebecca. It's nice to meet you, Blake."

"What's your next class?" he asks.

"English is next," I say.

"Who's the teacher?"

"The teacher's name is Mr. Williams," I say, glad that he's keeping the conversation going.

"Mine too. I'll walk with you," he says.

The teacher stands and starts talking, so I turn around. He hands out our books and gives us an overview of the course and how he plans to grade our work. I like history, and I hope he can bring history to life the way my teacher at home did.

The bell rings, and we're out the door. Blake is tall and thin with sandy-blond hair and brown eyes. He has a smile that lights up the room.

"Where's your locker?" he asks.

"My locker is in the first section near the front of the building. Where's yours?" I ask, keeping the conversation going.

"Not far from yours. The school assigns lockers when we enroll, and we keep the same locker every year. They don't get reassigned until we graduate. Here, this is the class. Let's sit together," Blake says, stopping outside the classroom. "Since we have classes together, can I get your number? We can do homework together." Once seated in the class I jot down my phone and pass it to Blake.

I make it through what could have been a very tough day. Fortunately, I made a few friends. The final bell rings, and it's time to walk home. I walk out the front door of the building, and there aren't any of the students walking. I start walking down the street and look around for anyone who might be watching me; it's all clear. The road, for some reason, is deserted. I pick up the pace and rush along, relieved that I don't see anyone.

I stop at the intersection next to the apartment building. There are a few people approaching and I stare at the light, willing it to change. My body begins to shake as I glance around for anyone coming from the back. The light changes, and I dash across the street and run into the building. Glancing around, I don't see the doorman. I rush to the elevator and push the button. I look around in all directions as I wait for the elevator door to open. The door opens, and I get in, pressing the button for the eighth floor. The door closes, and my body relaxes because I have the elevator all to myself.

I reach the eighth floor and step into the hallway. The key is snug in my hand and posed ready for the doorknob. Unlocking the door, I step inside, locking the door and securing the deadbolt. I reach for my phone and text Amanda to let her know I'm home and safe.

Walking to my room, I know that I have a lot of homework and should get started but my phone rings.

"Hello," I say.

"Rebecca, it's Blake; I didn't see you after school. Where did you go? I waited at your locker."

"I rushed out the door," I said.

"Did you have a bad day?" Blake asks.

"No, it was fine. I live downtown in a high rise," I respond. *Why did I tell him that?*

"Oh, I don't know of anyone who lives downtown. I think we all live in the suburbs and drive ourselves to school. I was going to give you a ride home."

"That's sweet—thanks for the offer," I say, smiling because he had looked for me after school.

"I'll call you later. I just wanted to see where you went. First days can be hard."

"Yes, they can, but you made it easy for me." I bite my lip, wishing I could take back my words. I don't want him to think I'm too needy.

"I'll call you later," Blake says, and we end the call. I smile, realizing that I have a friend. If he were to ask me out, would Amanda let me go? Where would we go on a date? Do I tell Amanda about him, or keep it a secret?

Pulling out my desk chair, I start on my homework. I'm happy to have something to occupy my thoughts. I focus on reading my history assignment. But it isn't long until my mind wanders back to the break-in and tattoo.

Will I forever be haunted by that tattoo? I ask myself. *Will I ever remember where I saw it? When did I see it, and where?* That ugly snake choking the heart, squeezing the life out of it . . .

Maybe that's what he wanted to do to me.

Chapter 14

It's been a week since school started. I've made several friends, but Blake is the kindest of them all. I do think that he likes me as more than a friend. Isy, short for Isabelle, has also been helpful to me. I usually sit with Isy and Lisa (Isy's friend) at lunch, but I think Lisa only tolerates me. Isy and Lisa are in choir with me.

I hurry to finish my homework. I don't know when Amanda will be home. She has been at work more than she's been at home. At least the school and my friends have been a distraction. I'm beginning to get used to the loneliness.

The phone rings and I answer it.

"Hey, girl, it's your sister! How was your weekend? Did Blake get up the courage to ask you out?" Maggie asks with a chuckle.

"No, sis, I don't know if Amanda will let me go out. I like him, and he has been so nice."

"Does he treat you the same way he treats other girls?"

"I've not thought about it, but he does nice things for me, and I don't see him doing them for anyone else."

"Like what?" Maggie asks.

"He brings me treats—little boxes of chocolate, trail mix, granola bars, and cupcakes from a bakery. He walks me to some of my classes and waits for me after school and walks me home."

"Oh, girl, he likes you. He'll ask you out soon, mark my words."

"How are you and Lance?" I ask, wanting to change the subject.

"He's a jerk. Just because he's the captain of the football team, he thinks all the girls want him. I found out he's been cheating on me. I broke up with him on Friday night after the game. He's been trying to get me back, but that isn't going to happen. I'd rather be alone than with a cheater," Maggie responds.

"I'm sorry—I thought he was a nice guy. That's what happens when you date a guy who doesn't go to your church," I say, knowing that I sound like my parents, and the thought of that brings a smile.

"Maybe so; he acts like he doesn't go to church at all."

"You should date one of the boys in Dad's old Sunday school class. Dad told me he was teaching those boys how to treat a girl," I tell her. I think of how the boys had given me the flowers at the graveside service. Their kindness and compassion had left a lasting memory.

"Maybe I'll do that," Maggie says. "Oh, and my parents were talking about you."

"What did they say?" I ask.

"I don't know. My parents were arguing, and then I heard your name mentioned at the end. It could be nothing, but I thought I would tell you."

"It seems strange; I don't know why your parents would be talking about me. Do you think they know something about my parents? I wonder if the sheriff talked to them."

"I just thought I'd tell you. Anyway, I have loads of homework, so I'll let you go. Take care, Becca!" Maggie says.

"Love you, Mags!" I respond, and we end the call.

I put down the phone and go to the kitchen. Why were Maggie's parents talking about me? Why would they be arguing, and do they know about my parents' deaths?

I start peeling potatoes and begin to sing "Somewhere over the Rainbow." Singing relaxes me and clears my mind. I turn on the oven for it to preheat and season the chicken breast. I try to prepare everything just like Mother did. It's almost six. I guess tonight will be another night that I'll eat alone. I've noticed that Amanda is eating all the leftovers. Does she eat when she gets home, or does she take it to work? Humming, I busy myself preparing the salad. The bright green salad with the slices of tomato and the purple onion look so pretty in the bowl.

A thud from the hallway outside the apartment sends shivers up my spine. I wonder if someone will break-in again. I always check the hall before stepping out the door. Amanda acts like she's forgotten all about the incident.

After all, it happened to me and not her. She's so into her work that I think she forgets I'm even here. Would it have been better had I gone to a foster home?

Pouring the dressing, I toss the salad and place it into the refrigerator to stay cold. I check on the chicken and stir the potatoes. Dinner is almost ready; I go into the living room and turn on the television. The noise of TV has become my companion. I smile when I hear the voices; they make me feel like I'm not alone.

I walk back to the kitchen to finish dinner when I hear keys clanging. Pausing for a moment, I stare at the door. Could it be Amanda coming home for dinner? I stand there frozen, my eyes glued to the door. The door eases open, and Amanda enters.

"You scared me," I say. "I wish you had said something. I thought someone was breaking in."

"So I come home to have dinner with you, and this is the thanks I get? I could have stayed at work and spent more time on my project," Amanda shouts at me.

"I didn't mean it like that. I'm happy that you came home," I finish the potatoes and take the chicken out of the oven.

"You must do something about this paranoia. I know something bad happened, but you have to let it go. Why is it that you choose to hang on to the bad stuff?"

"That's easy for you to say. You didn't find your parents dead and then days later have someone break in because they want to kill you too. It's just too much," I say, and the tears come streaming down.

Amanda stands and folds her arms in front of her. She doesn't say a word. After a few minutes, she walks to her room. I finish with dinner and set the table. I know that I'm a nervous wreck, but I can't help it.

After setting the table, I pour tea into the glasses when Amanda returns. She has changed into a pair of jeans and a cute sweater.

"Oh, dinner looks good. I have decided to have dinner with one of the partners this evening. I'm meeting her in fifteen minutes," Amanda says.

"But you said you came home to have dinner with me," I say.

"I did, but after your greeting, I'm going to go and meet her. She's been asking me, so I called her from my room, and we're meeting tonight."

"I'm sorry if I didn't greet you the way you wanted. I'll try to be better in the future. If you had just let me know you were on your way home, I wouldn't have been startled," I say, sitting down at the table to eat.

"Maybe you can think about how *I* feel. I do *everything* I can to make you happy, and it's never enough," Amanda says, going out the door and slamming it behind her.

"Well, all right. I'll be dining alone," I say to the back of the door.

Have I been terrible? I can't help my fears, and I still want to cry every time I think of my parents. Am I paranoid? Is Amanda leaving now a form of punishment? Has she done things to make me happy? It doesn't seem like it to me. It seems she wants to work all the time.

After getting ready for school, I go to the kitchen to eat breakfast. There's no sign of Amanda, but a note on the table. I pick it up and read:

I'm off to work. Don't cook for me tonight. I'm going out with friends. We'll be going to the farm on Friday after school, so pack your bags. We'll be leaving as soon as you get home.

I put down the note. I'm jumping up and down and smiling. I'm going to the farm. Maybe I can see Maggie. I'll call her as soon as I have breakfast. Why does Amanda want to go to the farm? Who are these friends she's going out with tonight?

Grabbing the cereal out of the pantry, I pour it into a bowl and add milk. I stand at the counter to eat. I rush through breakfast. I'll be hungry by ten. I have a granola bar from Blake in my purse, I grab my phone. I call Maggie before heading out the door. It rings, and Maggie answers.

"Becca, are you okay? You don't normally call in the morning," Maggie says.

"I'm coming to the farm on Friday after school. Do you think we can get together?" I ask, crossing my fingers.

"Sure! Why don't you come and spend the weekend with me at my house?"

"Are you cheering at a football game?" I ask.

"Yes, there's a game. I'll come and pick you up at the farm after the game. We'll go and grab a burger or something before going back to my house," Maggie says.

"Sounds great; I hope Amanda doesn't make me stay there with her," I say. I'm not looking forward to going to the farm—only seeing Maggie.

"Ciao!" Maggie says and hangs up.

I'm running late. I rush out the door and grab the elevator. I hurry across the lobby and walk out the door.

I step out of the building and onto the street, and my eyes search for anyone who looks suspicious. Is Amanda taking me to the farm and leaving me there? Maybe she's already tired of being a parent and wants her freedom.

I swallow a lump in my throat; things are getting stranger by the day. Is Amanda overreacting to how I greeted her? Is she using that as an excuse to be away from me? Why are we going to the farm?

I catch my breath when I reach the door. I look behind me to see if I was followed. Will I always live in terror?

I walk into the building while visualizing the tattoo and the heart it's choking.

Then I realize: It's my heart.

Chapter 15

Friday has finally arrived, and I'm sitting in my last class staring at the clock, waiting for the bell to ring. Will Amanda be at home, waiting for me? We haven't spoken or seen each other since the day she said I didn't greet her politely. Only notes back and forth are left on the table. Swallowing a lump, I expect the drive to the farm will be horrible without any conversation.

The bell rings. Rushing to my locker, I see Blake is waiting for me.

"I thought I'd walk you home if that's okay," Blake says, smiling.

"That'd be nice. I'll have to make it quick. We're going out of town, and I need to hurry. I think we're trying to beat the afternoon traffic," I tell him, pulling out the books I need. Blake's hands are shaking, and his movements are jerky. "Is something wrong?" I ask.

"No, I'm fine. If you're out of town, we probably won't get to talk. I look forward to our talks," Blake says as I slam the locker door.

We walk together to the front door. "Yes, me too, but it's only for this weekend," I say as we walk outside.

"If I were to ask you out, would you go?" Blake suddenly asks.

I stop and turn to look at him. "Are you asking me out?"

"Well, yes, I'm asking if you'd go out with me next Friday." Blake's face turns red, and he glances away from me.

"I'd love to go out with you. I'll have to ask for permission, and I'll let you know if I can go," I say, hoping to give him some reassurance.

He smiles at me, and we walk together. My heart swells with warmth. Tears of joy fill my eyes, and I blink them away. Blake cares enough about my safety to walk home with me. I've never told him about my parents dying, or that someone wanted to kill me. Would he still be interested in me if he knew all the details of my life?

"I'll miss you this weekend. I had planned to ask you out sooner, but I chickened out," he says, walking beside me.

"It's okay—after all, I won't be home to go this weekend. I'm sorry we won't be able to talk, but if I get a chance, I'll call you." I'll be with Maggie, but if Amanda doesn't let me go, then I'll have time to call him. But will my cell phone even have reception at the farm?

We reach the front of my building, and Blake stops.

"I'll miss you, Rebecca," Blake says.

"I'll miss you too. Thanks for walking me home. You'll never know how much it means to me." I look up at him and smile.

"I want to take care of you. You know, you seem like a bit of a mystery to me."

I smile at him. "Do you like mysteries?"

"Yes, I do most of the time. I'll see you on Monday. Call me if you get a chance," Blake says as he turns to walk away.

I walk across the lobby and press the elevator button. Staring at the floor indicator, the anxious feeling creeps up.

Will Amanda be home? What kind of mood can I expect?

The *ding* interrupts my thought. I enter and press the eighth floor button.

Amanda is standing in the kitchen wearing jeans and a T-shirt. I quickly change, and we're out the door in less than ten minutes.

The drive is quiet. *Why did Amanda decide to go to the farm?* I wonder fearfully. *Is she planning on leaving me there?*

She's probably happy to be getting rid of me. I find it strange that she never asks about school or if I've made any friends. She isn't interested in my life. So why did she agree to take me?

Will it even be safe to stay at the farm? The sheriff told us it wasn't safe. Have they found the person who killed my parents? If Amanda knows the farm is safe, then she must know something. Why is she withholding information? Does she not want me to know?

Amanda breaks the silence. "I went to the grocery and brought stuff for us to have food at the farm."

"Maggie wants to pick me up tonight after the game and take me to her house," I say.

"No, you'll be staying at the farm with me. We have some cleaning to do, since the house has sat vacant. I've arranged to sell the animals, so say goodbye to them. As soon as possible, I'll put the house up for sale; these nine hundred acres should bring a good price."

"But you said we could keep it until I graduate. What if I want to come back here to live?" I ask, shocked that she's selling the farm. Why is she doing this? What have I done to make her want to punish me like this? It's my farm, isn't it?

"I'm not going to keep up the taxes on all that land. It's just too much," Amanda says.

"I'm sorry, I didn't realize that. I thought my parents left money for me," I reply.

"Oh yes, they did leave money for you, in a trust account to be used for college."

"Then, I understand."

It seems Amanda is irritated that she can't get to the money, I think. *Am I selfish in wanting to keep the farm? It's the only place that I've ever lived until now.*

"I've made arrangements for you to stay at Mosleys on Sunday," she tells me. "You'll miss a few days of school, but I've taken care of that. I have an out-of-state business meeting. I have no one in Dallas who can stay with you, so you'll have to stay here. The meeting is important."

I lean back in the seat. Now I understand why we're on our way to the farm. She's selling it, and she needs a place for me to stay. Is she angry because she can't get to the money my parents left me? I feel tense as I wonder if she would harm me to get to the money. I don't want to spend the night on the farm alone with her. If I were to die, would the money go to her?

I take a sip of my bottled water. The landscape changes from the crowded city to large parcels with plowed fields and pastures with cows. We're getting close. Maybe only another twenty minutes and we'll be there. My heart leaps when I see the farm, but then it drops, knowing there'll be no greeting from my parents.

After they died, at first I couldn't bear to leave the place, but now the love and warmth that was there is gone. The house is now only a shell. I swallow the lump that's growing in my throat and blink to fight the tears. I can't let Amanda see me cry.

She turns onto the road leading to the house. I sit up and wait for the first little glimpse of the house—a sign of home. Just knowing that Amanda wants to sell the house makes my heart ache; what would my parents think if they knew? Farrow and Velvet—how can she just up and sell them? I understand that I can't take care of them if I'm not here, but why didn't she discuss it with me?

The sun is shining on the side of the house, and the trees are swaying in the breeze. My heart leaps with excitement. I know it won't be the same without my parents, but it is still home, and the house will still hold their love and warmth.

"Don't just get out and run off. I need your help unloading the car," Amanda says.

Why would she think that I would just run off? Of course I would help unload the car; my parents had taught me to be kind and courteous.

I step out of the car and reach for the bags in the back seat. My heart is aching, waiting to enter the house. I stand at the door and choke back more tears. Is this the last time I'll see this house? The weight of my backpack is pulling at my shoulders; it's the one Amanda bought, and I don't even like it anymore. The pain in my heart has moved to my stomach, and there's an odd feeling. Is it fear? Why do I feel fear?

"Take those bags to the kitchen and come back for your suitcase," Amanda shouts, pushing me inside the house.

I step inside and breathe in the air. Then I walk into the kitchen, remembering how we'd had such sweet times around the table. I place the bags on the counter and go back outside for my suitcase.

"It'll be good to sell this place and not be paying the utilities and upkeep," Amanda says, slamming the trunk.

I remain quiet, not wanting to cause her to get angry. We enter the house together.

"You change into something old and go take care of the animals. The buyers are coming tomorrow to pick them up. Remember, this is your goodbye to them. If there's anything here in the house that you treasure, you'll have to get it before you leave," Amanda says, standing in the den and looking around the room.

I take my suitcase to my room. I open the closet and pull out the old jeans and T-shirt that Mrs. Mosley thought was a disgrace. I put them on and head off to the barn.

Stepping out the back door, I breathe in the air and the scent of fresh-cut hay. The air feels lighter, and the tree limbs cascade above me as they sway slightly in the breeze. I smile at how simple and welcoming it all seems. I pause just outside the barn, noticing how quiet and peaceful everything is.

I stand at the barn door, and the dreadful morning I found my parents comes to mind. Slowly, I push open the door and enter. Immediately, in my mind, I can see my loving parents lying on the hay. I blink away tears. I walk around inside the barn, looking for anything that seems out of place or something that maybe shouldn't be there. I kick around some hay as I walk to the stalls.

"Velvet, is Mr. Carson taking care of you? Did you get a carrot or apple today?" I pull an apple out of my pocket that I brought from the apartment. After feeding and saying goodbye to the horses, I go back through the barn. There' something shiny just over to the left side of where my parents had been lying. Did the sheriff not search in here for clues? I walk over to the shiny object and bend down to pick it up. It's a small metal piece with a small ring on one end. The gadget is off someone's necklace or key chain; the metal piece is gold-colored and in the shape of a dollar sign, and it doesn't belong to my parents.

I look to the hayloft and slowly climb the ladder. The sound from up here that dreadful morning when the hay and dust fell . . . was the killer still here?

I step off the ladder and into the loft. I smile, remembering how I'd played here as a child. I walk from one end to the other looking for something—anything—that is out of the ordinary, but there's nothing unusual. Perhaps if there had been something here, the sheriff already found it.

Walking to the ladder, I get a bit dizzy looking down. I reach for the ladder, and more memories fill up my mind . . .

I was young and reaching for the ladder, and a man's arm extends from the ladder to help me. On the arm is the tattoo with the heart and snake. I don't see the face of the man, but the tattoo is the same one I saw on the suspect in jail.

Was this the killer? Who is he, and why does he want to harm me? I continue to fret. *How can we sell the farm now when things are starting to come back to me?* Maybe that's why Amanda wants to sell it so quickly: to keep me from remembering.

I walk back to the house with the dollar sign tucked in my pocket. I want to ask Amanda if she knows anything about the tattooed man, but she'd already told them at the police station that she didn't know him. Is it possible Amanda lied, and that she *does* know him?

I walk in the back door. Amanda is on the phone, and I stop. I shouldn't be listening—but what is she doing?

"I can't wait to sell this dreadful place. I have looked for some journals or logs where Bruce might have kept the money. I can't believe that he left everything to the child and nothing for me. How am I supposed to take care of her without the money?"

There is a pause before she starts speaking again.

"Yes, I realize that I have money, but that doesn't mean I want to spend it on her. I'm used to doing what I want when I want, and this child is in the way. She'll be back in a few minutes. There are a few more places that I want to look before she gets back." Amanda ends the call, and I ease out the back door. I don't want her to know that I overheard her call.

I run around the house, not wanting her to see that I was anywhere near the door. Walking a few feet farther, I enter the garden and notice the untended plants. This garden had been Mother's pride and joy; she had spent hours weeding and watering it. Now the garden is overgrown with weeds, and the plants are dying.

That's the way I feel without my parents to nurture me. I'm slowly dying. I'm not paranoid. *Amanda*, I think to myself, *someone killed my parents, and now trying to kill me. Maybe it's even you that wants to kill me. You're doing your best to erase the life that I had.*

I walk through the yard and stand under the big pecan trees and look up at the cascade of branches and leaves that form a cathedral-like cover. I always played under these branches, where I felt covered and protected. But these trees hadn't defended my parents, and they can't protect me.

Chapter 16

I stroll around the garden to avoid going near the door. Amanda mustn't know that I overheard her conversation. Who was she talking to, and what is her plan for the money from the property? I don't want her to sell it. I pass by the rose bushes. Mother had loved cutting the blooms and putting them on the table.

A loud crash from inside the house causes me to jump, and my heart starts pounding as I run to the back door.

I see Amanda staring at the floor. It's my mother's cookie jar, shattered, along with the fragments of cookies my mother had baked. Tears flood my eyes, and I look at Amanda.

"Oops!" Amanda says, turning to me and laughing. Her eyes are wild, and she is delighted with the damage.

"That was my mother's, and I loved it." I can barely get the words out of my trembling lips.

"How did that jar manage to get from the back of the counter to the floor?" I ask.

"It just fell on the floor. It's old and ugly," Amanda replies with a wild laugh.

Amanda is acting strange and wild. I back away from her.

"Let's have dinner," Amanda says, opening the refrigerator and taking out the food that we'd brought. I stand back and watch as she places things on the counter. Should I start making sandwiches, or wait for instructions?

"Here, you make the sandwiches. I'm going to the restroom." Amanda leaves the room.

Stepping over the shards of the jar, I wash my hands in the sink. I realize that I should program the sheriff's number into my phone—just in case.

After making the sandwiches, I grab the broom to clean up the broken pieces scattered across the floor. Mother and I used to make cookies and place them in the jar. There were always cookies to eat. Dad's favorite was peanut butter, and we made them often. I sweep the shards and bits of cookies onto the dustpan and dump it into the trash. It's gone, but not forgotten.

"Oh, the sandwiches are ready. That's good. I'm hungry. I brought potato chips and Cheetos—which do you, want?" Amanda asks, reaching for the bags.

"I like both, so whichever one you want is fine." I don't want to cause any problems. I don't want to do anything to set her off. She seems to go from very happy to mad in a matter of seconds. I don't know how to act around her.

"Potato chips it is. Let's eat. Oh, grab the sodas out of the fridge. We can drink out of the can," Amanda says, sitting down at the table.

I pull out my chair and sit across from her. She's sitting in Mother's chair, but I don't mention it.

"I've been looking for important papers, like your parents' wills, bank statements, car title, the deed to the farm, and other important documents. Do you have any idea where those things might be?" Amanda's wild eyes shift back and forth and she has a strange smirk.

"No, I don't have any idea," I say, knowing exactly where the papers are, but I'm not going to tell her.

"I have to find the papers so that I can put the farm up for sale. I want to meet with a realtor tomorrow, but if I don't find the deed or other papers, they won't even talk to me," Amanda says, chewing on her sandwich.

"I'm not sure—maybe you should check the closet in their bedroom." She won't find them there, but it will keep her occupied.

"Well, I'm going to keep looking. You clean up the kitchen," Amanda says as she leaves the room.

I sit at the table and munch on potato chips as I smirk to myself, knowing that she is looking in all the wrong places. I'll never tell her where to find the papers. Maybe if she doesn't see them, she won't be able to sell the farm. Why does she want the money, anyway? She has a good job.

I clean off the table and the kitchen. I walk through the den where Amanda is going through every nook and cranny. She's opening drawers and looking under furniture. I'm confident that she won't find any documents. In my room, I start on my homework. It's around nine o'clock by the time I finish, so I send Blake a text.

I finished my homework. Are you having a fun night?

I don't expect to hear back—because he's probably out with his friends—and I'm surprised when I do.

I just finished my homework too, Blake writes. *I'm going to work with my dad tomorrow, he's moving his dental office and I'm helping.*

Okay, I reply. *By the way, I won't be back to school until Wednesday.*

I thought you were coming back on Monday? I miss you. Maybe we can talk later.

We will. Goodnight, Blake.

Goodnight, Rebecca.

I plug my phone into the charger and change into my pajamas. I walk to the kitchen and Amanda is on her laptop. It looks like she's given up on her search—at least for now.

"Goodnight, Amanda," I say from the doorway.

"Goodnight. Maggie is picking you up around ten tomorrow. I'm leaving around eleven."

"See you in the morning," I say, walking back to my room.

I crawl into bed. I turn to the window; I have the view of the night sky from that window memorized. I know how dark the sky gets, and how the stars glisten, and how the grassy field below looks almost white. On a clear night, you can practically see the fence at the edge of our property.

I lay still and hear Amanda making noises in the house. She's slamming doors and using language I'm not allowed to say.

The sunlight beams in through the window and wakes me. The rooster crows and the cows moo. I jump into the shower and hurry to dress. It's early, but I like this time of the morning.

I dreamed about the man with the tattoo last night. Either he was a friend of my parents, or he worked for us. He was kind to me, and I know Dad liked him. I wish I could remember his name. Was it a dream I'd experienced, or a memory? The man with the tattoo was riding one of the horses, and he rode up to Dad. They talked and laughed. The man rode into the barn, and Dad followed behind him. I was playing at the swing.

Why do I remember this?

I step out of the shower and wrap the towel around my hair. I'm still thinking about the dream—or the memory, whichever it might be. I had been sitting at the kitchen table, and the man with the tattoo was eating with us. I was small and young—five, maybe. The man smiled at me from across the table. Dad turned to speak to him, and then said his name: Gordy.

Is that his real name, or a nickname? I wonder. *If Gordy and Dad had been such good friends, why had he not been around here for years? Perhaps I should dress and go to the barn. I seem to have memories there.*

In the bottom drawer I find an old pair of jeans and pull them on. They fit; I must've lost weight. I'd put them in that drawer because Mom had told me they were too tight to wear out in public.

I glance at my backside in the mirror, and they look good on me. I smile at my reflection.

At the back door, I pull on my boots, thankful they are still there and not in the pile Amanda seems to be adding to on the back porch. My heart feels squeezed. I can't seem to do anything to stop her.

I head for the barn. There, I feed the horses, and while they're eating, I brush them. I take my time and just nuzzle and talk to them. I climb up into the hayloft and think about the tattooed man, Gordy, standing here. He used to smile at me and give me a wave with his arm. I shake my head at the memory. When did he stop being friends with Dad? I don't remember him at the farm these last few years.

Someone drives up outside. I can see that it's a truck and horse trailer. I walk out of the barn, and Mr. Everman is getting out of the truck. He's been a friend for a long time. We go to church together.

"Good morning. How are you today?" I ask as he gets out of the truck.

"I'm doing just fine. Here's a check for the horses. I'm happy to be buying them; you loved them, and they're in great shape. If you ever want to see them, you know where they are," Mr. Everman says, walking to the barn.

"Would you like me to help you load them?" I ask.

"No, they're gentle, and Chip will be here any minute to help."

"I just fed them. If you don't mind, I'm going to the house. I don't want to see them leave."

Chip—who owns a farm nearby, and was a friend to Dad—arrives and gets out of his truck. He pauses when he sees me.

"Rebecca, I didn't know you'd be here. I'm sorry that we're taking your animals," Chip says.

"It's okay. I can't take care of them if I'm not here. At least I know that friends will have them, and I know you'll take care of them. What are you buying?" I want to know where each one of the animals is going.

"I bought the cows and two of the goats," Chip says.

"Okay. I'm going inside now. I don't want to see the animals leave." I walk back to the house.

I let the tears run down my cheeks as I walk into to my room. Everything my parents built is now being split apart. I change into navy slacks and a light-blue sweater from my time with Maggie. I'm hoping that Maggie comes early.

I get my suitcase ready and put my phone into my purse. I recheck the room, making sure I'm leaving it spotless. I take the check out of my jean pocket; it's made out to the "Estate of Bruce Wilds." Can Amanda even cash it? I slide it into my wallet.

Amanda closes the bathroom door. She's just getting up. I don't want her to know I have the check. Maybe Mr. Everman will leave before she comes out of the bathroom, and she won't even know that he's been here.

There's a knock at the back door, and I rush to answer. It's Maggie.

"Hey, girl, I'm so glad to see you," I say, eager to get away from Amanda.

"You've lost weight!" Maggie's eyes survey my body. "Get your stuff and let's go. We've got lots to do."

I pick up my suitcase and backpack, which are next to the door. The bathroom door is still closed. I shrug. I don't even want to see Amanda. I rush out the door and over to Maggie's car.

"Why are all these people here?" Maggie asks, looking around and waving at Mr. Everman.

"They're buying the animals. If it's okay with you, I need to come back here tomorrow afternoon," I say.

I watch as Mr. Everman drives away with the horses in his trailer. A pain hits me in the chest and tears fill my eyes.

We get into Maggie's light-blue BMW. "Sure, we can come back. But is it safe?" Maggie's voice cracks. She frowns and starts the engine.

"If the ice princess leaves, it's safe," I say, looking at her.

"What's going on? You're crying," Maggie says, hesitating before putting the car in reverse.

As we drive, I tell Maggie about overhearing Amanda's phone call and her searching the house for the documents and how Amanda wants to sell the house.

"Rebecca, it sounds like she's in it for the money. Is there anyone else who can take you?" Maggie asks.

"I don't think so, unless I have a long-lost relative." I startle myself with my answer. Is there by chance someone else who would be kind enough to take me?

"How do you find out if there's someone else?" Maggie frowns, and her words are soft.

"I don't know." I shrug my shoulders and turn to look out the window so that Maggie doesn't see the tears running down my cheeks.

"We have choir practice at church this morning. We're going there now. Anything you need before we get to the church?"

"I haven't had breakfast," I reply.

"That's not a problem. We'll stop for breakfast," Maggie says, smiling at me.

I sit back in the seat. I'm grateful for Maggie; I feel like I can handle almost anything, just by being with her. I look forward to choir practice and seeing all the kids at church. I smile sadly. I miss the life that I had.

Chapter 17

I can feel the tension in my body. Will Amanda dump me when she gets the money? I fear she'll dump me, just like my parent's belongings that she'd piled up on the porch. Everything is disposable to Amanda.

We arrive at church for choir practice. The large red-brick church with white trim and beautiful stained-glass windows is located near downtown. The parking lot has several cars parked near the door. Maggie parks the car and turns off the engine.

"The youth choir is singing for the service tomorrow. This is our practice," Maggie says, opening the car door.

There is a spring in my step as we approach the door. "I'm excited to see everyone, and to be singing again," I say.

Once inside the door, Maggie whispers, "We're practicing in the sanctuary." I turn and walk down the hall. The building is empty and I think we must be late. Listening for sounds is something that I catch myself doing often. Is it from the break-in, or finding my parents dead?

We're almost there, and it's still quiet. Maggie reaches for the door and pulls it open; I step inside. The youth leader and choir director are standing in front of the choir, and they're praying. I reach out with my arm to stop Maggie from entering.

"They're praying," I whisper.

We wait until the prayer is over, and then we enter. The choir director turns around and sees us.

"Welcome, girls. Rebecca, it's so good to see you. I'm glad you're here. I was wondering who would do our solo, and you've solved the problem," Keith, the music director, says as we approach the choir loft.

"Good morning, Keith," I say.

"Hey, Rebecca, glad you're here," shouts a male voice. Talking erupts among the youth, and Keith quiets everyone.

We begin singing hymns, and then Keith pulls out a few new songs for us to learn. My heart is full of joy. The music lifts my mood, and singing comes naturally. I can feel my body relax.

After practice, Keith asks me to stay and rehearse my solo, so Maggie and I hang back as the others leave. I'm a bit disappointed, because I wanted to talk to everyone.

"Rebecca," Keith says, "I know that everyone will want to hear you sing 'How Great Thou Art,' because you do it so well—probably the best that I've ever heard. I was also hoping you'd sing 'The Lord's Prayer.' Are you up for two songs?"

"Sure. Will I be singing them back-to-back?" I ask.

"No—I thought we would hold 'The Lord's Prayer' for the end," Keith says.

I practice both songs, and then Maggie and I leave. The parking lot is empty; everyone has gone.

"Are you hungry?" Maggie asks as we get into her car.

"Yes," I respond.

"Let's go to Cliff's," Maggie says, starting the engine. It's a short drive from the church to the center of downtown and the little hangout.

We arrive at the little diner, Cliff's, and Maggie parks the car in front at the curb. The diner is in the middle of downtown with a glass front. I'm excited to spend time with Maggie. We walk to the door and enter, only to find a group from choir practice already here and eating.

I have fun visiting with my friends from church. My old friend Erica—who is petite with freckles and straight brown hair pulled into a ponytail—is here, but she doesn't come over to speak to me. She's sitting at a booth in the corner. Perhaps she has moved on and forgotten about me. It's strange how close friendships can end so suddenly. Is that what happened with Gordy and my dad?

I want to tell Maggie about my dreams and memories of Gordy, but we just haven't had much alone time.

I nibble on my French fries, dipping them into the ketchup. Tyler and Tara are sitting in the booth with us. Tara is one of Maggie's friends, and Tyler is showing an interest in Maggie.

"How long are you here for?" Tara asks.

"I leave on Tuesday night, but I don't want to go," I say, biting my lip. Maybe I'm saying too much.

"I'd trade in a heartbeat. Nothing is going on in this one-horse town. I'd love to live in the city. What's it like there?" Tara asks, sipping on her soda.

"It's crowded and loud. Everyone's a stranger. It's lonely. I do like the school. It's new, big, and roomy. Some of the kids are nice. There's this huge mall with all sorts of stores," I explain, not wanting to say too much.

"I'd still like to trade, but I know we can't," Tara says, and Maggie gives her a funny look.

"Tara, so you want to live in the city. Just remember—things aren't always as they seem," Maggie explains.

"I want to move so badly, but my parents grew up here. I think that's what scares me—that I'll do the same and just be stuck here," Tara says.

"You worry too much," Tyler says, and we all laugh.

We finish eating.

"Are you ready to go, Rebecca?" Maggie smiles at me.

"Sure," I say.

"We have cookies to bake before tonight. See you guys later. You're going, right?" Maggie asks, looking at Tyler.

"If you're going to be there, I'll be there," Tyler says, smiling at Maggie.

Tara waves but doesn't get up.

Maggie and I walk out of the diner and over to the car.

"As you heard, we have to bake cookies for the hayride tonight," Maggie tells me, getting into her car.

"That won't take very long," I reply.

"Yes, it will, because we have a lot of talking to do as we bake. Now tell me more about you and Amanda," Maggie says as we begin the drive to her house.

I feel at home with Maggie. I've known her my whole life, but we were never close until now. I tell her all about Amanda and everything that has happened in the past few weeks. I even mention Amanda buying me things and how it started good and went downhill from there.

After we arrive, we go up to Maggie's room and sit on her bed.

"Where are your parents?" I ask Maggie.

"They went to Dallas. They won't be back until late. We'll be at the hayride by the time they get home."

"Why did they go to Dallas?" I ask.

"Mother needed a shopping day, and Dad has business. They go there a lot," Maggie says. "Now tell me what happened at the farm last night."

"I went to the barn to see the horses. Amanda broke the cookie jar. She seemed wild and out of control. She was slamming drawers and going through closets. I heard her on the phone talking about my dad's money. I was scared to go to sleep. I thought she might come in and kill me. Now I wonder if maybe she hurt my parents for the money. But I know the tattooed guy, who might be linked to the murders. His name is Gordy."

"You mean the man who tried to break in?"

"I don't know—maybe it's the same person. I can't remember why Gordy stopped working at the farm. I do remember the police said the man they arrested has warrants, but his name was Gene Maxwell," I say. "And I keep asking myself, why did Amanda want me to stay quiet at the police station? I think she knows more than she says."

"Rebecca, you need to be careful. I think there is something wrong. I'm not sure you're safe with her," Maggie tells me. "I think she's mentally imbalanced."

"Tell me about Tyler. He's interested in you," I say, wanting to change the subject. I, too, think that Amanda is out of her mind, but what can I do about it? I have to figure something out. I don't want to go home with her.

"I took your advice about dating a guy from your dad's Sunday school class. That guy happens to be Tyler. He's a real gentleman. I started talking to him this week—maybe on Wednesday. I'll see him tonight. It's the annual church hayride for the youth. Maybe he's interested; it's too early to tell," Maggie says.

"That's good. I think Tyler is a good choice. From what I saw today, I think he's interested," I say. *What if I don't go back to the city?* I worry silently. *I won't see Blake again.*

"There's someone very interested in you," Maggie says.

"Who would that be?" I question.

"Clay Matthews—he asks about you. I think he's interested," Maggie replies. I smile at her; Clay was also in my dad's class. Clay was a bratty kid growing up, always pulling my ponytail and shooting spit wads at me.

"We better go make cookies; we have six dozen to prepare," Maggie says, jumping up and walking out of her room.

"That's going to take a while." I get up and follow her to the kitchen. "So, what makes you think Clay is interested in me?"

"I told you, he asks about you all the time. You know Clay sings, right?" Maggie says, getting the mixing bowl out of the cabinet.

"What do you mean, he sings?" I ask, grabbing the giant spoon and turning on the oven.

"He has been singing a lot of solos at church, and I have to say, he's excellent," Maggie says, dumping the flour into the mixing bowl.

"So maybe he's attracted to my voice. Do you think that he'd rather be singing solos tomorrow instead of me?" I ask, stirring the eggs into the mixture.

"Gosh, Rebecca, don't you get it? You have something in common—a bond that causes him to be interested."

"But what about Blake? I like him."

"But Blake is in Dallas. What if you move back here?" Maggie says.

"And how can that happen?" I ask, still toying with the idea in my mind.

"I don't know, but there must be something in those papers. Do you think Amanda knows what's in the will?" Maggie asks.

"I'm not sure. I think no one knows what's in the will."

"Maybe someone else is supposed to have you. Maybe your parents left provisions for you to be with someone else. Maybe they agreed that whoever takes care of you must remain on the farm." Maggie's eyes get big as she says this.

"We have to go and get those papers tomorrow. I'm now dying to know what's in them," I say.

We place two cookie sheets in the oven, but we still need to prepare the next two cookie sheets to go in when these come out.

My mind is miles away from this kitchen and baking. What if I'm supposed to be with someone else? Who would that person be? Amanda is my next of kin—or is she? If it isn't her, who would it be? Is Gordy related to me? His name is not Gene Maxwell. Gordy is not short for Gene. I've never heard that name in my life. Could it be that the police got his name wrong? I need to call Officer Lawson and talk to him; I still have his card in my purse.

"Maggie, I just thought of something. I have to go and call Officer Lawson. I'm checking to see if they're still holding the guy who broke in. I need to see him again," I tell her.

"Please hurry. We have a production line going here," Maggie says.

"I'll be as quick as I can," I shout as I run for the stairs.

What will Officer Lawson think when I call and ask him about the tattooed man? I wonder.

I dial the number for Officer Lawson's cell phone.

"Hello, Officer Lawson speaking."

"This is Rebecca Wilds," I say. "I'm calling about the man who broke into the apartment."

"Yes, Miss Wilds, I remember you. What is it that you need?" Officer Lawson responds.

"When I saw the man in the police station, I remembered the tattoo. Now I remember the man also, but his name isn't Maxwell."

"And just how would you know that?" Officer Lawson asks.

"Because his nickname is Gordy, but I don't remember his real name."

"You're right; there were two men at the station. The man who broke into the apartment is Gene Maxwell, he has several warrants, but your tattooed man was clean as a whistle. Let me look at my files." There is a long pause while I wait for Lawson to return to the phone. "His name is Connor Gorman. He is retired from the Marines and says that he knows you. I called your aunt, but she didn't answer. Mr. Gorman says he was following Gene Maxwell because Maxwell was stalking you. It seems Mr. Gorman was trying to alert you of a problem."

"Connor—yes, that's his name, but we called him Gordy. He has deep-blue eyes, and his hair is shorter, but it's him. I do know him, who was the dark haired man?" I reply.

"Mr. Gorman says that he heard about your parents and confronted Amanda before the funeral. She refused to let him speak with you. He followed you to Dallas and was coming to speak with you when Maxwell was breaking into the apartment," Officer Lawson explains.

"What does he want to talk to me about?" I ask, crossing my fingers and hoping that maybe I'm supposed to be with him.

"I'm not sure. I wanted to clear it through your aunt before talking to you," Officer Lawson says.

"Thank you," I say before hanging up.

Connor—Mother had called him Connor. The last time I saw him, Mother had cooked a big dinner, and we said goodbye. Was he going to the Marines? And why does he want to see me? Does he know something?

I return to the kitchen to help Maggie with the cookies. She's getting behind with filling the cookie sheets, so I step in to help.

"Did you talk to the officer?" Maggie asks.

"Yes, he was helpful. It seems there were two men at the station that day. Apparently, the tattooed man was at the apartment to tell me that Maxwell was stalking me. His name is Connor Gorman. That's why we called him Gordy."

"I remember Gordy! He came to our church," Maggie says.

"You do? Maybe your parents know something about him," I suggest.

"Yes, we'll have to ask," Maggie says. "But for now, we have cookies to make."

"Yes, we do!" I smile and grab a cookie.

"Now, don't eat up all the cookies. We need six dozen," Maggie says.

"Come on, Maggie, you can't tell me you haven't eaten at least *one* cookie. I see the crumbs around your mouth," I say, and we both laugh.

But something is seriously wrong. Amanda is hiding something, and I have to get the papers.

Chapter 18

We take our six dozen cookies to the church. Barry, the youth director, is standing next to the trailer for the hayride. Maggie and I approach him as he's counting heads.

"What do you want me to do with these cookies?" Maggie asks.

"Maggie, you made me lose count! You girls take them over to Mrs. Ward—she's in charge of the food." Barry points across the parking lot to Erica's mother.

We walk away from Barry and start across the parking lot to Mrs. Ward—but then I stop. I turn to make sure that I'm out of everyone's earshot.

"You take them, and I'll wait for you here," I say, handing her my container of cookies. "Mrs. Ward hasn't spoken to me since my parents died. She wouldn't take me in, and now she treats me like I have the plague. There's no way I want to ruin tonight by having to face her."

"No, you're coming with me. Mrs. Ward needs to face you. You did nothing wrong, and she's avoiding you. Once you face her, maybe this nonsense will end," Maggie says, pushing me forward.

I walk over to Mrs. Ward. She has her back turned, and doesn't see me approach.

"Hello, Mrs. Ward, it's nice to see you," I say, seeing her startled face when she recognizes me. I hand her the container of cookies.

"Rebecca! I didn't expect to see you here. I never had a chance to tell you that I'm sorry about your parents," Mrs. Ward says, looking away from me.

"It's a big loss for everyone. My parents were wonderful people," I reply, turning to walk away.

"I'm sorry I didn't take you that day," Mrs. Ward says to my back.

I spin around and look at her. "I was devastated. I woke to find my parents dead. Then they tell me you're scared to take me. I sat in that dreary police room for hours while they searched for someone to help me. I thought you, of all people, would reach out to me. Erica and I were best of friends, and now she won't even look at me."

"It's my fault," Mrs. Ward says with a sigh. "I was just afraid that there was a murderer on the loose. I think Erica is just embarrassed that we didn't take you. Please forgive me for being selfish."

"I forgive you. I have learned a lot in the last few weeks. We need to move on," I say, and then I walk away, Maggie following.

"Gee, girl, I'm so proud of you. You told her, and you did it with grace," Maggie says, wrapping her arm around me and giving me a side hug.

"Now I don't have to walk on tiptoes around people. I didn't do anything wrong—and yet, some people are treating me like I'm a monster," I say.

"I think they don't know what to say. Everyone is sorry for what happened to you."

"I think I get it, but I don't like it," I say, and we walk back to the trailer.

Barry blows his whistle.

"Everyone get on the trailer. We have to eat before dark, so let's get a move on," Barry shouts.

Maggie and I get on the trailer. Most of the kids on the trailer are sitting near the front or on the other side. We keep to ourselves and stay in our place near the center of the trailer.

"This should be fun tonight," Maggie says. "I'm looking forward to spending time with Tyler, and I think you should get to know Clay."

"Why is everyone sitting on the other side?" I ask.

"I don't know, but I wasn't ready to join them," Maggie says. "I want to tell you to give Clay a chance. I think you'll find that you like him." I don't answer, and she continues. "I'm worried for you. Things with Amanda are getting serious. She could hurt you. Why'd she break that cookie jar? It makes no sense to me."

"I was scared last night when she wasn't acting normal. I was afraid she might kill me. I don't know what's wrong with her, but I don't want to go back to Dallas."

The trailer pulls off the parking lot, and we are on our way.

I turn and Erica is looking at me. I smile at her and turn back to Maggie.

"I wonder if things with Erica will ever get better," I say.

"Who knows? But you do have a lot of friends, Rebecca," Maggie replies.

"Yes, people are drawn to us—that's why we're sitting alone," I say with a smile, and Maggie laughs.

"That's partly my fault. I wanted to talk to you first. If Clay approaches you, I want you to give the guy a chance. Do you understand? It could be the start of something amazing."

"Will you give me a break? You keep pushing him on me. If it makes you happy, I'll give him a chance, but *only* if he approaches me," I say, smiling.

"Oh, trust me, he will. Just wait and see."

"I would never have thought that Clayton would be interested in little ole me," I whisper. Clay was an awkward and clumsy child; I can't imagine him being interested in anyone, but maybe he's outgrown his awkwardness.

"He doesn't like to be called Clayton. So call him Clay," Maggie whispers back.

"I'll remember that," I say.

There's a conversation going on among the others, and we listen in. It's mainly Kyle and Colton talking about the football game last night.

"I forgot to ask; did you win the game last night?" I say, looking at Maggie.

"Oh, yes, we won. Can't you hear them boasting? If we had lost, they would probably be silent," Maggie says.

We smile at each other, but my thoughts are still preoccupied.

I have to get those papers, and I have to find a way to not go home with Amanda. Would the Mosleys allow me to stay with them? Is that even possible? I should be enjoying my time, and not worrying about life. Why did this happen to me? Why my parents? What is it that I don't know?

"Rebecca, you look so sad," Maggie whispers.

"I'm thinking about those papers. I hope that there's something in the papers that'll keep me from going home with Amanda," I say, looking around and hoping that no one hears me.

"We'll look for them tomorrow," Maggie whispers. "Are you sure they even exist?"

"Yes, there are papers, but I wasn't going to tell her where they are. She'll never find them," I reply, smiling at Maggie.

We arrive at the campsite, and everyone gets off the trailer. I jump down and follow Maggie over to the stream. It's pretty, with clear water running over the rocks. We stand for a moment and watch it flow past. Without speaking, we turn and walk to the picnic tables where the food is displayed.

"Rebecca, I'm glad you came tonight," a voice says. I spin around to see Clay standing next to me.

"I'm glad that I came," I answer. "How are you, Clay?"

He's smiling, and his hands are shaking, so he shoves them into his pockets. He looks down at his feet and kicks a rock.

"I've missed you at church and school. I'm sorry about what happened to your parents," Clay says.

"Thanks, Clay."

"Is there any chance you could move back here?" Clay asks.

"I don't know, but I'd like to come back."

After a blessing over the meal, we fill our plates with hot dogs and chips. Clay and I find an old log on its side and make a bench out of it. It is over to one side away from the crowd.

"Save my place, and I'll get us some drinks," Clay says and walks away.

Maggie and Tyler walk by where I'm sitting.

"Are you okay here with Clay?" Maggie asks.

"Sure, I'm fine. Where are you going to sit?" I ask.

"Tyler found some chairs and grabbed them for us. I'll see you after we eat," Maggie says, and then she walks away with Tyler.

Clay comes back with our drinks and sits next to me.

"I want to ask you something," Clay whispers, and he looks around to see if anyone is near us.

"What is it?" I ask.

"I've liked you for a long time. I'd like for us to be more than friends," he says.

"Clay, my life is very complicated. I'm not even sure where I'm going to live. I've been living with my aunt, but that isn't working out. Maybe we could have something more if I were to stay here. If I don't stay here, I don't know how that would work."

"Even if you don't stay here, I still want to keep in touch. Give me your phone number and address? We'll figure out a way to make it work, and if you need help with anything, let me know. I'm here for you," Clay says.

I smile at him. He doesn't have a clue what my life is like, or what he's even saying. To be with me or to help me could be putting his life on the line. I could be in danger, and anyone near me could be in trouble too. Why can't I be a kid and enjoy this night?

Am I not being fair to Clay? I worry. *Why does he like me*?

After eating, Clay takes my hand, and we walk to the stream. We take off our shoes and wade into the water. The water is fresh and calming. The sound of the water flowing brings me peace. Clay wants time alone with me, and I am glad someone wants to look out for me.

"I remember helping your dad haul hay in the summer. You'd come out to the field and bring us homemade lemonade and cookies. You were always smiling and sweet," Clay says. "I used to watch you approaching and look at the sun dancing in your red hair. The curls bounced as you walked."

"Yes, you, Tyler, and Colton always helped out with the hay. I loved making the lemonade and cookies. The best part was making everyone happy," I say.

"It was always so hot and dry, and it was a much-needed break. It was your sweet smile that I liked the most," Clay says, taking my hand.

"I'm glad that you liked it," I say. I feel like Clay is pushing too hard and wanting it to be more. "We should probably go back. It's getting dark." I step out of the stream.

Clay grabs my hand and leads me back to the others.

We sit down in a circle around the campfire. Maggie and Tyler come and sit next to us. Barry brings his guitar and sits next to me.

"I thought we would sing for a bit," Barry says as he begins to strum.

Clay and I lead the others in singing. I'm stunned at how well Clay sings. His voice is deeper than I thought it would be, but with a mellow tone, and we harmonize so well. We sing a few hymns, and then Barry begins to talk.

"It's good to be here together. Sometimes when you're young, you don't appreciate what you have until you don't have it anymore. On a sad day, Rebecca's life was thrown into turmoil. She lost her family, and her life is now forever changed. I want you all to think about your home and your parents. Think about the comfort of your home, and how your parents take care of all your needs. As teenagers, we often get hung up in our own lives and what we want and forget to appreciate what others do for us. I want you to think of everything your home and your parents mean to you."

Barry reaches over and squeezes my hand when he hears me sobbing. I just let the tears stream down my cheeks. I'm thankful for the time I had with my parents, and all the things they taught me. The other kids may not realize what they have, but they need to think about it.

Barry hands me a tissue, and I wipe my eyes.

"When you go home tonight, I want you to thank your parents for all the things they have done, and continue to do for you. I'm proud of our group. I'm appreciative of the way you conduct yourself and the way you worked so hard at choir practice today. I know that we'll have a good service tomorrow because you'll do your best. Let's all stand and hold hands and sing together before we go back to the church."

We all stand, and Barry leads us in singing a song. It's a new song that I've not heard, so I remain quiet. Barry is holding one of my hands, and Clay the other. I feel warmth, love, and acceptance: things I don't have with Amanda.

Please, Lord, let me get those papers, and let there be a way out of my situation.

When the song is over, we get back on the trailer and begin the ride back to the church. There is a slight chill in the air, and Clay wraps his arms around me. I feel safe and snuggle up against him. Maggie smiles at me.

Chapter 19

I stand before the congregation at the end of the service and position the microphone. The music starts, and the choir stands behind me. The choir hums in the background as I sing. The song flows from me, and I feel like I'm in my element. As I begin to sing the last verse, the door to the sanctuary opens, and I look away, not to be distracted. In my peripheral vision, a man enters and walks up the aisle in slow, measured steps and sits down. He looks up, and I recognize his face. I almost forget the words and have to look down at the music. I hold it together until the last note is sung. The man who came in is Gordy.

The service ends, and I attempt to make my way over to Gordy. The members of the choir shove me out the side door and down the hallway. We enter the choir room to take off our choir robes. I'm rushing so that I can catch Gordy. Someone nudges me, and I turn around.

"You were great today. I'm sorry about everything. Can you ever forgive me for not being a friend when you needed one?" Erica says.

My mind is jerked away from my goal, and Erica's face replaces it. A flash of angry words and disappointment arise from my memory; I squash them—there's no time for that.

"Erica, don't worry about it. That was long ago. So much has happened since then. Right now, there's someone I must see before they leave." I give her a quick hug and rush out the door. Maggie's in the hallway.

"Rebecca, let's go." Maggie tugs on my arm and pulls me down the hallway.

"What's the rush?" I ask.

"I told my parents we're going to lunch with Tyler and Clay. I thought if we had a quick lunch, you and I could run and get the papers, and no one would know that we went."

"You mean you're afraid your parents wouldn't let us go?"

"Someone chose your farm to kill your parents. Will they be back? Will they kill again?" Maggie says, pulling me out the door.

"Hold up—I saw Gordy in the church. I need to find him," I say. I scan the parking lot and the front of the church. Where is Gordy? I must be too late.

"We're meeting Tyler and Clay at Bruno's for pizza, and then we'll go get the papers. I told Tyler it had to be a quick lunch, as we have errands to run," Maggie says, getting in her car.

"Okay . . . I was hoping to talk to Gordy. But I don't see him."

"Tyler called ahead and ordered the pizza so we won't have to wait for the food."

"It sounds like you thought of everything."

"We need to go. If we hang around, you'll start getting compliments, and we'll never get away. Your songs today were outstanding!"Maggie says.

"Did you see Erica?"

"I sure did, and I hated to break up the moment between you. We have to get moving so we can go to the farm without being caught," Maggie continues.

"I'm sorry to cause you problems," I say.

"Look, Rebecca, I would go to the moon and back for you. Let's enjoy a quick lunch and nab the papers," Maggie says.

"That sounds good to me. You're the best, Mags."

"So are you, Becca." Maggie smiles at me.

"I have to get those papers. Dad told me if anything ever happened to them to get this thick brown folder."

"What's in that folder? Do you know?"

"I'm not sure, but maybe there is something in that folder that will get me away from Amanda."

"I wonder where Gordy fits into all of this."

Maggie parks the car, and we walk into Bruno's. Tyler and Clay are seated at the table and have already purchased the drinks. We walk over to where they are seated.

"Pizza should be out soon," Tyler says.

"Thanks for ordering it ahead," Maggie says, sitting next to Tyler. "We have an errand that we have to do quickly."

Clay pulls out the chair for me, and I sit down.

"You forgot to give me your number last night. Can we do that while we wait for pizza?" Clay asks.

"Sure, give me your phone, and I'll put my number in your contacts," I say, proud that I've become tech-savvy.

Clay hands me his phone, and I give him mine.

The thought occurs to me that Amanda gave me this phone and taught me how to use it. She was nice to do that, but then everything changed. What happened? Did I miss something?

"You know that if you need anything, call me. I have a car and can take you places if Maggie isn't available," Clay says.

The waiter brings over the pizza, and we start eating.

The pizza is hot and the cheese is stringy. We eat and laugh about the cheese. For a brief moment, I forget that my life is in turmoil.

After eating, we say our goodbyes and head to the farm. My stomach is churning, and my hands begin to shake.

"You're quiet. What's on your mind?" Maggie asks as we take the road leading out of town toward the farm.

"I was thinking about the farm and wondering if maybe Amanda is there. Do you think she's watching to see if I lead her to the papers?" I wring my hands and notice that we're passing a yellow house. "We're almost there. We'll have to make it quick. You don't think Amanda is still there?"

Maggie turns to me as her eyes grow big. "Do you think that is a possibility?"

"With her, anything is possible. She's unpredictable."

Maggie turns on the lane to the house. I strain my eyes, searching for any signs of a vehicle or a person, but it all seems clear.

"I don't see anything," I say as she stops and puts the car in park.

"Rebecca, I'm scared. I didn't think about it until now, but with everything you've told me about her, she could do anything," Maggie says.

"Keep your phone with you at all times, and be prepared to run," I say. We walk to the back door. I unlock it, and we enter the kitchen. I don't stop to look at anything but head straight to the living room.

I yell over my shoulder, "Maggie, wait in there. The papers are tucked away—I don't want anyone to see where they are."

"No problem, I'll be the lookout," Maggie calls back.

I walk over to the bookcase that looks built-in, but it's free-standing and slides out to expose the hidden room. With my fingers, I search around for the remote lever. I don't find it. I try again this time, reaching deeper into the shelf. I finally find the switch and flip it up, releasing the rollers, and the bookcase moves forward. I step into the room, pausing only long enough to flip on the light switch.

Now I need to find that brown folder. For a moment I can envision Dad sitting at the desk and paying bills. I open the file drawer and remove all folders and place them in the box that I find in the corner. I pull out the checkbooks and bank statements and go through every drawer to see if there's anything of value or anything additional that I might need to take. I discover a bundle of letters and take them. Finally, I find the thick brown folder, and I grab it. I close the box and turn to leave.

I reach for the light switch, and notice something hanging on the wall behind the calendar. I move the calendar and discover the gold-framed record hanging on the wall. I read the inscription: "Jackson Nash, for selling a million albums." I turn out the light and leave the room. I push the bookcase back into place and secure the latch. Now the room is hidden. I return to the kitchen carrying the box. Maggie is leaning over the sink, looking out the kitchen window.

"Do you see anything?" I ask.

"No sign of any human, just a little squirrel scampering around. Did you get the papers?" Maggie says, spinning around.

"I sure did. Right here in this box," I say. "For some reason, I thought Amanda would jump out of hiding and demand that I give her the box."

"Girl, I've never been so scared, but we haven't made it away from here yet. So let's go before something happens," Maggie says as we hurry to the car.

"I was scared too. Thank you for bringing me," I say.

We turn off the lane and onto the main road. We only go a short distance when we notice that a black van is approaching and beginning to slow.

"Who is that, Rebecca?" Maggie asks nervously.

"I don't know. Lock the doors, and whatever you do, don't stop," I tell her. Maggie drives forward, and I turn to watch the van. The van turns in at the farm.

"Rebecca, who is it? And what do they want?" Maggie says.

"Do you think they know I got the papers? Are they spies for Amanda?"

"Maybe they're the killers." Maggie looks in the rearview mirror.

"Did they follow us?" I ask, grabbing the door handle.

"No, they haven't followed us. Are they going to break in again?"

"I don't know, but we can't go there alone again," I say, looking at Maggie with wide eyes. We drive in silence for a while before I ask, "Do you think the papers are safe now that we have them? Is there something in the papers that will free me from Amanda?"

"I don't know," Maggie replies.

Maggie turns onto the driveway of her two-story colonial house and looks over at me.

"We shouldn't have any problem sneaking the box inside because my parents aren't home," she says. "They went out for lunch, so they could still be a while."

"Will you help me go through these papers?" I ask.

"Sure. Let's hide the box in the guest room where you're staying and then pull out the will if it's in there," Maggie says.

Once inside the room, I go through the box and find the large brown folder. I take it out and sit, staring at it.

"What does it say?" Maggie asks, coming into the room.

"I don't know. I'm afraid to look. Even if there is something in the papers, I won't understand the legal jargon. Is there anyone we can trust who can tell me what it says?" I ask, looking at Maggie.

"Maybe a lawyer can explain it," Maggie replies.

"I know. Take me over to Judge Holcombe's. He doesn't live far from here," I say.

"You know this is a Sunday afternoon, and he just might not like being disturbed on his day off," Maggie says.

"This is important. You do understand that, don't you?" I argue.

"Come on, let's go." Maggie says. "He lives a few houses down, so let's walk. Hide the papers in your backpack in case someone sees us."

"Okay—thanks for going with me," I reply, shoving the papers into my backpack and rushing down the stairs.

Walking down the sidewalk to Judge Holcombe's house, Maggie and I both turn to look for the black van. Why had the van been at the farm? We reach a large white colonial house with massive columns in the front, black shutters around the windows, and a large black door. We walk up a red-brick sidewalk to the front door. I push the button for the doorbell; you can hear the large chimes echoing throughout the house. We wait. I'm scared to know what's in the papers. What if I'm supposed to be with Amanda? What will I do then?

The door opens, and Mrs. Holcombe, a kind, gray-haired lady in her seventies, looks surprised to see us. Her mouth falls open as she stares.

"Mrs. Holcombe, I'm Rebecca Wilds, and I have some legal documents that I need someone to look at and give me some advice. Could I please talk with Judge Holcombe?"

"Yes, Rebecca, I know who you are. You sang beautifully at church today. I wanted to tell you after church that it's good to have you back, but you disappeared. Please come in." She steps back and allows us to enter. "Just wait here and I'll get Herbert," Mrs. Holcombe says, leaving us standing in the foyer. The tall grandfather clock strikes as we wait. I jump and bump into Maggie. We laugh at how edgy we are.

Judge Holcombe, a kind gentleman in his seventies with graying temples and a bald head, comes into the foyer. "What is it that Edith's saying about some legal documents?"

"Yes, may I please explain?" I whisper, struggling to speak for fear of him saying no.

"You girls come into my study. I'll have to get my glasses. What kind of legal document is it?" he asks.

"Judge Holcombe, when my parents were killed, the sheriff didn't have my parents' documents. Sheriff Webster called my aunt, and I went to Dallas to live with her. Something isn't right with my aunt, and I'm afraid of her. I was hoping you could read the will or at least explain it and tell me who I'm supposed to live with." The words roll out of my mouth without a breath. I'm nervous and scared that this may not turn out the way I hoped it would. I can feel my knees knocking as I stand in front of his desk, looking down at him.

"So, what's the problem with your aunt?" Judge Holcombe asks.

I hand him the brown folder. "I think she's mentally unstable."

"That would be for the courts to decide. Let's see. Here's a standard will. So the attorney that drew up the papers is in Morgan; that's two towns from here. I wonder why they went to Morgan to have this done. It seems a bit strange to me that your parents didn't use an attorney here in town since we all go to church together."

"Well, maybe that's why they went to Morgan, so people in town wouldn't discuss it. You know how people around here talk," I say, hoping to get him moving along.

"You sang mighty pretty today. I've always liked to hear you sing. It's like Heaven's open, and the voice of an angel appears. You are very gifted, my dear."

"Thank you, Judge Holcombe, I do love to sing. And the papers . . ." I say, trying to get him to focus on the will.

"Well, I see that they left you the farm, the animals, and there is a trust for you. It says if they die before you reach eighteen that you are to be cared for by Connor Gorman. Oh yes, I remember Connor. He went away to the Marines—made a career out of the Service. He was a nice man. I think I saw him at church today."

It's all I can do not to shout for joy. I'm not supposed to be with Amanda! My body relaxes knowing that my life is about to change.

"Does it say anything about my aunt? Her name is Amanda Gordon."

"Let's see. Here is something . . . It states that the only living relative is Amanda Gordon, and your parents willfully and intentionally have omitted her from the will. That means that your parents left her absolutely nothing. So you might be right to worry about your aunt's stability."

"So what do I do now? My aunt is coming back for me on Tuesday, and I haven't talked to Connor; he tried to talk to me, and my aunt wouldn't allow it."

"Well, the will needs to go to probate, and you should be going to stay with Connor. The probate judge is Isaac Whipple, and here's his office number. Give him a call tomorrow morning. Tell him that Herbert said you need a rush job."

"My problem is I don't know how to reach Connor," I say.

"Well, let me give Sheriff Webster a call and have him track Connor down. He must be here in town since he was at church today." Judge Holcombe picks up the phone and makes a call. Maggie and I smile at each other.

"I'm relieved to know I don't belong with Amanda. My parents deliberately left her with nothing. Amanda made me think that she and Mother were close, but it doesn't sound like that to me," I whisper to Maggie.

Judge Holcombe hangs up his phone and removes his glasses. He's a gentle man with a kind smile. "Sheriff Webster says that Connor is staying at the hotel downtown," he tells us. "The sheriff is going to call him and tell him we need to speak with him right away. So wait here for a few minutes. Edith, would you mind bringing us something to drink and a snack? These ladies are going to be here for a bit."

Looking back at the papers, he continues, "There is more in the will. Your parents left the 980-acre farm and house to you, but out of the 980 acres, 100 acres is deeded to Connor Gorman. So you are, in fact, giving Connor 100 acres. All of that will be taken care of when you see Judge Whipple."

"So in exchange for taking care of me, Connor will receive a small portion of the farm?" I say—but I didn't realize I'd said it. I thought I was only thinking.

"Do you have a problem with the hundred acres?" Judge Holcombe asks.

Edith returns carrying a tray. She hands me a small plate with a slice of cake. She pats me on the arm and I smile at her. She serves us sodas and cake.

"You're such a lovely girl," Edith says to me. "I knew Herbert would want to help such a sweet girl. I'm so sorry you lost your parents. I do hope that you have someone nice taking care of you."

Judge Holcombe smiles at Edith. "We're trying to take care of her now." The phone rings, and he answers it.

"Yes, Sheriff. That sounds good. Yes, Rebecca is here waiting. Thank you." He hangs up. "Connor Gorman is on his way. He's been trying to speak with you ever since your parents died, but your aunt has kept him away. I think things are about to change for you, dear."

We sit and eat our cake. It's a delicious chocolate fudge cake that complements the soda. I eat slowly, savoring every bite of the sweet richness. Looking across the desk at the judge, he also relishes the dessert.

The doorbell rings, and Edith goes to answer it. Edith shows Connor into the room. Connor walks into the room slowly with his hands at his sides. His eyes are on the judge. "Judge Holcombe, the sheriff says you need to speak with me right away," Connor says, now standing in front of Holcombe's desk.

"Yes, I was going over the will of Bruce and Carol Wilds for Rebecca," the Judge says, nodding at Rebecca.

I stand and go pale as I face Connor. I haven't seen him in years, but the face is so familiar, and his deep-blue eyes make him look kind. Will he be willing to take me?

"Connor, I looked for you after church today," I say, looking into his face and remembering the intensity and gentleness of those eyes.

"Rebecca, I'm so sorry about your parents," Connor says as he gives me a big hug. "I've been trying to talk to you. I know that your parents wanted me to take care of you if anything happened to them."

"Why did you not come forward earlier?" I ask.

"I tried, but Amanda wouldn't let me. She was determined to keep you, but I knew you weren't safe with her."

"How did you know that?" I'm startled.

"I remember, Amanda," Connor says.

Judge Holcombe says to Connor, "I have the will here, and it strictly says that you are to be her guardian. It also says they are giving you 100 acres of the farm. How do you feel about taking care of Rebecca?"

Connor stands firm in front of Judge Holcombe's desk. His expression never falters as he replies, "I'm fine with taking care of Rebecca. I agreed to it years ago when Rebecca was just a small child. I take it we can live on the farm? I'm a single man—will they allow me to keep her?"

"The farm now belongs to Rebecca. I'm not sure what they'll say about a single man being her guardian," Judge Holcombe says.

"Since I got out of the Marines six months ago, I haven't settled. I've been living in an apartment and working in Morgan. I have a job as an engineer for Chapelton Mechanical. We could live on the farm, and I could drive to Morgan every day to work. Rebecca's life could resume as it was. What do you say, Rebecca?"

I'm stunned and elated at the thought of moving back to the farm. That would mean I could keep the animals and go back to my old school. "I think that sounds great. I know it's what my parents wanted. I remember you," I say, smiling at Connor.

So I won't be going back with Amanda. I won't be living with her. But I was still troubled. If Connor had been around, why hadn't I seen him at my parents? Why did he not come by for a visit?

Is Connor the one who came that last night and argued with my dad? I fretted. *Will I be safe with Connor, or am I rushing into trouble?*

"Well, it looks like we're finished here. Here is the will, Rebecca. Be sure and contact Judge Whipple tomorrow morning. After you meet with Judge Whipple, arrangements can be made for you to live with Connor," Judge Holcombe says.

"Will that happen before Tuesday night? I can't go back to live with her." I panic.

"I will talk to Judge Whipple about the urgency of the matter. Don't worry about it—we'll take care of it," Judge Holcombe says as he stands to lead us to the door.

"Thank you, Judge Holcombe. You and your wife have been so kind today. I appreciate your help. And thank you for the delicious cake," I say, shaking his hand.

Connor follows us outside.

"Where are you staying, Rebecca?" Connor asks.

"I'm staying with Maggie until Tuesday night. Amanda is supposed to pick me up."

"I'll alert the Mosleys that they aren't to release you to Amanda. I'll have the sheriff there if needed," Connor says.

Maggie and I start walking down the sidewalk. I turn quickly and ask, "Connor, do you have a black van?"

"No, I have a car. Why?"

"Just asking—and thank you for coming today."

"Give me your phone number," Connor says.

"Oh, yes—I guess I need your number, too," I say.

Walking back to the house with Maggie, a smile comes to my face as I think about moving back to the farm and seeing Velvet every day. Maybe I can even get Bruiser back.

Chapter 20

I lay in bed, unable to sleep. Tomorrow there will be discussions regarding my future. What will it be like going to court? Will Judge Whipple be as kind as Judge Holcomb? Will I have to go back to Dallas? Will I have to live with Amanda?

I turn over and pull the covers up around me, hoping to go to sleep. I lay still, and through the wall I hear the voices of Mr. and Mrs. Mosley. They're not talking; they're arguing. I lie still and listen.

"Remember, it's our duty and responsibility to help her," Mr. Mosley says.

"What do you mean 'our?'?" Mrs. Mosley shouts back.

"Okay, but as my wife, I expect you to help me with this," Mr. Mosley responds.

"I've been very cooperative up until now, but I want you to understand that she might be your responsibility, but not mine. What I do for her, I do because of Maggie."

"Yes, she and Maggie have bonded. They're like sisters," Mr. Mosley says.

"Well, I'll make the trip with you. I do like Rebecca—she's a sweet girl." Mrs. Mosley lowers her voice, and it's hardly audible.

"Thank you, Margaret. I'm grateful that you'll help," Mr. Mosley responds, lowering his voice also.

What does all of this mean? I wonder. *They're fighting about me. Why am I his responsibility? This seems so strange.* I try to quiet my mind so that I can sleep.

At some point, I must have fallen asleep because the alarm on my phone wakes me. The house is quiet; I must be the first one up. My phone shows that it's six. I rush to the bathroom to take a shower. I want to be at the courthouse on time.

I dress with care, choosing a simple black dress and heels. I dry my hair straight and then put curls on the ends with the curling iron. It's silly; I have naturally curly hair, but here I am curling it anyway.

I reach for the necklace that Maggie gave me and I put it on. I hurry out the door and go down the stairs. I see Mrs. Mosley in the kitchen when I enter. She is making coffee and is dressed in a red satin robe. Her hair is all tumbled.

"Good morning, Mrs. Mosley." I must have startled her, because she jumps.

"Good morning, Rebecca. You look lovely today." Mrs. Mosley smiles at me.

"I have business in town this morning," I respond, not wanting to say court.

"Yes, you're going to the probate court this morning. Judge Holcomb called us last night after you went to bed."

"Oh, what did he say?" I ask, stunned that someone called the Mosleys, but Judge Holcomb does know that I'm staying with them.

"Relax. Everyone is looking out for your best interests. I want you to know that I think you're a sweet young lady. Sometimes I may come across as harsh, but I don't mean it."

"Thank you, Mrs. Mosley. I'm thankful for everything you've done for me. You took me in when I was alone and desperate."

Mrs. Mosley smiles but doesn't respond.

"I'm hoping that Maggie can drop me off on her way to school," I say as I sit down on the barstool.

"Chuck will drop you off on his way to the office. Maggie has a test this morning, and I don't want her distracted. I'll be here when you finish so you can come back to the house," Mrs. Mosley says, taking a sip of her coffee.

"Okay. I'll remember that. I want to see the sheriff today to see if he has made any progress on the murder investigation," I say. Mrs. Mosley takes another sip of her coffee and closes her eyes as she enjoys the flavor. She could do a coffee commercial.

Then Mrs. Mosley reaches into the refrigerator and pulls out a bowl of fruit and a container of yogurt.

"Why don't you come around here and make four breakfast parfaits using the granola in this canister? While you're doing that, I'll toast a few bagels and get the orange juice."

"I love helping you in the kitchen." I jump from the stool and walk around the counter.

"Good morning, ladies," Mr. Mosley says as he enters the kitchen and grabs a cup of coffee before going to sit at the table.

"Breakfast is almost ready," Mrs. Mosley says.

I place the parfaits on the table and go back for the butter and jam that Mrs. Mosley placed on the counter.

"Good morning. I finished that paper last night and studied for my calculus test. I'm starving," Maggie says, sitting down at the table.

I take my seat, and so does Mrs. Mosley. We eat breakfast, and everyone is quiet, thinking about their day. My stomach is in knots, not knowing what to expect.

Why did Judge Holcomb call the Mosleys?

"Are you okay, Rebecca? You seem quiet this morning," Maggie says. When I don't answer, she adds, "Your hair looks amazing."

"Thanks, Maggie," I say, smiling at her. "May I be excused? I want to brush my teeth before I leave." I get up from the table.

"Take your time. I'm going to have another cup of coffee before I leave," Mr. Mosley says.

I hurry up the stairs, keeping my steps light so they don't make noise, and I want to know if there's a conversation when I'm gone. Stopping at the top, I listen, but the only sound is the scraping of utensils and the clank of a spoon in a mug.

I make quick work of brushing my teeth and straightening my bed.

Just as I grab my purse to head to the stairs, I see the top of Maggie's head as she comes up the stairs.

"Are you nervous?" she asks as she reaches the doorway.

I give her a weak smile. "I won't lie. Yes, I am. I don't know what to expect. I don't know if Amanda will be there, and what she'll say when she finds out they have the will she's been tearing the house apart to find."

Maggie puts her hand on my arm. "I wish I could go with you, but I have this test."

I reach to give her a quick hug. "Thanks, but I'll be fine. I have to learn to do things on my own now." The words hit like a thud; I'm on my own, alone, and responsible for my own decisions.

I hurry down the stairs, not wanting to be late.

"Oh good, I'm glad you're ready," Mr. Mosley says, standing at the bottom of the stairs.

"As ready as I'll ever be," I say, smiling back at him.

Why am I his responsibility?

"Then let's go," Mr. Mosley says, opening the front door, and we step out onto the porch.

"Rebecca, remember, I'll be here so you can come back when you're finished. Good luck," Mrs. Mosley says and closes the door.

The county courthouse is a large, stately building of a pink-looking stone with a large clock mounted at the top. It's two or three stories tall. I ascend the stone steps and enter the double glass doors. Once inside, I search for the probate court, but I can't find it. I walk up to a gentleman wearing a gray suit.

"Excuse me?" I ask. "I'm looking for the probate court. Do you happen to know where it is?"

"All of the courts are on the second floor." He points to the stairs in front of me, and I head over to them.

After ascending the stairs, I enter the door that says "Probate Court." An older woman with graying hair sits at the desk. Her hair is shoulder-length and turned under.

"Good morning," the woman says.

"I'm Rebecca Wilds. I'm supposed to see Judge Whipple."

"You weren't on the docket for today, so the schedule is off. We're still processing things, so we aren't ready for you. It just might take an hour. Please have a seat on the bench in the hallway, and I'll come and get you."

"Thank you. I'm sorry that I'm a disruption," I say, turning to go back into the hall.

"It's no problem, it's just that we aren't ready," the lady says.

I sit down on the bench. Things aren't ready; what is it they're doing? Connor comes up the stairs and enters the probate office. He didn't see me because I'm sitting past the door.

I'm surprised when Mrs. Higgins, the high school music teacher, comes out of the elevator and walks into the probate court door.

What's she doing here? I wonder. *Does she have a will that needs probated?*

Mrs. Higgins goes to our church, and Dad took me to her house for a piano lesson a few times.

I lean back on the bench admiring the ornate details of the old building. Dad taught me to appreciate the hard work of the skilled workers who built things long ago. Dad said they worked without the convenience of the tools we have today. All of the wood carvings in the building are beautiful, especially the stair rails. Dad had been good with his hands, and he'd liked making pieces of furniture. He would sand each piece and put hand-carved detailing on the front.

My stomach is churning, and I wish I had just skipped breakfast. I reach into my purse and pull out my cell phone. I want to call Blake, but he's in school. I wish I was at school too, and not waiting for the decision of my future. I toss the phone back into my purse and stand up to look for a bathroom.

I walk into the restroom and over to the sink. Standing in front of the mirror, my pale face shows the stress that my body is feeling. I wet a paper towel and hold it to my neck. I'm sick, weak, and can taste the acid in the back of my throat. I toss the paper towel in the trash and go back to the bench to wait.

Now the nausea is getting worse.

Maybe if I had something to drink . . .

I look around for a snack machine; there must be something here.

"Rebecca Wilds, we are ready for you now," the woman says, standing in the hallway.

I get up and approach her. "Ma'am, I think I'm going to be sick."

"Come with me," she says, leading me to her desk. She places her trash can next to a chair. "Sit down, and I'll get you a soda. It might help settle your stomach. I bet it's a bad case of nerves." She leaves and comes back with a soda. "Now, sip on this," she says. "They're waiting for you in his chambers and not the courtroom. That will at least take some of the pressure off."

I nod my head and take a few sips of soda. I want to hear what they have to say. Maybe as soon as this is over, I'll feel better. I stand with the drink in my hand and wait for her to point me in the right direction.

"Here, I'll go with you. If you think you're feeling worse, tell me, and I'll rush you to the bathroom. I think you'll find that this is painless," the lady says, patting me on the shoulder.

The lady being kind to me and patting my shoulder helps me to feel like I'm not entirely alone.

We enter the chambers. Sitting in chairs in front of the judge's desk are Connor and Mrs. Higgins. There is an empty chair between them, and I sit down, still holding the soda.

"Excuse the soda, but she's feeling a bit ill. It's probably a case of nerves," the lady says.

As I sit down, I let out a sigh of relief. I was afraid that Amanda would be here.

Judge Whipple is a tall, thin man in his fifties. He nods and says, "Let's get down to business. I'm Judge Whipple, and might I say that I don't have many cases like this one. Judge Holcomb and I have been discussing what might be best for everyone. Since you're a minor and Connor Gorman is an unattached male, we think it is not appropriate for you to live with him." Judge Whipple's intense eyes scan past each one of us for a comment, but everyone sits quietly.

The judge continues, "We have talked with Mrs. Higgins, and she has agreed for you to live with her. Mrs. Higgins lost her husband a few months ago and is living in that big two-story house alone." The judge pauses and waits—I guess to see if anyone comments.

Live with Mrs. Higgins? I thought I was going to move back to the farm and have my animals. This is not at all what I was expecting. I turn off my thoughts so that I can hear what the judge is telling us.

"Your parents left a trust account for you, but you can't touch the money until you're eighteen. Connor has agreed to pay Mrs. Higgins each month for your care. Both Connor and Mrs. Higgins will be your guardians. The Mosleys will take you to Dallas to check you out of school and get your things. At that time, you'll move in with Mrs. Higgins. Since you're a gifted singer and Mrs. Higgins is a music teacher, I thought the two of you might be a match. What do you have to say?"

Do I tell him the arrangement is fine, but not at all what I was expecting? I think. *Do I tell him I want to live at the farm?*

"I think it's wonderful. I love Mrs. Higgins," I say.

Wait a minute—they didn't mention Amanda.

I sit up in my chair and clear my throat. "What about my aunt, Amanda? Does she know about this? What's she going to do when I get my things from her apartment?" I grip the arms of the chair as all the things that have happened rush at me.

"What if she gets mad and won't let me leave?" I continue. "Or won't let me have my things? She's already trying to sell the farm. She sold the animals!" My voice rises at the end.

Mrs. Higgins puts her arm around me. She smells sweet, like honeysuckle blooms on a summer day. She whispers softly, "Rebecca, be calm, everything is going to work out."

"I'm aware of what she's tried to do. We, Mr. Gorman, and Mrs. Higgins, have an idea. Perhaps you might sell a few hundred acres. You would have plenty of money for your care and college." He leans forward and smiles at me as he speaks.

I take a deep breath and realize that I no longer feel sick.

"Very well, Mrs. Higgins, you can get back to class. We'll draw up all the papers, and you can pick them up after school," Judge Whipple says, and Mrs. Higgins leaves the chambers.

I sit back in my chair.

What's next?

"I don't know what the land is worth. I know we have seven hundred acres," I say, turning to Connor. "What do you think?"

Connor pats my hand, which is still clinging to the chair arm. "I agree with the judge. Even if you sell a hundred acres, there's plenty left. I'll continue to farm just as I have been. It'll be your father's legacy to you."

I nod. "I will agree to sell a hundred acres," I say. "It was over nine hundred acres. If Connor receives a hundred acres, and if I sell a hundred, I'll only have seven hundred acres left. I don't want to sell any more than that. Please don't sell the house."

"Very well; you will find that seven hundred acres are plenty. The money from the sale of the hundred acres will be used for your care until you reach eighteen. If there is any money left that will go for your college education. Now that Mrs. Higgins is not in the room, do you have any reservations regarding living with her?" The judge questions.

"No, your honor, I think it's a good arrangement." I swallow hard. I hardly know Mrs. Higgins, but any arrangement is better than where I am now.

"Very well, I appreciate your time and patience. You will remain with the Mosleys until they obtain your items, and they will deliver you to Mrs. Higgins. I understand the previous arrangement with your aunt is not working out." Judge Whipple frowns and waits for a response.

I nod; my throat isn't working right now.

"Very well, you can go. Mr. Gorman, if you will wait a few minutes, we'll have your paperwork ready," the judge says to Connor as I head towards the door to his office. "Rebecca," he calls, "if you need anything, you know how to reach me. I'm only a phone call away."

"Thank you, Connor. I'm going over to the sheriff's office to see if there's anything new on the case," I reply.

I step out of the judge's office.

"Are you feeling better?" the secretary asks.

"I'm feeling much better. The soda helped. Thank you for giving it to me. You've been very kind," I say, and then I leave her office.

I'm relieved as I walk down the stairs and out of the courthouse. I'm so excited that I don't have to live with Amanda that I want to hop down those stairs, but the dress and heels won't allow it. I'm sad that I won't be seeing Blake or attending school with him.

I'm confident that I've taken care of business. With my shoulders back, I cross the street and walk to the building with the sign that reads "County Sheriff's Office."

"Good morning, Lucille," I say as I enter and stand in front of her desk. "I'm here to speak with the sheriff. Is he in?"

"Well, good morning, Rebecca. Yes, the sheriff's in his office. Go right on in. I'm sure he'll be happy to see you," Lucille says.

I enter the sheriff's office, and he's going through a mound of papers on his desk.

"Good morning, Sheriff. I would like to talk to you about my parents' case. Do you have a few minutes?" I ask before sitting down.

"Rebecca, come on in and have a seat. How are you doing?" the sheriff asks.

"Do you know who killed my parents?" I ask, plopping down in the chair across from his desk.

"You sure get down to business fast. No, I don't, but I'm working on it. I thought you were in Dallas?"

"I was. A lot has happened. I found my parents' will. I just left the probate court, where Judge Whipple arranged for me to live with Mrs. Higgins—you know, the music teacher at the high school."

He nods; his expression shows he's interested.

"Now she and Connor Gorman are in charge of me," I add.

"Good people," He says, and it makes me feel better.

"I was wondering . . ." I pause, trying to put my question into the right words. "Did my aunt call you about this case?"

The sheriff frowns for a moment, then his expression clears, but he is still serious. "No, I haven't talked to her since the funeral. Why do you ask?" he says, leaning forward in his chair and putting his elbows on the desk.

I grip the chair arms for reassurance, lean forward, and almost whisper, "Did she tell you my dad was a famous singer? That his name was Jackson Nash, and there are a lot of people who are angry because he left the music industry?"

The sheriff's eyes widen at my question. "Your father was Jackson Nash? I had no idea. He was—and is—still my favorite singer. I wondered what happened to him." The sheriff frowns. "He changed his looks—his hair, and beard. I guess we don't look closely at people anymore." He shakes his head in disbelief. "I should have known this."

"Don't feel bad, I just found out who he was myself, and he was my own father." I forced my fingers to relax their grip on my purse. Then I continue, "When you told me that you haven't talked to my aunt, it surprises me. She told me she was going to talk to you. She was supposed to tell you about the man who broke into her apartment. He was caught. By any chance, do you recognize the names Gene Maxwell and Connor Gorman?"

"Yes, both of them. Connor—he's a good guy. I can't believe he did anything wrong, but that Gene Maxwell is a convict. I've arrested him before, and he has been to prison. From what I understand, he's about to go back. You think he might have killed your parents?" the sheriff says.

"I don't know. I'm just confused. I don't know who I can trust," I reply, leaning back in the chair.

"From what I know, Connor is a good guy. But we arrest good guys all the time for doing bad stuff."

"Sheriff, Connor has been back for six months. He's supposed to be a close friend of the family, but since he's returned, I haven't seen him until now. Why would he come back and not contact my family? Someone came to the house that night. I don't know who it was, but could it have been Connor? These are just questions I have. I don't know anything. Do you know anyone who drives a black van?"

"A black van . . . I can't say that I do. Why?" The sheriff studies me. "You know more than you think you know—for example, Connor's return. Why was he arrested in Dallas? All these are questions I need to get answers to." The sheriff writes something down on a sheet of paper.

"How's Bruiser?" I ask.

"He's doing great. He's riding with Officer Clark today and likes being in law enforcement. He's making a good detective. I think he might be in love. He's been visiting my neighbor's lab—a female."

"I'm happy for Bruiser," I say. "Anyway, I should be going. Since I'll be living here again, I'll be dropping by to check on the case. Please find the killer." I stand and walk to the office door.

"I'm still working on it. Thanks for the information."

"Goodbye, Sheriff." I leave his office. I walk through the outer office and out onto the street. I walk down the sidewalk, and all I can think about is what the sheriff said.

"I know more than I think I know." What exactly does that mean?

Chapter 21

I walk down the sidewalk on my way to the Mosleys. I need time to process everything that's happened. Most of all, I want to think about what I know.

Is there anything I know that might be valuable to the case?

I want to go through the box from the farm. I want to see what's in the bundles of letters.

As I walk, shooting pain in my big toe gains all of my attention. My shoe is rubbing, and with each step, the problem worsens. I must have a blister. Why did I decide to wear heels today? I knew before I left that I'd be walking back to the house. The walk is less than a mile, but I'm in heels. By the time I reach the Mosleys, I'm limping. I enter the front door.

"Mrs. Mosley, its Rebecca. I'm back."

"Rebecca, what's wrong? Why are you limping?" Mrs. Mosley asks, coming to me.

"It's my fault. I wanted to look nice, and so I wore heels." I step out of my shoes and bend down to pick them up.

"Go upstairs and change. I've prepared a little lunch for us," Mrs. Mosley says.

"Thank you. I'll be right back." I rush up the stairs.

I change into a pair of jeans, and not wanting to keep Mrs. Mosley waiting, I rush back down the stairs and into the kitchen.

"I made you a glass of iced tea. I thought you might be thirsty after the walk," Mrs. Mosley says. I wonder why Mrs. Mosley hadn't come to court, and why she hadn't offered to pick me up. She seems so concerned and caring now, so why didn't she come?

"Thank you. Can I help with something?" I ask.

"No, have a seat at the table. We're having a salad and tuna sandwiches. I'll bring them to the table," Mrs. Mosley says.

"I was so nervous this morning and thought I was going to be sick," I say without thinking. Why am I sharing my thoughts with Mrs. Mosley? I'm not sure she cares, but I'm glad she's kind now.

"I'm sorry that you're facing such major changes in your life. No child should ever have to go through the things you've gone through." She places our salads and sandwiches on the table.

I smile at her as she sits down across from me.

"Let's say grace. Lord, thank you for watching over Rebecca and being with her in court today. Thank you for this food. Amen." Mrs. Mosley reaches for her sandwich.

"Did you know before I went to court that I wasn't going to have to live with Amanda?" I ask, taking a bite of my salad.

"I knew that you probably wouldn't be living with her, but the rest was up in the air, so I didn't want to raise your hopes. I understand you'll be staying with Mrs. Higgins," Mrs. Mosley responds.

"Yes, she seems nice. I do feel odd going to live with a stranger."

"You know her from church, and weren't you in her choir?" Mrs. Mosley asks, patting my arm.

"I was supposed to be in choir with her this year, but my parents died before school started. I've seen her at church, but I never talked to her. I did take a few piano lessons from her." I continue to talk, "I heard you last night. I wasn't snooping. I was lying awake, and I heard you and Mr. Mosley arguing about me. Why is he responsible for me, and you're not? Why does he feel a sense of responsibility?"

Mrs. Mosley chokes on her bite of salad and starts coughing. My timing might not have been the best.

Mrs. Mosley wipes her mouth with her napkin and looks at me with wide eyes. "Oh dear, you weren't supposed to hear that. I'm so sorry you heard us arguing."

"I wasn't snooping—I just heard it. What does it mean?" I stare at her for an answer.

Mrs. Mosley looks down at her sandwich for a long time. For a minute I think she isn't going to answer.

"Well, sometimes I think I'm too harsh with you, but it isn't you. It's the situation." Mrs. Mosley seems a bit hesitant to go on.

What does she mean "it's the situation?" Does she not want me here?

Mrs. Mosley looks sad as she speaks. "When Maggie was less than a year old, I tried to have another child, and I lost it."

"Oh, I didn't know. I'm sorry." I reach for her hand, but she moves it away. She looks like she's in a trance, maybe reliving the time.

"Not only did I lose the child, but I had a hysterectomy. I went into a deep depression. Amanda was attending the college where Chuck was a professor. All of us—your parents, and Amanda—went to church together. Amanda started flirting with Chuck at the college. She then she was doing more than flirting. In the beginning, he resisted her, but eventually, he gave in after her continual attempts. He and Amanda had an affair, and Amanda got pregnant. Amanda was living on the farm with your parents at the time. When your parents found out she was pregnant, they went to the college to complain about Chuck having an affair with a student. He lost his job and his teaching credentials. Amanda was wild and completely out of control. I don't think your parents saw just how bad she was. She went away and had the baby."

"What happened to the baby?"

Margaret looks down at her hands, and then up at me with pity. "Bruce and Carol adopted the baby and sent Amanda to a college out of state."

"Hold it! Bruce and Carol adopted it . . . Am I the baby? I'm adopted?" I say, turning to look her straight in the eye. I'm so stunned that my eyes are probably as big as baseballs.

There's a long silence, and there's pain in her eyes. "Yes, you're adopted. Your biological parents are Chuck and Amanda."

"Chuck and Amanda are my parents? That's why Mr. Mosley said he was responsible for me, and you aren't." I'm stunned. I grab the edge of the table to steady myself. I grab my chest to stop the pounding of my heart.

"Sometimes when I'm with you, I don't see you, but the situation. You're a product of my husband having an affair. You're also my daughter's half-sister."

"Wow! That's a lot to take in. Amanda is my real mother?" *That evil woman is my mother?* "My parents were my aunt and uncle?" My head is spinning. "So, Maggie is my half-*sister*. Bruce and Carol were not my birth parents."

"That's correct. Carol wanted you more than anything in this world. She couldn't have children, and you were her last hope. No one here in town knows because Amanda had the baby in California. Your mother went to California with her and stayed until you were born."

"And Mr. Mosley, how did he feel about the arrangement?" I ask. *Did he want to keep me?*

Margaret sighs and says, "You would have to ask him. I see him looking at you sometimes. I watched him when you were singing your solo. He couldn't keep the grin off his face."

"Where did I get the red hair?" I ask. I've always wondered about my red hair and blue eyes. No one in the family had my color of hair.

"Chuck's family—his grandmother had beautiful curly red hair. There are some pictures of her hanging in his study. His grandmother was also an accomplished pianist and singer. So that's where you get your musical talent. Unfortunately, Maggie didn't inherit that musical talent." Mrs. Mosley smiles at me.

"I don't know what to say. I'm more confused now than ever. The people I loved most in the world were not even my parents. Amanda certainly doesn't know how to love a child. Does Maggie know that we're half-sisters?" I turn to Mrs. Mosley with wide eyes.

"Maggie doesn't know any of this. I prefer to keep it that way. She thinks her dad hung the moon. I don't want her to know he had an affair. She's drawn to you. When they first brought you to church, I couldn't keep Maggie away from you. She's always loved you."

I smile at Mrs. Mosley. "That's why you wanted me to come back here today. You wanted to tell me. I'm glad you did, but it only raises more questions for me."

"Why would it raise more questions?" Mrs. Mosley stands and takes our plates over to the sink.

"Why did Amanda take me after my parents died? She didn't want me then, and she doesn't want me now," I say, getting up from the table and following her.

"I think Amanda thought she had a chance at being a mother. I think she wanted someone or something to love her. But Amanda isn't capable of feelings," Mrs. Mosley replies.

"So, you do see her true colors," I respond, pouring another glass of tea.

"I certainly do."

"Tell me, why did they ask for you and Mr. Mosley to take me to Dallas if they don't know that he's my father?" I ask, taking a sip of tea and watching Mrs. Mosley pour herself another glass.

"They ask us to take you to Dallas because you're staying with us. No one knows that you were adopted. No one knows that my husband feels responsible. I prefer to keep it that way."

"Thank you for telling me. Maybe I would be better off not knowing any of this, but I'm glad I have a sister," I say.

"Rebecca, things are hard, and I want you to know that you can come to us if you ever need anything. You're not my child, but you're Maggie's sister." Mrs. Mosley smiles at me.

"Thank you for everything you've done, and thank you for telling me. I now hate Amanda more than ever. Does she know that I'm moving out?" I ask, leaning against the kitchen counter.

"She knows nothing. She hasn't even called to check on you since Maggie picked you up. She has no parental skills whatsoever," Mrs. Mosley says.

My thoughts are spiraling. *So did Mr. Mosley want me? Did he ask Margaret to take me?* Then I realize something. *While Mrs. Mosley is talking freely, I need to see if he could have been in the barn.*

"When did Mr. Mosley leave to go on that fishing trip?" I ask.

"He left the day before your parents were killed. He knew nothing about it until he returned home almost a week later," Mrs. Mosley says.

"So, he didn't ask you to pick me up at the sheriff's office?"

"No—Lucille called me and told me about your parents being killed and asked if we would let you stay here for a few days."

"Well, thank you for saying yes," I say, blinking to hold back my tears.

Mrs. Mosley's arms wrap around me, and she pulls me into her warm lean body.

"My heart goes out to you. You've not had it easy since your parents died. Now you hear that the ones you loved most are not who you thought they were."

"Thank you, Mrs. Mosley. I think I'm going to need a friend. I often feel all alone. If it weren't for you and Maggie, I think I would give up."

I feel her cheek next to mine. I can't seem to stop the tears.

"It's okay to cry. I'm here, and you'll be my daughter, just like Maggie. It'll be between the two of us. And please, call me Margaret. I think we can drop the formality. If anyone asks, we'll tell them you're almost like family for us." She backs away and holds my shoulders. She looks at me smiles.

"Thank you, Margaret. If you don't mind, I think I'm going upstairs to rest. This day has been more than I anticipated. My head is still spinning from all the information," I say, walking out of the kitchen.

"I'll wake you for dinner. By the way, we're leaving early tomorrow for Dallas. We want to be at the school when school starts. We'll check you out of school and then go to the apartment to get your things. We want to be in and out of there quickly with no chance of seeing Amanda."

"That sounds good. I do have a friend that I'd like to say goodbye to," I say, still walking to the stairs.

"We'll try to get there early enough for you to see them before class starts," Mrs. Mosley says.

"That would be wonderful. I'm going to try to take a nap."

I walk upstairs, lie down on the bed, and close my eyes—not to go to sleep, but to think. My mind replays Margaret's words. *Her husband had an affair with Amanda, and I'm the result?* A feeling begins to creep into my body and overtakes my brain. *Who am I? I don't belong anywhere.* Tears creep from the corners of my eyes, and I don't even try to stop them.

Chapter 22

I'm intrigued by the bundle of letters in the box I retrieved from the farm. I pull a stack that's tied with a dark ribbon and set it on the edge of the bed. Untying the navy-blue grosgrain ribbon, I wonder why these letters have been kept safe. The first envelope has a return address, and it's from Amanda in California. All of them are from Amanda. I go to the oldest and work my way to the present.

In the first letter, Amanda is asking—almost demanding—money. She writes, "After all I've given you, the least you can do is send me money when I ask."

What does she mean, "after all she's given them?" Could she be talking about me? Is Amanda blackmailing Bruce and Carol because they adopted me? I reach for another letter. It reads:

> *Carol, I still haven't received any money from you. If you want to keep Rebecca, you better send it soon. I'm sure that an attorney could help me reclaim the child that is rightfully mine.*

By the time I read the last message, I have a good understanding of why my parents had little to do with her. She continually made demands.

I tie the ribbon around the stack of letters and toss them back into the box. I'm tired, and I have other concerns on my mind. *What will happen when we go to Dallas? Will Amanda be at the apartment? Will I be able to see Blake? Will I be able to tell him how much he means to me? Will I ever see him again?*

My parents always told me that they loved each other so much that their love produced me. It was a sweet thought, but I'm not sure of who I am now. A small part of me is angry that they lied.

Maggie opens the bedroom door and walks over to the bed. "Hey girl," she says, "how did it go today?"

"Well, I don't have to go and live with Amanda."

Maggie sits down next to me. "That's a relief."

"I'm staying here. I'll be living with Mrs. Higgins. Your parents are taking me tomorrow to get my things," I say. My heart swells with pride; I'm looking into the eyes of my sister.

Maggie's mouth drops open. "Mrs. Higgins? Why are you going to live with her? I don't see the connection."

"I guess they couldn't find anyone else to take me. I can't stay with Connor because he's an unattached male."

Maggie shrugs and laughs, "I know the will named him as the person to care for you, but did you want to live with him?"

"Not really, but I had this fantasy in my head that I'd be able to live on the farm, and things would go back to normal. But for me, there'll never be normal. What my parents and I had was magical, and you only get that once in life," I say.

"Not to change the subject," Maggie starts, "but Clay wants to know if you'll go on a double date with Tyler and me on Friday night. There is a dance after the football game. It's homecoming!"

"Do you think Mrs. Higgins will let me go?" I say. I don't know what my life will be like living with this older woman. She's not old—probably in her early sixties.

"Well, let's hope so. I'll let Clay know that you'll go if you get permission. You'll need a nice dress for the dance. I think I have one that you can wear," Maggie says.

"I need you to know that I like Clay, but I'm not into him. I still like Blake."

There's a tap on the door.

"I hate to disturb you girls, but dinner's ready. Come down and eat before the food gets cold," Mrs. Mosley says and smiles.

"We'll be right there. Thank you, Margaret," I say, and we smile at each other.

"Whoa, what's this, Margaret stuff?" Maggie asks me.

I shrug, not wanting to explain the afternoon that I had shared with her mother. "She told me to call her Margaret. I guess she's tired of being called Mrs. Mosley."

"Yes, I've heard her tell people that Mrs. Mosley is Dad's mother."

It's early when Margaret taps on the bedroom door and tells me to get up and get ready. I rush to the shower; I need to look my best when I see Blake. I'll text him on the way and tell him I want to see him. I should have called him last night, but I wasn't sure how much information to give him.

Maggie comes down to the front door to tell us goodbye. She has another test today. We each have a brown paper sack with our breakfast inside. The Mosleys each have a thermos of coffee, and I have a small bottle of orange juice. I quickly eat my muffin and sip on the orange juice before grabbing a bottle of water.

"We should be at the school by eight. Classes don't start until eight thirty, so that should give you time to see your friend," Margaret says.

"That's assuming that we make good time," Mr. Mosley adds, looking at Margaret.

Did Margaret tell him that I know? Would he act any differently if he knew that I know he's my father? What would it be like to have him for a dad? I pause. *That's funny—he* is *my dad. Had I lived with him instead of Bruce and Carol, would my life be different?*

I reach for my phone and text Blake.

Blake, I'm on my way to Dallas. I'm withdrawing from school. I'm moving back home. I'll explain later. I would love to see you. Can you meet me at the front door? I should be there around eight.

I put my phone back in my purse. Blake may be angry that I haven't called him. He knows nothing about my situation, and he never asked. Blake took me at face value. He protected me and bought me things, and somehow I want him to remain a part of my life.

"Chuck, did your key chain break?" Margaret asks. My interest is piqued.

"Yes, it broke. I'm not sure when or where I lost it," Mr. Mosley replies.

"Maggie bought that for you, and you loved it. I'll see if I can find you a new one that's just like it. I think I saw one at Tatum's Jewelers just last week," Margaret says.

I lean forward and look out the windshield. "What does it look like?" *I'm curious—could the dollar sign I found be from Mr. Mosley's key chain? I don't think he was ever at the farm . . .*

Mrs. Mosley says, "It was a big gold dollar sign."

Not wanting them to see my expression, I turn to look out the window and say quickly, "That's nice." *Maybe other people have the same key chain*, I rationalize. M*argaret said he'd left for the fishing trip before they died. But what if he was actually there?*

There is a something I'm missing here, like a missing puzzle piece.

"Rebecca, you're quiet," Margaret says.

"I'm fine—just wondering if I'll get to see my friend and if we can get my things without running into Amanda," I say.

The rest of the trip is quiet. We're on the major interstate, and traffic is getting heavier as we near Dallas. I stare at the passing landscape and see that familiar buildings are getting close. I feel the excitement building as we turn the corner and into the school's parking lot. A glance at the dash tells me its seven forty. I've got time before school to find Blake.

"We'll go into the school office and get the papers sorted. You can go see your friends," Margaret says as we enter the building.

I scan the faces of the kids standing around and soon see that familiar smile: Blake. He walks toward me with a slow, even pace. He's smiling, but his eyes look sad.

"Rebecca, I've been worried about you. Are you okay? Are those people with you your parents?"

"No. They're friends," I reply. "How are you, Blake? I'm sorry I didn't call. So much was going on, I couldn't talk."

"It's okay. Are you going to live with that couple or stay here at the apartment?"

"I'm leaving school." I choke down a sob and feel a heavy sadness. I was just starting to make friends. "I was living with my aunt, but things didn't work out. I'm moving back to my home school and living with one of the teachers."

"I remember you said your parents died."

"I guess I did mention that. I hope you'll still talk to me," I say, swallowing hard. I look into his eyes, and my body warms. I get all jittery and excited when I'm near him.

"Still talk to you—you're joking, right? You know I like you. I'm not giving up on you," Blake says, looking distressed.

Blake had protected me and welcomed me when I was alone. Now I'm leaving him behind. I feel like I need him and his strong confidence and quiet nature.

Mr. Mosley walks over to us. "We need your books, Rebecca."

"They're all here in my backpack." I take off my backpack and hand it to him.

Chuck eyes Blake before returning to the office.

"Rebecca, I'm going to miss you. There's so much I want to say," Blake says.

"Blake, I need you in my life. Please don't give up on me. Call me so we can talk," I tell him, throwing my arms around him and hugging him.

"Becca, this doesn't seem right," Blake says. "I don't understand."

"Please, Blake, call me," I say, and then I follow the Mosleys out of the building.

I slide into the back seat of the car, and the bell rings. Blake is now in class. *Will he keep his promise and call me?* I wonder.

Tears fill my eyes. I don't want to lose him; I've already lost so much.

At the apartments we grab empty boxes out of the back of the car. We take the elevator to the eighth floor. My hands tremble as I place the key into the lock. Shaking, I turn the knob and ease the door open. I'm terrified that Amanda will be waiting inside. I turn off the alarm; the alarm was armed, so I know that Amanda isn't here. We go straight to my room and start gathering my things.

"I'm scared to be here. I'm afraid Amanda will appear at any minute. If she sees us, she'll go wild," I say, taking things out of the drawers.

Margaret gives me a reassuring smile. "It'll be fine. Amanda's out of town, remember."

"That's what she says, but is it the truth?" I ask, unplugging the computer.

"It does feel cold and strange here." Mr. Mosley grabs the computer and sets it aside.

"So, you feel it too," I say, grabbing the last of my shoes and throwing them in a box.

"You have a lot of clothes. I'm glad you have some nice things," Margaret says.

"Amanda bought them," I reply.

Margaret smiles,"Well, at least she did one thing right. She's good with a credit card."

There are footsteps outside in the hallway and we look at each other. Our eyes reflect the panic. We each let out the breath we were holding when the sound of the steps disappears down the hall.

"Let's grab these boxes and get out of here before we hear footsteps again," Mr. Mosley says, grabbing a load of boxes.

We grab the boxes and leave the apartment. I slam the door and don't even bother to set the alarm. I have no desire to look back. I'm glad that evil place is no longer a part of my life.

Now I have to find out if Mr. Mosley killed my parents.

Chapter 23

I sink into the seat surrounded by the boxes of my belongings and close my eyes, settling myself in for the long drive ahead of us.

Will they take me to Mrs. Higgins, or will I spend the night with the Mosleys? How did the sheriff miss the key chain on the ground when they searched the barn—didn't they take enough care? What kind of detectives are they? These thoughts bring the heat of anger to my face. *Am I the only one who cares about finding the truth about what happened to my parents?*

The sound of the car door shutting startles me. I stare outside. We've stopped at a gas station.

"We should be home in less than an hour," Margaret says, turning to me. "Your friend seemed nice. Do you think you'll see him again?"

"I certainly hope so. Blake's been so kind and considerate. He helped me hold myself together when I was falling apart." My voice cracks. I clear it and swallow. The lump in my throat slowly moves back down.

Margaret looks startled. "What do you mean, when you were falling apart? Does he know about your parents?"

"No, I was afraid for his safety after the break-in. I thought if he didn't know anything, he would be safer."

Mr. Mosley gets back into the car. "We're almost home, and I'm getting hungry. That muffin we had for breakfast just wasn't enough to hold me until lunch," he says.

"Are you hinting that I prepare lunch when we get home?" Margaret snaps. She turns to glare at Mr. Mosley.

"No, I'm suggesting that we stop for pizza!" Mr. Mosley shouts, shooting a stern look back at Margaret.

"Rebecca, would you like some pizza?" Margaret asks, rolling her eyes and turning to look at me. There is clearly a lot of tension between them.

"I think that would be nice," I say.

There are still problems between the Mosleys. Not only is there tension, but Chuck shows Margaret no gentleness or compassion.

Was Mr. Mosley shocked when he returned from his fishing trip to find that I had been staying at his house? Does he care that his two daughters seem to get along nicely? Would Maggie be resentful if she knew the truth?

I spend the afternoon going through the boxes from the apartment and repacking them. When things don't fit the way I want, I take everything out and repack them. Frustrated, I leave them alone and wander downstairs to wait for Maggie.

Margaret is in the den with a book on her lap. She isn't reading, but she wipes her eyes with a tissue. She's been crying.

Making my last steps louder on the stairs, she turns and gives me a weak smile.

"Do you need something, honey?" Margaret sits up and places her book on the table next to the chair.

"I was just going to ask if I could help you prepare dinner," I say.

"That would be lovely. Let's go to the kitchen," Margaret says, getting out of the chair and leading that way. I want to ask her if she's upset, but I'm afraid she'll think I'm prying.

Is my being here causing problems for her?

"I didn't realize it was late, and this roast will take a while to cook. I wanted to cook it in the oven, but I waited too long. I'll get out the Instapot and cook it in that. Will you get two potatoes, onion, and three carrots?" Margaret asks as she pulls the roast out of the refrigerator.

The doorbell rings, and Margaret and I look at each other.

"I wonder if that's Amanda," Margaret says. "I thought she would be much later."

"I don't know." My eyes grow big.

Margaret presses the button on the intercom. "Hello?" Margaret says.

"I'm here to pick up Rebecca," Amanda answers.

Margaret startles me when she responds with a stern voice, "She isn't going with you! The courts have removed her from your care."

"Oh no, she's coming with me," Amanda replies.

Margaret frowns and raises her voice. "As I said, the courts have removed her from your care."

Amanda pounds on the door and yells, "Open the door—*now*! I'm picking her up!"

Margaret shouts back into the intercom, "I'm not opening the door. You need to leave because Rebecca is going nowhere with you."

Margaret frowns and her eyes look big. I'm trembling, and I see that her hands are shaking. Worry lines form on her forehead. She turns off the intercom and stands quietly, waiting to see what happens. I hand her the potatoes, onion, and carrots.

"Wash the vegetables good and then cut them to put around the roast," Margaret says as she opens the Instapot.

I wash the vegetables with shaking hands. Amanda was mean, and I know she won't give up that easily.

We put the roast and vegetables into the Instapot and turn it on. There a shuffling noise coming from the den, and we peek around the corner. Amanda is standing at the terrace doors.

"Quick, go upstairs and into your bathroom and lock the door. Don't come out no matter what. Now hurry, and go around the other way so she won't see you," Margaret says, and she spins around and grabs for the phone as I exit the room.

I rush down the hall and up the stairs. *What will Amanda do next? So it's about money. I'm not even sure there is any money. The judge said there is a trust account that I can't touch until I'm eighteen . . .*

At the top of the stairs, I stop for a moment to listen. Mrs. Mosley is calling the police and whispering.

Just as I turn, the sound of breaking glass and footsteps hurry my feet into the bedroom. In the bathroom, I lock the door. I sit on the cold tile floor and wrap my arms around my legs, pulling my knees up under my chin. Fear creeps through me. I begin to rock back and forth when I hear a crashing sound downstairs, and the security alarm goes off. What about Margaret? Will Amanda hurt her?

I sit, straining to listen for any sounds. The shrill of the alarm is so loud that I cover my ears. Did Margaret call the police? Where is Mr. Mosley?

The alarm is still going off. I'm unable to hear anything else. I wring my hands as I sit and wait. The waiting seems like an eternity. Maggie should be home soon. What will happen to her? "Please, Lord, protect them," I whisper.

I look around in the bathroom for something that I can use for protection. I need to be ready in case Amanda breaks down the door.

I search for anything that will scare Amanda away from me. I reach for a can of deodorant; I can at least spray the deodorant in her face and maybe blind her for a few minutes. I plug in the curling iron so that it will get hot, and then I wait.

My mind is racing, and I have visions of Amanda hurting Margaret and maybe even Maggie as she arrives home from school.

Where's the sheriff? Didn't Margaret call him?

I wait and wish that I had grabbed my phone. Margaret had told me not to leave the bathroom, no matter what.

How long do I wait? Is Margaret hurt, and does she need me? Should I go and help her?

I wring my hands and keep pacing back and forth.

Suddenly, everything is quiet. The alarm is no longer sounding. *Is someone here? Is the sheriff here? Is it safe for me to come out?*

I wait and lean against the door, hoping to hear something—anything.

There are shuffling sounds outside the bathroom door. If it were Margaret, she would say something.

My hands tremble, and I can hardly hold the can in my hands. I wait with my ear plastered to the door and listen for any clue. I hear a shuffling sound. What can it be?

There's a knock on the door.

"I'll break the door down if I have to, but you're coming with me," Amanda shouts through the door.

Margaret told me not to open the door no matter what, so I stand ready. If Amanda breaks through the door, maybe she will be stunned from the jolt and I can escape.

Amanda hits the door, and I step back away from it. The door withstands the force. I hold the can of deodorant and get ready. I brace myself for what is about to come.

A force hits the bathroom door, and the door shakes but holds firm. I stand ready. The door is slammed again, and this time the door springs open, and Amanda falls inside. I reach down and spray a load of deodorant in her face. Then I quickly grab the hot curling iron and start hitting her with it. She has a butcher knife and is swinging it in all directions.

"Stop it! You're coming with me!" Amanda shouts, feeling around to grab me. Her eyes are closed and watering. Every time she reaches out for me, I burn her with the curling iron. I manage to get between her and the door. I spray her face one last time before letting go of the curling iron. I run out of the bathroom and through the bedroom into the hall and down the stairs. I reach the bottom of the stairs and rush to the front door. I grab the doorknob, and a groaning sound comes from the top of the stairs. I turn to look; Amanda is feeling her way for the stairs. Her face is red and swollen. I fling the door open and rush out onto the front lawn. I'm screaming as I run.

I stumble and take off down the street, screaming for help. I keep my eyes straight ahead, afraid to look back.

Where is Margaret? What has Amanda done to Margaret?

I need to get help.

I continue to scream and run toward town. I rush across the street and make it around the corner. I continue to cry, and a bright red pickup truck stops at the curb.

"Miss, can I help you?" A man in his fifties leans toward the passenger window.

"I need the sheriff. I've been attacked, and so has Mrs. Mosley!" I shout. I'm shaking, and my knees are knocking. *Where is Amanda—did she follow me?*

The man says, "Get in, and I'll take you to the sheriff."

Without thinking, I jump into the truck. I need to get help for Margaret. Where is Margaret, and who turned off the alarm? I'm shaking and sobbing. For all I know, Margaret could be dead.

We drive to the sheriff's office, and the man goes inside with me.

Just inside the door, I start shouting, "I need the sheriff! Quick, where's the sheriff?"

"Hold on, child, what's the matter?" Lucille shouts.

"Amanda broke into the Mosleys' house. I think she hurt Margaret," I say.

"I've already dispatched the sheriff to the Mosleys. Carl, can you go to the Mosleys? Lucille says, looking at the driver of the truck.

"I'm going with him." I say following him out the door. I didn't realize that Carl is a deputy but off duty.

I get back into the truck. Carl looks over at me.

"This Amanda, is she armed?" Carl asks, reaching into his glove compartment. He pulls out a pistol and lays it on the seat.

"I don't know. Amanda was swinging a butcher knife. I managed to get away from her by spraying deodorant in her face," I say, worried about Margaret. "I burned her with a curling iron and got out of the house. Someone turned off the alarm."

"The company monitoring the security system might have reset the alarm. If they did, they should have dispatched the sheriff," Carl says.

We arrive back at the Mosleys' house, and the sheriff pulls into the driveway. I start getting out of the truck.

"Rebecca, you need to wait in the truck," Carl shouts.

The sheriff gets out of his truck approaches us. "What's going on?" he asks.

"It's Amanda, and she's gone wild. She broke into the Mosleys' house, and I think she might have hurt Margaret," I say, getting back into the truck.

"Where is Amanda?" the sheriff asks.

"She was on the stairs when I left. Her face and eyes are swollen shut," I say, slamming the truck door. Sitting back, I watch as the sheriff approaches the house.

The sheriff goes inside, and Carl waits outside the door. I turn and see that Amanda is sitting in her car that's parked at the curb. I jump out of the truck and yell at Carl, pointing to Amanda's car.

"Carl, that's her sitting in her car. You have to stop her—don't let her leave!" I yell.

"Hey, Sheriff, she's out here," Carl shouts into the house.

"I need an ambulance at the Mosleys, stat," the sheriff says into his phone as he exits the house. The sheriff and Carl rush to the driveway. Amanda has started the engine, and they are squatting behind Mrs. Mosley's car in case she's armed. I'm still standing near Carl's truck, but out of Amanda's range of vision.

"Get out of the car with your hands up!" the sheriff shouts.

Carl creeps around to the passenger side of Amanda's car. The sheriff distracts her, and Carl runs around to her side of the vehicle. She opens her car door, and Carl grabs her from behind.

"I've got her, Sheriff," Carl shouts.

The sheriff handcuffs Amanda and places her in the back seat of the squad car. Then he walks over to me.

"Want to tell me what happened here?" the sheriff asks, frowning.

"Amanda came to pick me up, and Mrs. Mosley told her I wasn't going with her. Mrs. Mosley sent me upstairs to hide in the bathroom. I was in the bathroom for a long time with the alarm blaring. Then Amanda came upstairs and broke in the door. I sprayed her face with deodorant and burned her with a hot curling iron. I managed to get away from her and went for help. Where is Mrs. Mosley?" I say, spinning around to go back and look for her. The sheriff grabs me by the arm and pulls me back.

"Don't go in there—it's a crime scene. Margaret must have fought to protect you." The sheriff pushes me back as the paramedics bring Mrs. Mosley out on a stretcher.

"I know you want to go to the hospital, so ride in the ambulance," the sheriff says.

"Someone needs to call Mr. Mosley and tell him to meet us at the hospital," I say, and then I wait as they load Margaret into the back of the ambulance.

"It's a good thing you ran for help, or else Mrs. Mosley might not still be alive," the sheriff says.

"You need to sit over there and buckle up; it's a bumpy ride," the paramedic says to me as the door slams shut and siren blasts.

Chapter 24

The waiting room for the Emergency department is a large white-tiled room. One wall is windows and has a large glass sliding door. I'm sitting and waiting to hear about Margaret. I'm not allowed to be with her because I'm not family. If I had my phone with me, I'd call Maggie. Maggie would want to be here.

Did the sheriff not contact Mr. Mosley because he isn't here? I wonder. *Why didn't he come?*

I pace the floor of the waiting room. The television hanging above me is on a game show that I'd never watch, so there is nothing to do but pace and wait.

My shoulder is hurting. It stings and burns. I try to adjust my shoulder; perhaps I pulled a muscle while fighting with Amanda. There's blood all over the front of my shirt, and even on my shoulder.

Is this blood from Margaret? I didn't get close to Margaret it can't be from her, I'm bleeding!

I need to call Maggie.

The sliding doors open, and Maggie comes in with a startled look.

Maggie approaches me. "Rebecca," she says, "what's going on? What's happened? The police are at the house, and they told me that my mother is at the hospital. I came straight here."

"Maggie, I'm sorry. Amanda came to pick me up. Your mother told her that I wasn't going with her. Then she sent me upstairs to the bathroom, and Amanda broke into the house," I say without catching my breath.

Maggie looks around and then crosses her arms. "Did Amanda hurt her?"

I stand in front of Maggie. This is all my fault. "Yes, she's with the doctors now. They won't tell me anything because I'm not family."

"Well, I'm family, and I'm going to find out something," Maggie says, and then she turns and walks to the nurses' station.

I stand back, and the nurse nods her head and allows Maggie to step inside the locked doors. I sit down and wait near the entrance for Maggie to return.

I wait for what seems like hours, and finally Maggie comes out to where I'm sitting. She's been crying and is still wiping tears from her eyes.

"Rebecca, she's bad. Her head is wrapped in a bandage, and she's unconscious. The doctor said she's in a coma but stabilized, and they're watching her for any brain swelling. We can go back and sit with her, but the doctor said it would be best if we wait out here." Maggie makes it over to the chairs, and we both sit down.

"Where's your dad, and why isn't he here?" I ask.

"I don't know," Maggie replies. "Did someone call Dad?"

"I thought the sheriff said he would."

"You don't have your phone?" Maggie asks.

"No, I rode in the ambulance. I didn't have time to grab it."

Maggie uses her phone to call her dad's number. There isn't an answer.

"That's strange that he isn't answering. Maybe he's gone to the house, and the police are still there searching," Maggie says.

"They would tell him your mother is here, right?"

"They told me, so I'm sure they'd tell him," Maggie replies. "Tell me exactly what happened. I want every detail."

I go through the entire story, explaining everything that happened. I even tell Maggie about the alarm and spraying Amanda's face.

"So Amanda did this to my mother?" Maggie turns and frowns at me.

"Yes, I'm afraid so. I was able to run for help." I reach over and take Maggie's hand.

"It's a good thing you ran for help. The doctor said that if it had been much longer, Mother might not have made it."

"I'm glad I was able to get help." Then something occurs to me. "Maggie, I left the curling iron plugged in, and we started the Instapot. I hope we don't burn down the house."

"Don't worry about it—the police are there. If they smell smoke, they'll take care of it," Maggie says, redialing her dad's number. "I don't understand why he isn't picking up." Maggie's hand is shaking as she continues to redial the number.

I take the phone from Maggie. "I'll dial the number for you."

Mrs. Higgins and Connor Gorman walk through the double glass doors and into the waiting area. Connor has a worried look. "Rebecca," he says, "we heard what happened. Are you okay? Were you hurt?"

"I think I'm fine. My shoulder keeps burning, but other than that, I'm okay."

"Why didn't you say something sooner? You're bleeding," Maggie says, touching the spot on my shoulder. "I thought that blood was from Mother, but you're bleeding too."

Connor looks at my shoulder and goes over and talks to the nurse. The nurse calls me to come back into the examining room. I follow her.

"You need to take off your shirt and put on this gown," the nurse says, handing me the hospital gown. I reach to pull off my shirt, but it's stuck.

"I'm afraid my shirt's stuck to my shoulder," I say, holding the gown in my hand.

"Your shirt being stuck has probably helped to stop the bleeding. Let me wet the spot on your shirt so you can take it off. Be gentle when you remove it," the nurse says, squirting water on my shirt. I gently lift my shirt over the wound and toss my shirt aside. I put on the hospital gown, but the injury has started to bleed, and blood is pouring onto the gown.

With all the blood, I can't tell the size of the injury.

The doctor enters the room. "So you've been out in the waiting room with this wound?" he asks.

"Yes, but my shirt had stuck to the wound and stopped the bleeding. I knew my shoulder was burning, but I thought the blood had come from Mrs. Mosley. I didn't realize in all the excitement that anything had happened to me."

"Let me take a look." The doctor examines the wound. "We'll have to suture this. There is a large gash. Is this cut from a knife?"

"Yes—she had a large butcher knife. I guess she took it from the kitchen," I say, but I don't know how anything happened.

"You wait here. I'll have the nurse prepare the suture tray." The doctor puts a compress on my shoulder and tapes it into place before he exits the room.

Sitting on the exam table, I look around the sterile room. The table is hard and every movement causes the stiff paper under me to crackle. Even the hospital gown smells of some disinfectant. The events of the night spin through my head like they're on fast forward.

The doctor and nurse enter the room, and the doctor asks me to lie down.

"I'm going to give you a shot to numb the wound before we suture it. Just take a deep breath," the doctor says.

I hold my breath but flinch when the needle goes in. The shot hurts, but I didn't feel any of the stitches. Once he finishes, he bandages the wound.

"This is a large gash. It took thirty stitches," the doctor tells me. "Is there someone here that will be taking you home?"

"Connor Gorman and Mrs. Higgins are in the lobby. They're my guardians," I say

The doctor leaves the room, and the nurse helps me with my wet and bloody shirt.

"What an ordeal. I'm sorry you had to experience something so terrible," the nurse says.

"This isn't nearly as bad as finding my parents' bodies in the barn," I say without thinking.

"Oh my, I didn't realize you're the girl who found her parents." The nurse clamps her lips closed and tilts her head, looking at me. "I'm so sorry—I didn't mean to upset you."

"It's okay," I reassure her. "I know you meant well."

"The mess with the Mosleys was caused by my aunt." I get off the table. I wince when I put my arm down for leverage, and pain shoots up to my shoulder.

"Careful there, I'll put your arm in this sling so you won't be tempted to move it," the nurse says.

"I hope the police have your aunt in custody," the nurse continues as she follows me.

"Yes, she's with the police now," I reply. I enter the waiting area and see Mrs. Higgins and Connor waiting. The doctor is talking to them, and I approach to hear what they're saying.

"No one will be going to the Mosleys for a while. It's a crime scene. I'll take them by the store to get the essentials," Connor says as he turns and wrinkles his brow.

"I need to see her tomorrow afternoon. Keep the wound dry. The prescriptions are for infection, pain, and a sedative. She'll need to take them. You can go now," the doctor says, and he turns to leave.

"I'm going to Mrs. Higgins's now?" I ask, looking around for Maggie.

Connor smiles at me. "Yes, that's correct. Maggie can come with us. She'll need somewhere to stay."

Maggie comes out of the restroom and approaches. Mrs. Higgins touches her on the shoulder. "Did you talk with your dad?" she asks. Maggie shakes her head no, and Mrs. Higgins gives her a little hug.

All of us leave the hospital together. Maggie seems to be in a daze, and Connor and Mrs. Higgins have taken charge. Maggie and I are like little robots, doing as we're told.

Connor looks at me in the rearview mirror and smiles. "Rebecca," he says, "do you feel like stopping at the store?"

"Not really," I answer. I lean back in the seat, and my head spins.

"When we get to the house, the girls can write down what they need, and you can go shopping," Mrs. Higgins says, looking over at Connor.

Connor laughs. "Shopping for a girl will be a whole new experience."

We drive past the Mosleys' house and see that police cars are still there. Maggie's eyes are glued on the house, but there's no sign of Mr. Mosley's car.

Maggie leans over. "Where's Dad?" she asks. "With everything going on, you'd think he'd be here. I feel like my life is falling apart. I now know how you must have felt when you came to our house that day."

"What will it be like at Mrs. Higgins?" I whisper.

Maggie shrugs, and we sit back for the short drive.

Chapter 25

We arrive at Mrs. Higgins's home, a large two-story house just a few blocks down the street from the Mosleys.

My shoulder is stinging and burning, and I try to adjust the sling, but every movement causes pain. The only thing that gives me relief is to stop moving. I let out little breaths.

"Are you okay?" Maggie whispers.

I give her a weak smile and small nod.

Mrs. Higgins, a charming woman in her sixties, shows us to our room. My room is the largest, and it looks out over the front yard. It's got a canopy bed and a large window seat. Maggie's place just next door is a bit smaller, and there is a bathroom between the two rooms that we'll share.

"I take it you girls haven't eaten," Mrs. Higgins says with a lilt in her voice.

"No, we've been at the hospital the whole time," I reply, looking at Maggie.

"Here's some paper. Prepare a shopping list for Connor. Remember, it might be a few days before you can get your things. Be sure to include clothing sizes," Mrs. Higgins says as she leaves the room.

I giggle. "I guess that means underwear, makeup, PJs, and the works."

Maggie chuckles as we complete the list of items we need. It's fun thinking about Connor shopping, and how awkward he'll be selecting everything.

"This could be a disaster. He'll probably go to Wal-Mart, so the quality might not be as good." Maggie hands me her list.

"I wrote down lipstick. I wonder what color Connor will select." I say and we laugh. "It's only for a few days. We can rough it!"

Maggie's room is a soft sage green with beautiful dark-wood furniture. "Will you be okay here tonight?"

Maggie shrugs. "I guess I don't have a choice. Where's my dad? Why hasn't he returned my calls? Does he know about Mom?"

I turn to Maggie and ask, "Do you think that Amanda got to him too?"

Maggie tears up.

I wish I could take back what I just said, I fret. *Why would I say something like that to Maggie, knowing that she's already a nervous wreck?*

"I'm so sorry. Please don't cry, Maggie. I want you to know that you'll always have me. I know that isn't much, but just knowing I had you made all the difference to me," I say as Connor comes to retrieve our list.

"Okay, girls, I'm off for the shopping adventure. You two settle in while Mrs. Higgins prepares dinner for us," Connor says as he leaves the room.

"Maggie, I'm sorry about what I said. Can you forgive me?" I say, placing my hand on hers.

"You know I'm thinking about all the terrible things that might or could have happened to him. Yes, I forgive you. It's you and me, kid," Maggie says and squeezes my hand.

We smile at each other.

Maggie jumps off the bed, pulling me off too. "Come on—I want to check out your room."

For some reason, I'd thought that coming to Mrs. Higgins would be dreadful, since she's an older woman living alone. Her house looks normal. The room she gave me is large and beautifully furnished. I expected her house to look like a museum filled with antiques, but it's a nice mixture of antiques and new pieces. I think it's very tastefully decorated, but coming from the farm, what would I know about decoration?

The room is huge and decorated in a lovely pink color. It has oversized furniture and a large window seat, and I walk over and sit down. Leaning into the window, I try to see down the street. *Where is Mr. Mosley, and why hasn't he called Maggie?* I wonder. Of course, the Mosleys' house is not visible from this window.

Maggie looks around the room and then walks to the door. "I'm going to lay down for a bit," she says. "I feel tired." She walks back to her room.

My shoulder hurts with every move I make. I lean back and close my eyes, hoping to gain some relief. I must have fallen asleep because I never heard Connor come back with our things.

"Okay girls, dinner is ready. Please come down quickly before it gets cold," Mrs. Higgins calls.

I jump up from the window seat, and my shoulder starts to throb. I grab my shoulder and take a deep breath, hoping to ease the pain. Why does it hurt so much?

I rush down the stairs and walk toward the clanging of dishes since I'm not familiar with the house. I find my way to the dining room and the table with pink floral china plates and crystal glasses. There's a pink-and-white flower arrangement in the center of the table.

"Please sit down and make yourself at home," Mrs. Higgins says, sitting down. Connor sits down across the table from me, and Maggie sits down at the other end.

Mrs. Higgins has prepared a lovely meal. We have stuffed pork chops with a cherry glaze, mashed potatoes, green peas, and rolls. The food is delicious, and she serves a fruit punch to drink. It's difficult eating with my shoulder hurting, but Connor looks over at me and sees that I'm struggling to cut my pork. "Rebecca, if you don't mind, I'll cut your meat for you." Connor comes over and cuts up my pork. He returns to his seat.

"Maggie, I noticed your car was in the driveway at home. How did you get to the hospital?" Connor asks.

"The sheriff dropped me off," Maggie says with a trembling voice.

"If you give me your keys, I'll walk down to the Mosleys and drive it up here so you girls won't have to go and get it tomorrow morning."

I look at Maggie before responding. "Connor, that's very thoughtful."

I look over at Mrs. Higgins and smile. "Thank you, Mrs. Higgins, for preparing a lovely meal."

"You're welcome, dear. You've had an upsetting day. The least I can do is put you to bed with a full stomach." Mrs. Higgins smiles and looks over at Maggie.

"Thank you, Mrs. Higgins," Maggie responds. Maggie is quieter than usual and shows no expression.

Mrs. Higgins serves a scoop of lime sherbet for dessert. Then I offer to help her with the dishes.

"No, Connor will help me with the dishes. You go up and get ready for bed. You'll need some rest after the day you've had. Let me know if you need anything. Don't shower, because you have to keep your shoulder dry," Mrs. Higgins says, picking up the plates. Maggie and I go upstairs.

"Maggie, I'm worried about you. You hardly said a word at dinner," I say, placing my hand on her shoulder.

"I'm so scared. What am I going to do? My mom is in a coma. What will I do without her?" Maggie begins to cry.

"Stop it, Maggie. I've been praying for Margaret, and you keep praying too. You know all the people at church are probably having pray vigils for her. You must be strong and trust that God will take care of her. You have to be strong for her," I say, hugging her.

Maggie wipes her eyes with the back of her hands. "Thanks, Rebecca—I'm just scared."

"We'll go to the hospital together in the morning. Just get plenty of sleep so you can help your mother." I shake my finger at her and walk out of her room. Back in my room, I unpack the items I need for bed. I laugh when I see the things that Conner picked out for us. The pajamas look like something Mrs. Higgins would wear—not a teenager. I can't wait to see the makeup and other items he purchased.

The bed is big with many big fluffy pillows and looks inviting, and I get in.

An hour later I'm still lying in bed. The pain in my shoulder is so severe that I can't sleep. I get up and walk over to the window seat and the sky looks clear. There's a crescent moon tonight. Gazing at the moon, I wonder what the future holds for Maggie and me.

"I thought I heard something in here. Are you having problems sleeping?" Mrs. Higgins says, entering the room.

"My shoulder is hurting and keeping me awake. I normally sleep on my side, but it hurts too much," I say, looking at Mrs. Higgins in her long pink robe.

"Let me fix you some tea. The doctor gave me a mild sedative to help you sleep. You've had a lot of trauma in your life, and I hope that things will turn around for you," Mrs. Higgins says, leaving the room.

I smile. Mrs. Higgins has been so caring and kind to Maggie and me. I was so afraid to come here, but she seems so kind and sweet. She returns with a tray loaded with a teapot, cups, and a plate of cookies.

"We'll have tea and a little chat together. Come sit here in the chair." Mrs. Higgins places the tray on the table, and we sit down in the chairs across from each other.

"I thought you might want to call me Bess," Mrs. Higgins says as she pours our tea.

"Bess?" I ask.

"My parents named me Bessie. I never cared for the name, so I always went by Bess. It isn't a pretty name, but it's my name." She hands me my cup of tea, and I take it. "Careful, it might be hot."

I take a sip; it tastes of strawberry and peach.

"This is good. It has a fruity taste. I like it," I say, taking another sip.

"Won't you have a cookie? They're sugar cookies I made yesterday." She passes the plate to me, and I take a cookie.

"May I ask you something, Bess?" I say.

"Certainly, what is it?"

"Why did you agree to be my guardian? You don't know me."

"Oh, Rebecca, the things that were kept from you—and I guess it's all up to me to tell you."

Whatever it is, she's having a hard time saying it, I think. With all I'd learned in the past few days and weeks, I hope it isn't something awful. I bite on the cookie and take a sip of tea to help swallow.

"I'm Bruce's Aunt. You're my great-niece. At least my adopted niece, but Bruce loved you as his own."

Luckily I swallowed before she announced that. "You're related to Dad and me? How come I wasn't told?"

"He never spoke about me?" Her expression turns sad. "He used to come here to write and play songs. He didn't want anyone knowing who he was."

"Wait! You're Bess," I say. Mrs. Higgins smiled and nodded. I take another bite of the sugar cookie and smile. I hold up the cookie. "This is good!"

"Thank you. That cookie was Bruce's favorite."

"Mine too. He must have brought them home after he visited you. We'd share them with a cup of hot chocolate to dunk."

Bess leans back against the chair and gives me a look. "They were that bad you had to dunk them to eat them?" She crosses her arms and gives me the teacher look.

"No . . ." What am I to say? "That's not why we dunked them. We loved hot cocoa and cookies. We just did it to see who got to the bottom of the cup first."

She gave me that look like I'd told her the dog ate my homework. "Honest," I say. I crossed my heart and kissed my finger. I hoped it worked.

She gave me a big smile. "I was just kidding. We did the same here."

Whew! I sighed. She was going to give me a heart attack, but there was a twinkle in her eye. We'll get along just fine.

"I'm glad I still have some family." I smile at Bess.

"Yes, a family is good, and you're all that's left of mine. I guess we girls need to stick together," Bess says, sipping her tea.

"I think I'm going to like it here," I say, yawning.

"I hope you love it here. We'll do some fun things together. You like music, right?"

"I love music."

"Then we'll get along just fine. Do you still play the piano?" she asks, putting down her cup.

"Yes, I love to play," I say, yawning again.

"That's great. I can see the sedative is starting to work. Why don't you let me tuck you into bed? I'll put pillows around your shoulder to protect it while you sleep," Bess says, putting down her cup.

I walk to the bed and climb in. It's lovely having someone to tuck me in and even give me a little kiss on the forehead. I close my eyes, and the sedative worked because, by the time Bess left the room, I was already asleep.

Chapter 26

Bess left the house early but left breakfast for Maggie and me. Maggie hardly says a word while we eat. I'm a bit worried about her when we get into the car to go to the hospital. Maggie gets in behind the wheel and just stares into space as she pulls out of the driveway. I'm afraid to ride with her because she doesn't seem aware of her surroundings.

"Maggie, you're driving. Please focus," I say, but she doesn't even act like she hears me.

"I know, Rebecca," Maggie replies, but not in the way I expected. Normally she would tell me that she isn't stupid and to leave her alone.

"Let's go to the hospital first and check on your mother. We'll ask if they've seen your dad, and if not, we'll search for him," I say. I want her to know I have a plan, and that she isn't alone.

"I wouldn't even know where to start looking," Maggie says.

"Sure you do. This is a small town—people here know everyone's business. All we have to do is ask. Someone must have seen something," I reassure her, but her face is blank.

As we're driving I say another prayer for Mrs. Mosley. Maggie might lose it if there's no improvement. Maggie parks the car. I turn around and look for Mr. Mosley's car is in the parking lot, but it isn't there.

We walk into the Emergency entrance and speak to the nurse at the desk.

"We're here to see Mrs. Mosley," I say to the nurse, but I keep my eyes on Maggie as she stands quietly in a daze.

"She isn't here. We moved her to a room early this morning. Go down this hallway and take the elevator to the third floor. She's in room 320," the nurse says before turning away from us.

Like robots, we walk down the hall to the elevator. I hit the elevator button without saying a word.

Maggie's in a bad state; I can tell. *Is she in shock?*

We get onto the elevator, and I push the button for the third floor. As the elevator door closes, I keep my eyes on Maggie. *What do I do? Should I say something to one of the nurses?* The elevator door slowly opens, and we step off. We walk down the hall a short distance to room 320 and enter the room.

Mrs. Mosley lies in bed with tubes and monitors hooked up everywhere. My heart sinks; she's still in a coma.

"Rebecca, she isn't any better. What'll I do without her?" Maggie says and begins to cry.

"Stay here, Maggie. I'll be right back." I rush out the door to the nurses' station. I'm not sure what to say, but I recognize one of them. It's Mrs. Clark, who I know from the church.

"Mrs. Clark, I need to talk to you for a moment," I say, leaning over the counter.

"Yes, Rebecca, what can I do for you?" she asks, looking up from the computer screen and standing to speak with me.

"It's Maggie Mosley; I think she's in shock. She's walking around in a daze. I think Maggie is hardly aware of what's happening," I say.

"From what I understand, yesterday was a nightmare. Was Maggie there when her mother was attacked?"

"No, she was at school," I respond, turning to make sure Maggie is still in the room with her mother.

"It's only understandable that she would be upset," the nurse says. "I can leave a note for the doctor that he needs to evaluate her emotional state. I think the doctor will be making his rounds any minute. Be sure you stay until the doctor comes by."

"Okay, we'll stay. Has Mr. Mosley been here?"

"No, we haven't seen him. I've been wondering why," Mrs. Clark replies, sitting back down at her desk.

"Thank you for your help." I turn and walk back to the room.

Maggie is sitting in the chair next to her mother; she's staring at the wall. It looks like she's in a daydream. I enter the room and walk over to Maggie.

"How are you holding up?"

"What will I do without her? Why won't she open her eyes? Where's my dad?" Maggie cries again.

I put my hand on her shoulder to comfort her. I stand next to her chair and pray that Mrs. Mosley will wake up. I have to do something to help this situation.

Dr. Harris, from the emergency room last night, comes to the door and stops to look at Maggie before entering.

"Good morning, girls. How is our patient this morning?" Dr. Harris says, entering the room and watching Maggie.

Maggie sits and stares into space, not even realizing that the doctor has entered the room.

"Rebecca, will you go and get Nurse Clark and have her come in? I need you to wait in the hall afterward." Dr. Harris nods toward the door.

After getting Mrs. Clark, I make my way down the hall to the small waiting area. I sit down, folding my hands in my lap to steady them.

Maggie isn't handling this very well. I don't know what—if anything—the doctor can do, but I think she needs his attention. Mrs. Clark returns to the nurse's station, so I get up and walk toward the room.

"Rebecca, don't go in just yet," Mrs. Clark calls to me. "The doctor is evaluating Maggie. I'm looking for a room for her. I think we're going to keep her and give her a sedative. She's in a bad state. Thank you for bringing this to our attention."

"Mrs. Clark, you say you're going to keep her. You mean like, admitting her?"

"Yes, Rebecca. Some people don't handle stress as well as others. I think she needs a little help handling all that's happened. A day or two on medication will make a big difference."

Dr. Harris comes to the nurse's station and nods at Mrs. Clark. He looks over at me.

"Maggie isn't coping well. We'll keep her here overnight," Dr. Harris says as he writes out orders.

I'm choking and can't breathe. I spin around on one foot and head to the elevator. I mash the button and stare at the arrow above the door, waiting for it to turn green. My eyes are stinging, and the tears are about to betray me.

The elevator door dings, opens, and I step inside. I press the button for the lobby and hope the door closes before anyone else joins me.

What do I do now? I wonder. *I guess the only thing left to do is find Mr. Mosley. I can walk to the sheriff's office and see if perhaps they have found him. Did he go home last night? Is he at work? Why hasn't he come to the hospital?*

I walk out of the hospital and down the sidewalk. I'm walking too fast and trip on an uneven spot on the path. I fall to the ground, and a part of me wants to lie there and cry, but that won't solve anything. I pull myself up and look around to make sure that no one saw me. I dust off my clothes and start walking. I push the tears aside with my palms and wipe my hands on my jeans.

I've walked a couple of blocks when someone yells my name. I turn, and Judge Holcombe pulls his car up to the curb.

"Judge Holcombe, good morning," I say. *Did he see me fall? Can he tell I've been crying?*

"Where are you going in such a rush?" he asks.

"To the sheriff's office—I want to know if he found Mr. Mosley."

"Get in. I'll drive you," Judge Holcombe says.

"Thank you for the ride," I say, not wanting to look at him.

"I see you've been crying."

"Yes sir, I have. Mrs. Mosley is still in a coma, and Maggie was so upset that they had to admit her. We don't know where Mr. Mosley is—he hasn't even been to the hospital." Judge Holcombe makes me feel so comfortable that it all spews out of my mouth before I can stop it.

"Well, I can see things are a mess. Maybe the sheriff knows about Mr. Mosley. I didn't realize he was missing."

Judge Holcombe drives to the sheriff's office and parks in front of it. I reach for the door handle.

"Rebecca, you can't handle all of this on your own. Come to my office, and I'll have Mrs. Holcombe pick you up. Together you ladies can do some investigating. None of this is your fault. How are things with Mrs. Higgins?"

"Bess has been wonderful. I think I'll like it there," I respond as I open the car door.

"Glad to hear it. Remember; come back to my office unless the sheriff takes you home."

"Thank you for the ride, Judge Holcombe. I'll see you soon," I say, closing the car door. I rush to the door and enter the sheriff's office.

"Rebecca, what brings you here?" Lucille says when she sees me.

"I want to see Sheriff Webster," I say, attempting to walk past her.

"Hold it—he isn't here. What do you need with the sheriff?" Lucille shakes her head.

"I want to know where Mr. Mosley is, and why he hasn't been to the hospital." I stomp my foot and place my hands on my hips.

"Come and sit. Let's talk," Lucille says, ushering me over to her desk. I sit in the chair across from her.

"Have they found Mr. Mosley?" I ask, looking into Lucille's eyes.

"Not to my knowledge, but they're looking for him. How is Mrs. Mosley?"

"She's in a coma. She has tubes and machines connected to her. They admitted Maggie because she was so upset," I say, fidgeting in my chair. "Look, Lucille, I feel this need to do something. I can't sit here and chat, knowing Mr. Mosley is out there somewhere, and Mrs. Mosley needs him."

"Girl, what are you going to do? You can't drive, so you have to walk everywhere. You can't solve this. This isn't your fault, and it isn't up to you to fix things. That's why we have the police force, and they're searching."

"But Lucille, I can't just sit around and do nothing," I say, fighting the tears.

"I tell you what. I'll call Oscar. He's the deputy on duty. I'll ask him if he'll drive you around to look for Mr. Mosley. Oscar is searching in the downtown area and can be here in a matter of minutes."

"Okay, that sounds good, and then maybe he can drop me off at the hospital when we finish," I say.

"Look, Rebecca, I know you blame yourself for what happened, but it isn't your fault. The trouble Amanda caused has been brewing for many years. That woman was never anything but trouble. She's locked up, and this time she'll get what's coming to her." Lucille picks up the phone and calls Oscar. "Oscar, Rebecca—the daughter of the Wilds—is here, and she wants to ride around with you looking for Mr. Mosley. I figured you could use an extra set of eyes. Swing by and pick her up." Lucille puts down the phone.

"Thank you, Lucille. You've been so kind to me, and I appreciate it. I want all of the Mosleys to be okay."

"They will be, Rebecca; give it a little time, and everything will go back to normal."

"Is there such a thing as normal? For me, there'll never be a normal," I say, twisting in my seat.

"Yes, I understand that, Rebecca. I'm so sorry. There'll never be a normal, but you can at least find happiness, and when you do, hold on to it." Lucille smiles at me and pats my hand. She turns and looks at the front door as Oscar enters the office.

"Okay, young lady, let's get going. I was about to swing by the city hall and see if Mr. Mosley showed for work today," Oscar says, standing behind my chair.

"That sounds like a good plan," I say, jumping up and walking toward the door.

"We'll see you in a while, Lucille. Let me know if anyone finds Mosley," Oscar says, and we walk out of the sheriff's office and get in the squad car.

I sit in the back and look at the buildings and the cars around town as Oscar drives. My eyes are peeled for Mr. Mosley or his car, but we make it to the city hall, and there's no sign of him or his vehicle. Oscar parks the squad car. He slides out of the seat and turns to look at me. Oscar is the oldest deputy on the force. He's a kind and friendly man who everyone loves.

"I'm going inside to see if Mr. Mosley called in today," he says to me. "You wait here and keep your eyes peeled for any sign of him."

I nod and lean back in the seat. Is there any chance that Amanda got to Mr. Mosley before she reached the house? If that's the case, why has no one found him or his car?

Sheriff Webster's voice comes through on the radio.

"I found Mr. Mosley's car out on Mission Loop. No sign of him, but it's his car." I cringe. Mission Loop! The farm is on Mission Loop. What's he doing so close to the farm?

Oscar slides into the seat.

"Did I miss something on the radio?" Oscar asks.

"Sheriff Webster found Mr. Mosley's car on Mission Loop. No sign of Mr. Mosley," I say.

"This is Oscar, Mosley didn't show up for work, or call in," Oscar says into his radio and starts the car.

"I've got a team here helping me look for Mosley. You hang tight in town," Sheriff Webster responds.

"Where can I take you, Rebecca?" Oscar asks.

"Take me to the hospital. I want to check on Mrs. Mosley." I lean back in the seat.

I walk into the hospital, and the halls are empty. I press the button for the elevator; the door immediately comes open. I get off the elevator on the third floor and walk to Mrs. Mosley's room. I pull a chair up to the bed. I sit down beside her and take her hand in mine.

Mrs. Mosley and I shared a moment together when she told me I was adopted. She said she would always be there for me. She was kind and compassionate. It's my turn to do the same for her.

"Margaret," I whisper, "you were there for me. I want you to know that I'm here for you. Please open your eyes, because Maggie needs you. Wake up, Margaret."

I sit there for hours, stroking her hand and whispering to her and pleading for her to come back.

There is a tap on the door; Sheriff Webster is standing in the hall. He motions for me to come with him.

"We found Mosley." Sheriff Webster has a frown on his face and looks worried.

"That's good, isn't it?" I say.

"Maybe, but it comes with more questions," Sheriff says, leaning against the wall.

"What kind of questions?" I ask. *Why's he telling me this?*

"His car was on Mission Loop near your farm. Do you have any idea why he was out that way?"

"Sheriff, I never knew of Mr. Mosley coming to the farm. I never saw him there, but that doesn't mean he wasn't ever there. Remember the dollar sign I gave you? I found it in the barn after my parents died. It came off of a key chain that I believe belonged to Mr. Mosley. That could be proof that he was there. Is it possible that he killed my parents? Is it possible that there is a connection? You said you found him?"

"Yes, we first found his car out on Mission Loop and started searching. He was lying out in Gil's pasture on the creek bed."

I widened my eyes. Gil's property is next to our farm, and the creek runs through both properties.

"The medics are bringing him here," the sheriff continues. "I think someone ran him off the road. He ran, and they shot him. I'm not sure who did it, or why."

I fall back against the wall and gasp for breath.

The sheriff grabs my hand and points toward the waiting area. "Let's go into the waiting area. I need something to drink."

By the time we reach the waiting area, I'm beginning to calm down. The sheriff gets two sodas out of the machine and motions for me to sit with him.

"You know, I think I remember seeing that key chain in his hand. I think while he's here, I'll have them run his DNA. Then I can compare that to the evidence that we found in the barn," Sheriff Webster says, nodding with a smile. I'm thinking he's beginning to fit the puzzle together.

"So, you think it could be him?" I ask, almost afraid to hear the answer.

"I'm not ruling it out, but his disappearance at the most inappropriate time does cause concern. Where exactly did you say you found that dollar sign?"

"I found it in the barn, near the pile of hay where my parents were lying. The sun was shining through the open door, and the light hit the dollar sign and made it sparkle. So I dug into the loose dirt and found it."

"You said loose dirt. So it wasn't deep?" The sheriff looks into my eyes.

"No, it wasn't buried, but it had a little dirt covering most of it. Maybe someone stepped on it. I don't know, but it wasn't hard to find. It was just lying there," I say, taking a sip of my soda and realizing that I'm hungry and haven't eaten today.

"I'm going downstairs to check on Mr. Mosley. How is Mrs. Mosley?" he asks as he stands to leave.

"She's still in a coma." I stand and follow him to the elevator.

"I'll keep you posted on our progress," the sheriff says when we reach the elevator.

"What's going to happen with Amanda?" I ask.

"There'll be a hearing next Wednesday. Since Mrs. Mosley is in such bad shape, we're going to ask that Amanda be held without bail."

"So, there's a chance she could be released?" I take in a deep breath and hold it. *They can't release her. She's dangerous!*

"It's possible, but I don't think so," the sheriff says, and then he steps into the elevator.

"Thank you, Sheriff." The elevator door closes, and I turn and walk back to Margaret's room.

I sit in the chair next to her bed and take her hand.

"Margaret, you need to wake up. Maggie needs you," I whisper, but Margaret doesn't move. "Margaret, if you can hear me, squeeze my hand," I say, and I feel the twitch of her fingers.

I smile knowing that Margaret is on her way back to us.

Chapter 27

I'm sitting with Margaret, flipping through the pages of a year-old magazine that I'd plucked from the table in the lounge as I'd passed by. In the recipe section, pages have been torn out, and the edges of the magazine are frayed from wear.

The door makes a light whisper and Bess pokes her head around it.

"Is she still in a coma?" Bess asks.

"Yes, but her hand twitches when I talk to her," I say, standing up and walking over to Bess.

"Rebecca, have you been here all day?" Bess asks as she looks around the room.

"I've been here most of the day. A lot has happened," I say.

"Come on, let me take you home. I bet you're hungry."

"Yes, I am, but I need to check on Maggie before I go."

"Where is she? Isn't she coming with us?" Bess asks.

"She was admitted. Maggie was in a trance, so I asked the doctor to take a look at her," I explain, walking out of Margaret's room with Bess.

Bess shakes her head. "I thought she was acting strange. I should have paid more attention. How's your shoulder?"

"It's hurting a lot. I think I injured it again when I fell today," I say, entering Maggie's room.

Maggie is still sleeping, so I squeeze her hand and leave her room. Bess and I walk to the elevator.

"What do you mean, you fell today?" Bess asks, and we step into the elevator.

"I was running down the sidewalk outside the hospital. I was on my way to the sheriff's office, and there was a hole in the sidewalk, and I tripped and fell. When I fell, I landed on my shoulder. I felt something warm and wet, so I think it might have bled."

"I hope you didn't tear any of the stitches. I don't see any blood on your shirt, so that's a good sign. Did you have someone look at it?" Bess asks as we walk to the car. "Why were you going to the sheriff's office?"

We get into the car, and Bess pulls out of the parking lot.

"No, I didn't mention my shoulder to anyone. There was just a lot going on, and I want Margaret to wake up. If she doesn't come out of the coma, what'll happen to Maggie? I went to the sheriff's office to find out about Mr. Mosley." I say this so fast that the words run together.

"You look tired. Did you eat today?"

I don't answer. We walk to Bess's car.

"Rebecca, none of this is your fault," Bess says as we drive to her house. "You act like you caused all of this, but you did nothing wrong."

"That's what everyone says, but Bess, if I wasn't at their house—"

"Rebecca, stop! What happened isn't your fault," Bess tells me again, pulling the car into the driveway.

"I know that's true, but I can't help but feel responsible," I say, getting out of the car.

"You didn't answer me. Did you eat lunch today?

Bess unlocks the door, and we enter the house. I follow her into the kitchen.

"No, I didn't have time for lunch," I say.

Bess nods. "You said a lot had happened today. What did I miss?"

"First, Maggie got admitted," I begin, "and then I fell. I went to the sheriff's office and rode around in the squad car with Oscar. I heard on the police radio that they'd found Mosley's car, but not him. Later, while I was at the hospital with Margaret, the sheriff told me that they found Mr. Mosley out near the farm on Gil's property. He has been shot, and they've transported him to the hospital."

"Mr. Mosley has been shot? Good heavens, what'll happen next?" Bess puts her hand on her chest to steady her heart. "Well, it's been a hectic day. Do you need something for pain?" Bess asks.

"No, I think I can handle the pain. It isn't as bad as yesterday."

"Well, I'll fix something to eat. I know you're hungry."

"Let me help you."

Bess pulls the bread out of the pantry.

"Since it's just the two of us," she says, "I think we'll eat in the breakfast room. You can talk to me while I get the food ready."

"Sure, whatever I can do to help," I reply. "You told me there are a lot of secrets surrounding me, or something like that. So what has been kept from me all these years?"

"Why don't we prepare dinner, and then we can talk? I thought we would just have grilled cheese sandwiches and tomato soup. Will that be enough for you?" Bess turns to the stove.

"I'm hungry, but I don't know if I can eat much. I feel like my head is spinning, and I have a rock in my stomach. I didn't tell you everything that happened."

"You mean there's more?" Bess looks at me with shock.

"Yes, I found this dollar sign in the barn after my parents died. I thought maybe whoever killed them had lost it, and that the sheriff's office hadn't seen it when they were investigating. On my trip to Dallas to get my clothes, I discovered that Mr. Mosley had a key chain that was missing a dollar sign." I eye Bess for a reaction.

"Go ahead, girl, you have my interest. I'm listening," Bess says, stirring the soup.

The wheels in my head are turning, and my head is spinning. *Why was Chuck near the farm? Was he there when my parents were killed?*

"Anyway, I reminded the sheriff about the key chain and informed him that Mr. Mosley had lost his." I fidget in my chair.

"I can see you've had a busy day. After dinner, we'll take a look at your shoulder," Bess says.

"So the sheriff tells me that he's going to get Mr. Mosley's DNA and compare it to the DNA from the crime scene."

"Were you told that Chuck Mosley is your biological father, and Amanda is your biological mother?" Bess frowns and turns to glance at me as she stirs the soup.

I walk over to Bess so that I can see her face. "Yes, Margaret told me. I wonder why Margaret is so nice to me. I know that my existence must have put a strain on her marriage."

"Margaret is a nice lady. She's always known for doing the right thing," Bess says, putting the sandwiches on our plates.

"I like her, and I want her to come out of this coma. The only thing is, she might wake up to an entirely different life." I turn and walk to the table.

"Let me get the soup into the bowls, and then we'll be ready to eat," Bess says.

We sit at the table, and I take a bite of my sandwich.

"Are there more secrets, or is my adoption the only secret?" I ask.

"You know about Bruce being Jackson Nash?" Bess glances at me as she sips her soup.

"Yes, I know that. Amanda told me."

"Well, he made a lot of money. After you were born and they adopted you, he took that money and put it in a trust for you. The trust mentioned in the will is millions of dollars. Amanda wants you thinking that she can get that money."

"The trust is worth millions of dollars? Are you sure? Does that mean I'm rich?" I shake my head, not able to process what it all means.

"So maybe Amanda killed them? She wanted the money? But how can she get it?" I continue, taking a bite of my sandwich.

"I'm thinking Amanda was going to kill you because she's next of kin, being your mother's sister and go to court and get the money. You see, she didn't know that I too am too am related." Bess rolls her eyes and looks at me for my reaction.

"So when that man, Gene Maxwell, broke into the apartment, it was to kill me?" I ask. "Amanda must have hired him to get rid of me. She told the police she had never seen him. Maybe they were working together." I take a bite of my sandwich, and my head is spinning even more. I have so much new information to process.

"Wait! You're also my relative. Are you after the money too?" I ask, realizing that I could have entered another web of lies. *Bess seems nice—but is she?* I choke on my soup.

"I have no interest in the money. I have my home, savings, and a good job. As long as I have my music, I'm content. The Amanda and Gene theory is just what Connor and I think. I was afraid that Amanda was up to no good. Connor was trying to come and warn you. Connor and I were trying to get custody of you, but we didn't have the will."

"Do you think that Mr. Mosley and Amanda are working together?" I ask.

"I don't know. I can't say if Chuck and Amanda are together," Bess answers.

"So, is my life still in danger?" I ask. I think about all the times I've been alone.

Bess shakes her head. "I can't answer that, but I have a feeling that as long as Amanda is around, you're in danger."

"Oh Bess, I lived such a simple life, and now it's nothing but turmoil."

"It won't always be this way. Once they discover who and why your parents were killed, this will settle down. You'll have a calm life after that."

"Are there more secrets?" I ask.

"Amanda was wild. All during high school, she was getting into trouble. She was arrested for armed robbery, but Bruce's money got her out of trouble. She is capable of anything. I was afraid for you while you were with her. I called Connor every day and told him he had to help you."

"So, where does Connor fit into all of this? I remember he worked at the farm when I was young," I say, finishing my soup.

"Connor is also my nephew. Connor and Bruce were cousins. Not only were they cousins, but they also grew up on the same street. They were always together. Connor and Bruce are both good guys."

"Were you close to them when they were growing up?" I ask.

Bess shakes her head. "Not in the beginning. When they were young, I was away at college, and then I got a job in another state. I guess they were preteens when I finally relocated and moved closer to family. By then, Bruce was already into his music, and knowing I was a music teacher, he asked me to help."

"So you and Dad became close through the music."

"Yes, music was part of it. We just connected. After Bruce lost his parents, he came to live with me."

"So, you were everything to him," I say, finishing my sandwich.

"I wouldn't say everything, but I would say we had a connection."

"Thank you for telling me. What do you think about Mr. Mosley? Do you know anything about him?" I ask.

"There was a time when he was pretty wild—at least that's what Bruce and Carol told me. He was a college professor and got involved with a student. Of course, the student was Amanda. He lost his job because of it and almost lost his wife and daughter. I doubt that Maggie knows any of it. Something tells me that Margaret has sheltered Maggie from knowing the truth about her Dad."

"Why do you think that Margaret stayed with him?" I ask as I finish my food.

"Well, Rebecca, I'm not sure, but I think she loved him. I think she was also a young mother who was scared of raising a child on her own."

"Yes, I do think she loves him. I think he's often mean to her. I've seen it a few times how he talks to her and disregards her. A man shouldn't treat the woman he loves like that," I say, carrying my dishes over to the sink.

"Thank you for helping. Here—will you wash off the table?" Bess says, handing me a dish towel.

"Yes, I want to help with the dishes, too," I say, wiping off the table.

"Stay here so you can talk to me. I do enjoy your company," Bess says, smiling as she washes the dishes.

"Thank you for telling me all the secrets."

"Oh, Rebecca, who said that, was *all* the secrets? We'll save the rest for another time."

"Do you think that maybe Gene Maxwell hurt Mr. Mosley?" I ask.

"What makes you say that?" Bess asks.

"Gene Maxwell was paid by Amanda to break into the apartment—not that the police are aware of that. Maybe she paid him to get Mr. Mosley out of the way. Maybe she's jealous that he stayed with Margaret. I don't know, but Mr. Mosley is shot, and I can't imagine who did it," I say, leaning on the counter as Bess washes the dishes.

"Well, Rebecca, it isn't for you to figure out. The police will be investigating. If that Gene Maxwell is around, I'm sure they'll find him. If Amanda had anything to do with it, it'll all come out," Bess says, drying the dishes and putting them away.

"I hope you're right. I want Margaret and Maggie to be back to normal. I love both of them," I say, watching Bess.

"I know you do. We'll keep them in our prayers. I guess you want to go back to the hospital tomorrow?" Bess says as we leave the kitchen.

"Yes, I want to. Will you take me there tomorrow morning?" I ask.

"First, let's have a look at that shoulder. I hope we didn't lose any stitches," Bess says as we walk upstairs.

"I missed my doctor's appointment this afternoon," I say as we reach the top of the stairs.

"I got a call from Dr. Harris's office saying that he had an emergency and needed to reschedule. So your appointment is tomorrow morning," Bess says as we reach the bathroom.

"I bet the emergency was Mr. Mosley. I know that Dr. Harris was with him in the Emergency room.

"I'm glad I put all the bandages in your bathroom. It makes things easier." Bess says, reaching for the bandages.

I take off my shirt, and Bess removes the bandage.

"Yes, I can see it bled, but not a lot. I don't see any torn stitches. I don't think there's any damage. When you see the doctor tomorrow morning, you need to tell him about the fall," Bess says.

"Isn't his office by the hospital?" I ask, putting my shirt back on.

"Yes, in the building next to the hospital. Don't worry; I'll go to the doctor with you. I'll take you to the doctor and then go to work. I want to give you money for lunch. I don't want you going all day without eating."

"Okay. I hope that Maggie is better tomorrow, and that Margaret isn't in the coma." I say, leaving out of the bathroom.

"It may take Margaret a while to come out of the coma. She might have a bit of swelling around the brain. The swelling will take several days to go down. So don't be disappointed if she isn't awake," Bess says, walking out of the bathroom and into my room.

"Do you like watching movies?" Bess asks.

"Yes, I do," I respond. I figure it will fill a long evening that could otherwise be boring.

"Let me pop some popcorn and we can watch a Hallmark movie. But let's get ready for bed first," Bess says.

"Sounds like a plan," I say, and then my cell phone rings.

"I'll leave you alone to talk on the phone. Let me know when you're ready for the movie."

"Okay, and thanks Bess," I say as she leaves the room. "Hello?"

"Becca, its Blake."

"You did call! I've missed you."

"Are you all settled in school?"

"No, things have happened." I try to hold back my tears, but they betray me. I'm crying.

"Rebecca, why are you crying? What's wrong?"

"The Mosleys—the people who brought me to school that day—have been hurt. He was shot, and she's in a coma. I now have new guardians. The reason I was in Dallas is that my parents were killed. I'm sorry I never told you."

"Are you in danger?"

"No, I'm fine. I can't believe all the violence. It all started with me finding my parents dead. I slept through the whole thing. I can't imagine why they were killed. It makes no sense to me." I blurt it all out before I have time to think. Until now, I haven't told Blake anything about my life.

"I knew you had been through a tragedy. I just sensed when you were here that you needed someone. I want to come and see you on Saturday. What do you think?"

"You're coming to see me on Saturday? Let me ask if that's okay. Can you hold on?"

I put down my cell phone and walk to Bess's room. I tap on the door. Bess opens it.

"Bess, my friend from Dallas—Blake—wants to come and see me on Saturday. I told him I'd ask if it is okay. What can I tell him?"

Bess crosses her arms in front of her. "Do you like this boy?"

"Yes, I like him. He's so kind and supportive. He was there when I needed someone. I never told him about my parents."

"I think that'll be just fine. What are your plans?"

"I'm not sure. Can I tell you later?"

"I just want you to be happy." Bess closes her door.

I rush back to the phone.

"Blake, she said yes. I can see you on Saturday."

"That's great. I'll take you to lunch, and you can show me around town. Maybe we can take in a movie before I have to drive home."

"That sounds great. See you on Saturday."

I end the call by dancing around the room. Blake is my first official date.

I change into my pajamas and skip down the hall to Bess's room, still excited from talking to Blake. I tap on the door. Bess answers the door in her fuzzy pink robe.

"I'm ready for the movie," I whisper.

"Rebecca, you look pale, is something wrong?"

"I'm fine. You see, the last thing I did with my parents was watch a movie before going to bed," I say, and the tears betray me. I begin to cry again.

Bess puts her arms around me and hugs me. The warmth of her hug calms me. Bess genuinely cares about me. I brush the tears off of my cheeks. I see tears in Bess's eyes and know that she too feels my pain.

"We don't have to watch a movie, dear. We can go downstairs and play the piano. I'd love to hear you sing," Bess says, attempting a smile.

"I think I want to give the movie a try. I never know how it will be, and I can't avoid movies for the rest of my life. By the way, thank you for saying that I can see Blake on Saturday. When I was in Dallas, he was my rock," I say.

With Bess, I still have a family. I feel like with her, I'll be able to face anything.

"Then a movie it is. If it gets too emotional, we can always turn it off," Bess says, smiling.

"Thank you for being so understanding. Thank you for caring about me and taking me in," I say, I'm always thanking her for the beautiful things she does for me. Just that thought sends warmth to my heart.

As we sit in her den, eating popcorn and enjoying the movie, I see that life can again be magical.

Chapter 28

I'm worried about the Mosleys and why was Chuck near the farm.

After my doctor's appointment, Bess drops me off at the hospital. I'm eager to check on Maggie and Margaret. I rush past the nurses' station and into Maggie's room. To my surprise, she's sitting up in bed, eating her breakfast.

"Maggie, I'm so glad to see you're awake!" I walk to the bed and stand at her side.

"I must have been a mess." Maggie smiles at me.

"You were just in a trance," I say.

"I'm better now—at least while I'm taking the medication. I talked to the doctor yesterday afternoon, and I'm leaving the hospital. I have an aunt in Morgan that's coming to pick me up. I'll be there for a few days," she says, taking a sip of her juice.

"I'll miss you. I was hoping you would come back to Bess's house, but we can talk on the phone," I say. Things look pretty grim for Maggie right now, with both of her parents injured. Something tells me that she doesn't know about her dad.

"I heard you've been sitting with Mother. Will you keep an eye on her while I'm gone? Tell her I haven't abandoned her," Maggie says.

"I will. You get well, and hurry back to us." I hug her.

"We aren't sure how long it'll be before Mother is better. I'm not as strong as you. My Mother is in a coma, and I fall apart. You lost both parents and have held it together."

I smile at Maggie, but don't say anything. Now I know for certain that she doesn't know that her Dad's been shot, or that she could lose both of them.

If she does, will she be able to handle it? Will I ever get to see her again? She thinks I held it together, but little does she know that my heart is bleeding.

"I need to take a shower and dress. Will you come back and say goodbye before I leave?" Maggie pushes back the hospital tray and slides off the bed.

"Sure. I'm going to check on Margaret. I read that it's good to talk to people in a coma. It helps to bring them back. I've been talking to her, and I felt her fingers twitch," I say.

"That's good news isn't it?" Maggie says as I walk out of the room.

I walk next door and enter Margaret's room. It's dark, and I walk to the window and open the blinds. I turn to Margaret and say, "Its morning, and time to wake up. I bet you'd love a cup of coffee to start your day. Here—let me fluff your pillow and adjust those covers." I walk to the bed and lift her head, removing the pillow. I squeeze the pillow and smooth the pillowcase, then lift her head and replace it.

"I bet that feels better. Can you smell that coffee? It even makes me want some, and I don't drink coffee." I slide the chair next to the bed and sit down. I take her hand in mine.

"Did you sleep well last night?" I continue. "I hope you had good dreams, but it's time to wake up. Maggie and I need you more now than ever. I need you to wake up. Can you hear me?" I squeeze her hand and search her face for any sign that she might be waking.

There's a tap on the door; a neatly dressed woman is standing at the door.

"Hello," I say.

"I'm Sarah, Margaret's sister from Morgan. How is she?" she asks as she approaches.

"No change," I say.

"I don't think we've met," Sarah says.

"I'm Rebecca Wilds," I say, not wanting to tell her more.

"Oh, yes, Rebecca. You were staying with them. Margaret talked about you," Sarah says, pulling up a chair and sitting next to me.

"I guess you came to get Maggie," I say, turning to her.

What has Margaret told her, and how much she knows about me?

"Yes, she'll be with me until Margaret gets better," Sarah says.

"I'll move my hand if you want to hold Margaret's hand," I say, pulling my hand away.

"No, I'm fine. I won't be here long. I'm waiting for the doctor to prepare Maggie's discharge papers," she says coldly with no expression.

I reach for Margaret's hand and gently squeeze it. I want her to know that there is someone here who cares. I want her to know that someone wants her to wake up. We sit in silence, and there is tension coming from Sarah. She must resent my presence. Will Maggie's visit with Sarah will be anything like my visit with Amanda? Something tells me it won't be pleasant.

I turn to Sarah and get a good look at her. She frowns back.

"Margaret never mentioned you. Oh, wait. You have a child," I say, wanting more information.

"No, I don't have a child. My husband has a twelve-year-old son, but he doesn't live with us," Sarah says, fidgeting in her chair. She's wearing a pristine suit with matching shoes. She shifts in the chair and gets up. She keeps her back to me and, without a word, walks to the door.

"Tell me how you're related to Margaret?" I ask; she's uncaring, and so unlike Margaret.

"I'm Chuck's sister," she says.

But earlier, you said you were Margaret's sister . . .

"Chuck is here. Have you seen him?" I ask.

"No, I haven't—he's on the first floor, and a nurse was with him," she says with her back still to me.

"What's his condition?" I ask, wanting to know everything. *Will she tell me?*

"I'm not sure. I didn't get the details."

"I hope it isn't bad," I say. Maybe I shouldn't discuss anything near Margaret. She could be listening.

"I think I'll go and check on him," Sarah says, walking out of the room.

"Margaret, how can you stand Sarah? She's as cold as a popsicle," I say, and I feel her hand twitch. "Can you hear me?"

I wait for a second, and then I feel her hand move.

I wait for another reaction, but there's nothing. Had I imagined that Margaret moved her hand?

"Margaret, right now would be a good time for you to wake up. You can have a warm cup of coffee and see the sunshine. You know, you protected me from Amanda. You're my hero," I say. Her eyes flutter; this time I did see it happen.

Do I tell the nurses, or keep talking?

"I suppose you're ready for that coffee. Open your eyes and I'll get it for you." I wait for a response. All I want is any movement—or any sign—that she can hear me.

Slowly, her eyes flutter again, and she opens them. I squeeze the button for the nurse. I want to jump and shout and say she's awake, but I'm afraid to make any noise.

The nurse appears at the door.

"Her eyes are open," I say.

"I'll get the doctor," she replies, running out of the room.

A team of people enter the room and ask me to leave. I'm hoping that this is a good sign. I stick my head in Maggie's room, but she isn't there.

Has she already left with Sarah?

Margaret is out of the coma but sleeping, so I sneak downstairs for a peek at Mr. Mosley. I want to talk to him. Why was he near the farm—who shot him, and why? Was the person who shot him also the person who killed my parents? Mr. Mosley must know something. He has to know. I have to know, and I have to talk to him.

As I approach his room, Oscar is sitting in a chair outside the door. I walk up to Oscar.

"What are you doing here?" I ask him.

"I should ask you the same thing," Oscar responds, looking at me with a smile.

"How is he? Is he going to survive?" I ask, trying to look around him and into the room. It has to be Mr. Mosley's room.

"I think he's going to make it." Oscar crosses his arms and looks at me sternly.

"So, it is Mr. Mosley's room. Can I talk to him?" I make a sad face, almost pleading.

"Nope, can't let you do that." Oscar shakes his head.

"Now, Oscar, you know me—right?" I say, hoping to persuade him to let me enter.

"Yes, but that doesn't change the fact that you can't go in." Oscar stands and faces me. I cross my arms and plant my feet sternly.

"Please, Oscar. I need to know if he knows anything about my parents. Why was he out near the farm?"

"The sheriff has already questioned him. It's an active investigation, so step back and let us do our job," Oscar says, with a frown and crossing his arms in front of him.

"Would you tell me if it had anything to do with the death of my parents?" I ask.

"I would, but at this point, it's an investigation," Oscar says.

"So, you're not going to let me enter?" I try one last time. Oscar has a soft heart and is often easily persuaded; if I plead, I might be able to get him to change his mind.

"Not now," Oscar says and sits back down.

"How about I buy you a soda?" I tease.

"Don't try bribing an officer. You must be patient. You know what they say about good things coming to those who wait."

"Oscar, you're a good man, but I wish just this once you would turn your head."

"Rebecca, it isn't going to happen." He shakes his head and laughs at me.

"Fine, Oscar, you know I'm dying to know details," I say, spinning around on one foot.

"Have a nice day, Rebecca," Oscar says as I walk away.

Do they know more than they're telling me? I wonder. *Why would they be guarding his room? Is it to keep him in or someone out?*

Chapter 29

Leaving Oscar, I hang my head and drop my shoulders. I'm disappointed that I couldn't persuade him to let me talk to Mr. Mosley. I pass the cafeteria, and the scent of food fills the air, reminding me that I haven't eaten since breakfast. My stomach growls and I change directions and enter the cafeteria.

I slide my tray past the choices, but nothing is connecting with my hunger. I get to the end, and a tired-looking man stares at me.

"What'll it be?" He asks the question as if it were a single word.

"I'll have a hamburger, please," I say.

He nods and slaps the circle of beef on the grill. The smell makes my mouth water.

"Okay," I mutter to myself, "food's on the way."

I pay for the burger, bag of chips, and a soda and move to the self-serve drink dispenser. I fill my cup and move to the station to dress the hamburger. I apply mustard and grab some pickles. I find an empty table next to the window. Using the wad of napkins to scrub the table, I sit.

Before I can even take a bite, Sheriff Webster's car pulls into the parking lot

Holding the burger, I ignore the action outside and take a bite. The juice runs down my hand and onto my arm. The combination of meat and mustard fills my mouth. The cook had sprinkled just the right amount of salt and pepper to make it tasty. My taste buds are piqued. It's so good.

A movement outside grabs my attention. More police cars pull into the parking lot.

What's going on here? Why all the police activity around the hospital? Can it be they know more than they're saying?

I want to run down the hall and start asking questions. If I couldn't get Oscar to talk to me or let me in Mosley's room, no one else will either. Sometimes it just sucks being a kid. They think I'm just in the way, but I do know things.

I finish my burger and am halfway through the bag of chips I'd saved for later; the frustration of not knowing and no one telling me anything has me distracted. Out the window, a squirrel runs along the branch of a giant oak tree. The faces of the people in the cafeteria are mostly people either from around town or from the church.

A nurse approaches me; it's Mrs. Collins, the big mouthed woman from the church.

"Mrs. Collins, please sit," I say, munching on my chips.

"I heard you talking to Oscar," Mrs. Collins says, turning to see if anyone is within earshot.

"I didn't know anyone heard us talking," I respond.

"I work in the nurse's station right by Mr. Mosley's room. Why is it you want to talk to him? "

"I'm concerned. I want to know how Mr. Mosley is doing."

"Everyone in town has been talking about what happened," Mrs. Collins says, taking a bite of her salad. "Mr. Mosley's in stable condition. We expect a full recovery. I hope that answers your questions and will put you at ease."

"I'm so glad to hear that. I was worried that Maggie would lose both of her parents as I did."

Mrs. Collins leans forward. "They're both recovering nicely." Then she looks around to make sure no one is near us. "So why did you want to talk to Mr. Mosley? All of this happening—Mrs. Mosley getting attacked, and Mr. Mosley shot. What's going on around you? You seem to have brought a lot of drama to our town." Mrs. Collins shakes her head, and her brows furrow in judgment.

What do I say? Bess said that this isn't my fault.

Emotion wells in my chest, and it's hard to breathe. I want to get away from her. She turns and looks over her shoulder, and then back at me.

"All this drama around you, and now the Mosleys have been attacked, along with their daughter." The smile disappears, and her gaze pins me like one of the bugs in the science room.

"What do you know or have that someone wants to kill for?" Mrs. Collins asks with a determined look.

The question hits me like a brick. None of this was my fault. I was just a casualty. I push back my chair and stand. My hands crush the bag, and chips fall to the table. Grabbing the tray before Mrs. Collins can stop me, I say, "I'm sorry, but I can't talk now." Anger floods my face. Mother had said that Mrs. Collins is a "busybody."

I rush out of the cafeteria. I need fresh air.

Why do people not see the things I see? I know that Amanda and Gene Maxwell are evil people, and that somehow, Mr. Mosley is mixed up with them. I see it all so clearly, but no one else sees it.

I rush down the hall and run into Sheriff Webster.

"Wow, where are you going in such a hurry?" Webster asks.

"I need some fresh air. I'm so frustrated, I can't stand it," I say, trying to move past him.

"Wait a minute; you seem pretty upset. Let me walk with you."

"Only if you can keep up; I'm not slowing down!" I shout. I reach the main door, and I'm shaking so much that my hands can barely grab the door handle. I step out onto the sidewalk, the air hits my face, and the tears begin to flow.

"That's what I thought. You're crying. Now, tell me what's going on," Webster says, looking down at me.

"Everything's going on," I say. My whole body is jerking from crying so hard. I stand and wipe the tears away with my hands.

"Go ahead, cry. I'll still be here waiting when you finish," Webster says.

It takes a few minutes for the sobbing to stop, and for the tears to stop flowing. Standing here, I take comfort that Sheriff Webster is with me and there is concern on his face.

"Are you ready to talk to me?" Webster asks.

"Maybe, but not right here in front of the whole town. I don't want everyone talking about this," I say.

"Fine—follow me inside. We can find an empty room. Something tells me I want to hear what you have to say."

I follow him inside, and we walk down the hall to an empty room.

We go inside and close the door. I swallow a lump in my throat while the sheriff moves two chairs next to each other.

"Have a seat," he says, and I sit down. He sits across from me. "What's eating at you?"

"I think you know," I reply. "It's losing my parents, Amanda attacking Mrs. Mosley, and you finding Mr. Mosley out near the farm. Now Maggie has gone to stay with her aunt. It's like the cycle continues. The worst part is I know and see things that no one else does. I can connect dots that no one else even sees."

"Remember when I told you that you know things that you don't even know, you know?"

"Yes, I remember it clearly. Those words echo in my mind. I do know things—the trouble is; no one else does. Even worse is no one will listen to me," I say, wiping away a stray tear.

"I'm ready to hear what you have to say," Webster says as his eyes appear to be fixed on me. *It's comforting that someone is ready to listen.*

"Maybe it isn't enough. The only thing new I have to say is that Mr. Mosley was out near the farm and was shot, and so were my parents. Do you see a connection?"

Webster stares at me. "Possibly, but you do know that even if I suspect something, I can't tell you until I can prove it."

"So you see the dots. I'm not the only one." I stare back at him, searching his face for the answers.

"I see the dots, and they are beginning to connect. Be patient with me. The web of lies is coming untangled. Soon the truth will surface. We're nearing that truth."

"I hope so—I need answers. Thank you for sharing that with me."

"Rebecca, I'm sorry all of this has happened to you."

"Thank you, Sheriff." I stand, and we hug.

I walk out of the room and down the hall. I hit the button for the elevator and wait for the door to open. I hope that Sheriff Webster isn't giving me false hope. I hope he's nearing the answer.

I walk to the nurses' station and wait to speak with a nurse. There seems to be a lot of extra activity, and everyone seems extremely busy. I don't want to say or do anything that might cause problems for Mrs. Mosley.

"Can I help you?" says a nurse who I don't recognize; she's young and in a rush.

"I'm going in to see Mrs. Mosley. If she asks about Maggie or Mr. Mosley, what do I say?"

"Tell her they'll visit her later. She doesn't need to know more, and there's no need to upset her. Keep her talking and thinking about positive things. Don't stay long—she needs her rest."

I shake my head and turn to enter Mrs. Mosley's room; I pause just outside the door and take a deep breath. I want to calm myself, and I hope that my eyes aren't swollen from crying. I need to join her with a smile on my face and appear happy.

"Rebecca," Mrs. Mosley whispers when she sees me approach the bed. I reach for a chair and move it next to the bed.

"How are you feeling?" I sit next to her. "Would you like some water?"

"That would be nice," she says, and I hold the glass for her and guide the straw to her mouth. She sips the water and smiles at me.

"How do you feel?" I ask her again.

"I have a headache, and things are foggy. I don't know what's real, and what are things I've maybe dreamed or imagined."

"I want to thank you for protecting me. You're my hero." I smile at her.

"I didn't do anything. I don't remember much about that day. Maybe I don't want to remember. I don't like ugly things, and I think it was probably ugly."

"Yes, it was. Maybe not remembering is your mind protecting you," I say, afraid of where the conversation might lead us.

"I remember you talking to me before I woke up." Margaret looks at me and smiles.

"I did talk to you. Do you remember anything I said?"

"I just remember good-smelling coffee, and maybe something about a popsicle." She smiles.

"Yes, I said both of those things. So it's the food you remember. You must be getting hungry."

"No, I'm not hungry. I'm glad you're here. Something tells me I don't want to be alone right now."

"Hospitals are scary. I never liked the smells."

The nurse comes into the room and takes her vitals. Then the nurse turns to me.

"Remember, she needs rest." The nurse leaves the room, and I sit quietly as Margaret falls asleep. When she dozes off, I get up and walk out of the room.

It's a while before Bess will pick me up. I go down to the first floor and sit in the main lobby to wait on Bess. While I'm sitting, thoughts flood my mind. *What does Margaret know? She knew about me even before I was even born, and she knows about my adoption. So she knew about Amanda. Does Margaret know other things? What was the real reason she took me into her home?*

My phone rings, and its Blake. I answer.

"Hello, Blake."

"Rebecca, how are you?" Blake sounds unhappy and distant.

"I'm fine, but you don't sound like yourself. Is something wrong?" I ask.

"I'm sorry, but I can't come tomorrow as we planned. I thought I had it all arranged, but my dad signed me up to play in a golf tournament with him. Can we move it to the following weekend?"

"Yes, we can. Are you looking forward to the tournament?" I ask, not wanting to show disappointment.

"Not really. I was looking forward to seeing you. You were going to tell me what happened to you."

"Listen, Blake, why don't you call me tonight, and I'll tell you everything," I say. This is not the place for me to talk.

"Okay, I'll call you tonight."

"That sounds good. Talk to you later. Bye." I end the call.

I'm in no condition to see him tomorrow. I'm still trying to figure out Mr. Mosley's connection. Is he connected to my parents' deaths, or did he happen to be in the wrong place at the wrong time?

The sheriff mentioned a web of lies. I've certainly lived in that web. At this point I don't even know who I am. Even the people who raised me weren't my parents, and Bruce was Jackson Nash. Am I the cause of Bruce and Carol's death? Is it all about the money in the trust? When will I have answers?

Chapter 30

I walk into Margaret's hospital room, and she's sitting up in bed.

"Rebecca, come in," Margaret says, and I enter. "What are you doing here on a Saturday morning?"

"I wanted to see how you're doing. Bess dropped me off on her way to the beauty salon. How do you know it's Saturday?" I ask, sitting down next to the bed. I smile, happy to find her sitting up. She must be doing better.

She points to the big calendar on the wall. I nod.

"How are you feeling?" I ask.

"I'm doing better. My headache is almost gone. Dr. Harris says that I can't go home until I've been two days without a headache. So I'll be here a while longer," she says.

"At least you're getting good care while you're here." There is shuffle of feet in the hallway, and I turn to the door.

A tall woman with shoulder-length dark hair enters the room. She's attractive and wearing a diamond ring on her finger that's as big as a quarter.

"Margaret, I just got home from my trip. I heard Maggie's message on the answering machine. I wish she'd called my cell phone. I would have dropped everything and come immediately," the woman says as she approaches the bed. She leans over and hugs Margaret.

"Sarah, it's so good to see you," Margaret says as the two women embrace. I'm taken aback by the name.

"Wait a minute," I say, jumping out of my chair. "You said, Sarah. Who is this?" I blurt out.

Margaret looks at me like I'm crazy. "This is my sister, Sarah."

"No! She can't be Sarah." I fall back into the chair and hold my head as the room spins.

"What's wrong with you, Rebecca?" Margaret leans over and places her hand on my knee.

"Sarah . . . is your sister? She's Sarah?" I say, trying to make sense of things. "A lady picked up Maggie yesterday. She said she was your sister, and that her name was Sarah. I didn't like the woman. Even yesterday, I felt like something was off. She came into the room and showed no interest in you. First she said she was your sister, and then she was Chuck's sister. I was confused."

"This is important. Did you see Maggie leave with her?" Sarah asks.

"No. I went to Maggie's room, and they were already gone. Maggie would have stopped in here before leaving, and that didn't happen. I just felt like it was all bizarre. Why would Maggie leave with her?"

"Strange indeed. Why would someone come here and pretend to be me?" Sarah reaches for her cell phone. "I'm calling the police."

"Who would take my Maggie? Why?" Margaret burst into tears.

I stand up to comfort Margaret.

"We'll find Maggie. You need to be calm. Getting upset is not going to help you get well. Take a few deep breathes and take a sip of water. The police can handle this," I say, handing the glass of water to Margaret. She hesitates, but takes a sip.

"I know, you're right," Margaret replies. "I need to be calm about this. I don't want to delay my recovery. The sooner I get well, the quicker I'll get out of here. Where could that woman have taken her? Why would someone take our Maggie?"

"I don't know, but I'm sure the sheriff will find out," I say, trying to reassure her.

Sarah puts her cell phone in her pocket.

"The sheriff's on his way," Sarah says. "He'll be here quickly, because he is downstairs. Maybe the hospital has surveillance cameras that will help them see what happened. This is a small town. It might be someone you know." Sarah takes Margaret's hand. "I bet this has something to do with that lowlife you married."

I sit on the edge of my chair, stunned by Sarah's comment. Why does she feel that way about Mr. Mosley?

"Now, Sarah, this is not the time to start on that." Margaret pushes aside the bedside table and attempts to get out of bed.

"I don't think that's a good idea," Sarah says, pushing her back into the bed. "You just came out of a coma. You need to rest, and please try to stay calm. The sheriff will be here soon."

"Sarah, we've got to find Maggie." Margaret begins to cry.

"Margaret, we'll find her. You know me—I won't stop until I do." Sarah settles Margaret in the bed.

My lips form a straight line as I try to think of a way to help. "Should I tell the nurse that she's upset?"

Sarah nods. "That's an excellent idea."

A few minutes later, Dr. Harris and two nurses enter the room. Sarah and I step out into the hall and wait while they calm Margaret and give her a sedative.

Sarah leans against the wall and grips her phone in front of her. She's frowning. "I'm glad you remembered that the woman yesterday said she was me. Think hard—have you ever seen her before?"

The elevator dings, and Sheriff Webster steps out.

"No, I've never seen her. I didn't think Maggie would leave without telling me bye, so nothing about it seemed right. With all that's happened, I wasn't thinking clearly," I tell Sarah as I watch the sheriff enter the room and approach.

"I hope the sheriff can find her quickly." Sarah takes a few steps toward the sheriff.

The sheriff stands with his hands on his hips. His eyes search our faces.

"I'm Sarah Gray, Margaret Mosley's sister."

Sheriff Webster reaches out and shakes Sarah's hand.

"Someone came to the hospital yesterday, pretending to be me, and took Maggie," Sarah says, quickly trying to move things along.

"There's a waiting room over there. Let's go and sit so I can get all the information." Webster nods towards the waiting room. We follow him down the hall.

We sit before anyone speaks again.

"After Chuck was shot, we called in extra police—they're here now. We have the State Police and the Texas Rangers, and we even have some drones to cover the rural area," Sheriff Webster says as he leans forward and worry lines form on his brow. "Rebecca, did you see the woman?"

"Yes, Sheriff, I did. I even talked to her."

The sheriff starts writing in his notepad. He continues to ask questions, and he reassures us that he'll find her. He leaves, and we walk back to Margaret's room.

There's a nurse attending to Margaret, so we wait outside the door.

Sarah crosses her arms in front of her. "So someone shot Chuck?"

"Yes, that's what they say. I haven't seen Chuck. There's a guard outside his room, and he wouldn't let me enter."

"A guard, I wonder what that's all about." Sarah starts pacing.

"They wouldn't tell me anything. I did try to bribe the guard into telling me something, but he wouldn't. Tell me about Mr. Mosley." I gaze into Sarah's face and lock eyes with her.

"Why? Who are you, exactly, and why do you want to know?" Sarah places her hands on her hips.

I let out a deep sigh. "I'm Rebecca Wilds. My parents were killed, and Margaret let me stay with her. Margaret told me that I had been adopted, and that my biological father is Mr. Mosley."

"Oh, so you're the one Margaret mentioned. She said she tried her best to resent you, but you were so sweet that she fell in love with you." Sarah's eyebrows raise, and her lips turn up at the corners.

Hot tears fill my eyes, and I blink to hold them back. My heart feels heavy, "I love Margaret too. I want nothing but the best for her."

"That's good, because if I find out otherwise, you'll have to deal with me," Sarah says.

The nurse comes out of Margaret's room with a worried look, and she turns to Sarah and me.

"You ladies need to take your conversation somewhere else," she tells us. "We have Margaret calm and resting. You can come back later today."

"Fine, Rebecca, you're coming with me," Sarah says, turning toward the elevator.

Frustrated that I might not be able to help, I put my hands on my hips. "I can't, because Bess is picking me up anytime now."

"Who's Bess?" Sarah frowns and turns her head to look at me.

"Bess is my guardian."

Sarah crosses her arms. "Girl, I thought you said you were staying with Margaret? If that's the case, why do you have a guardian?"

"It's complicated. I do have a guardian. I wasn't with the guardian until after Margaret's attack," I say.

"Then we'll go downstairs and wait for her. I need you with me. You know things that will be beneficial. I have to find Maggie." Sarah hits the button for the elevator so hard I think it's going to break.

"I've told you all that I know." I step onto the elevator with Sarah.

Sarah pushes the button for the first floor. "You've seen the woman, and that's valuable."

"Yes, that's about all I know."

We step off the elevator and walk to the small waiting area just inside the main door.

"You live in this town. You know things that will help me," Sarah insists.

We sit down to wait for Bess.

"It's a good thing I came today, and that you were here with Margaret," Sarah continues. "Who knows how long it would have taken for us to figure out that Maggie is missing?" She has been a tower of strength, but a tear slips down her cheek.

I place my hand on hers. "I know it must be so hard. Your sister and her entire family are in turmoil. I can't help but think that the whole thing is because of me."

"Don't blame yourself. I'm sure we're going to find out that Chuck is the root of all of this." Sarah removes her hand from mine and wipes away the tears.

"You don't like him," I say, swallowing hard and feeling my muscles tense.

"No, I don't, and I never will. My sister would be better off without him. Poor Maggie thinks her Dad is such a good guy." Sarah studies my face.

"Oh, there's Bess." I jump up and rush to the door to meet Bess.

"You didn't have to wait for me downstairs. I was going to visit with Margaret," Bess says, entering the hospital.

"Something has come up. I'm Margaret's sister; you see, we have been alerted that Maggie was taken. I want Rebecca with me to search for her."

Sarah stands in front of Bess with her arms crossed. Sarah radiates confidence and authority.

"Taken—what do you mean taken? Maybe you should leave this to the police. I don't want Rebecca to be in any danger." Bess seems worried.

"I'll protect her. She saw the woman who took Maggie, and that's very beneficial," Sarah says, fidgeting.

"Who are you exactly? Why Rebecca? Hasn't enough happened without involving more people?" Bess begins to shake and dabs her eyes with a tissue.

I tire of waiting for her answer. "I do want to help Maggie. Please, Bess, Sarah doesn't know her way around town. I saw the woman, and I can be of help. You know I want to help Maggie." My voice cracks and I'm impatient. I cross my arms and tap my foot as I wait for permission.

"We're wasting precious time. We need to be looking instead of standing here talking," Sarah says and turns to Bess.

"It's up to you, Rebecca. If you want to help, you have my permission," Bess says to me.

"I want to help Maggie," I say, almost pleading with Bess.

"Will you bring Rebecca home?" Bess asks Sarah.

"Yes, I'll take care of her," Sarah says, walking forward.

"Keep your cell phone on so I can call and check on you," Bess says.

"Come on; we're wasting time. Let's go," Sarah says, grabbing my arm and moving toward the door.

"Be careful," Bess shouts as we exit the hospital.

I turn around and see Bess standing on the sidewalk with a confused look, waving as we leave.

I slide into the passenger seat of Sarah's sleek silver Mercedes. I fasten my seatbelt. Where does she plan to look? Where do you look for a kidnapper? Something tells me she isn't going to be standing on a corner.

"Let's grab a bite of lunch. It will give us a chance to think and make a plan. Any good places we can go?" Sarah backs the car out of the parking space.

"What kind of food do you want?" I ask.

"Hamburger is fine—it'll be fast and filling."

"Take a left and go down two blocks," I say, as several cars drive by us with "State Trooper" written on the side.

"I see the sheriff wasn't lying about the state police being here. Hopefully, with all the law enforcement, we'll find Maggie quickly," Sarah says as we drive the two blocks.

"Turn right, and this is the place," I say. There are a lot of police cars parked in front of the restaurant.

We enter the front door, and there are police officers seated at the big table in the center of the dining room. We take a booth near the middle. We're near the officers and can be aware of their activity. I spot Clay sitting by the windows but hope that he doesn't see me.

"Here's the menu. We have to go up front to order." I shove the menu in front of her, and Clay makes his way to my table. Most girls would be excited if Clay liked them, but there is something about him that makes me nervous. It's like he tries too hard. He slowly slithers to the booth with a faraway look. In my mind I see his tongue moving like a snake, and I'm uncomfortable.

"Rebecca, what've you been up to?" Clay asks, leaning on the edge of the table and ignoring Sarah.

"Why do you ask?" I avoid eye contact by glancing at the menu.

"I haven't seen you at school. Rumor has it you're back and living with Mrs. Higgins. I heard about your aunt attacking Mrs. Mosley."

"I'm sure the rumor mill is abuzz with activity now that all these officers are in town," I respond. I'm irritated that he came over to be nosy, and my voice gets shrill at the end. The officers turn to look at me because I was so loud. Clay leans in closer, and I feel like he undresses me with his eyes.

"Yeah, wonder why all those guys are here," Clay says, nodding toward the table with the officers.

"If you don't mind, we're in a hurry. We need to order our food and eat," Sarah says, sliding out of the booth and forcing Clay to move. "Rebecca, I'll order. You stay here and save our place. Tell me what you want."

Clay steps away and lingers near the booth. He gives Sarah a sour look, shoves his hands in his pockets, and walks a short distance away.

"Thanks for getting rid of him. I want a number five with no onions," I say, winking at Sarah.

"You want a soda?" Sarah asks.

"Sure, anything is fine."

Clay is still watching Sarah and me.

Sarah walks to the front to order, and Clay comes back to our booth.

"She was rude," Clay says, putting his hands on the edge of the table and leaning over.

"Maybe she thinks you were. You came over and leaned on our table and acted like she wasn't even here. You should go before she comes back." I give him a frown. Clay shrugs his shoulders and goes back to his booth. I don't turn around, but I can only imagine that he's staring at me. I'm sure he didn't like my response.

Sarah returns to the table with our soft drinks. I peel the paper off my straw and insert it into the lid.

"I see your friend returned." Sarah smiles at me.

"Yes, Maggie tried to set me up with him, but I think there's something a bit off about him."

"I agree with you on that. I would have thought Maggie would be a better judge of character." Sarah takes a sip of her drink.

"He's her boyfriend's best friend."

"Well, that explains it. It's all about keeping it close." Sarah smiles at me.

"I'm glad that you also see that Clay is strange."

"Rebecca, maybe he isn't strange, but just feels awkward around you. Some boys just get nervous around girls," Sarah says.

A waitress delivers our hamburgers, and we eat without talking.

My thoughts are on Clay and how strange he makes me feel. Why didn't Maggie see it before?

Sarah is sending a text, and I watch her. She is so strong and sure of herself. So well put together.

The officers' radios go off, and they all storm out of the restaurant like they're going to a fire.

"Something's happening. We need to finish and get out of here. Can you see which direction the police are going?" Sarah asks, tossing her last French fry in her mouth.

"Yes, I can see," I say, keeping my eyes peeled out the front window.

"Let's go—we're following them," Sarah says, sliding out of the booth.

"Isn't that against the law?"

"Quiet, someone might hear you," Sarah whispers as we walk to the car.

Chapter 31

It's been a long afternoon driving around searching for Maggie or any clues to her whereabouts. Sarah and I were unable to keep up with the troopers, but we know that they drove into a rural area.

"Do you think they found Maggie?" I ask.

"I'm not sure, but something has happened. Margaret is expecting me to take care of things for her. I can't go back until I find Maggie. Is there anywhere else that we can look?" Sarah asks.

"This is a long shot, but we could go to my farm. That's where all the bad stuff started." I glance at Sarah to see her reaction.

"We might as well give it a try. It can't hurt anything."

"Sarah, it was out in the country where they found Mr. Mosley shot, so whoever is doing the shooting might be out there. We could be putting ourselves in danger." I frown, if Maggie's there, I want to know. We must find her.

"Let's check it out. Keep your cell phone in your pocket. Be prepared to call for help. Now give me directions," Sarah says.

"Stay on this road until you get to FM 2130 and turn right. We'll stay on that road for fifteen miles."

"I trust that you won't get us lost out here in the boonies," Sarah says.

"I know this area well. There's a road ahead we call the Loop. It's coming up just past the end of the white fence." My eyes are peeled for anything out of the ordinary.

"I see the fence and the sign. Turn right?" Sarah asks.

"Yes."

We make the turn, and Sarah slows the car down a little as we near the backside of the farm.

We round the curve where the land in front of us stretches out, and police cars are lined along the road and parked in the pasture. I stiffen, and my heart beats faster.

"Rebecca, look at all those police cars," Sarah says, slowing to almost a stop.

"I wonder why the police are there." She throws me a quick look before she continues driving. "Do you think they found Maggie?"

My breath is shaking. "I don't know. Maybe they got an emergency call." I try to swallow the lump in my throat. I choke a cough.

Sarah glances at me.

"I'm okay." My hands are still shaking, and my knees join the action.

"You're really scared. Are you holding something back? Something you aren't telling me?"

She slows the car to a crawl. All I want to do is jump out and start running, but I can't.

"That's the back of my farm. Keep going around on the Loop," I say, glancing back.

"It looks like everything is happening back there. Do you think the police found Maggie?" Sarah seems worried.

"I don't know. Just keep going," I say, but maybe someone is at the house or the barn. Is it safe for us to go there alone? I try to swallow, but my mouth is dry. I choke and begin to cough.

"Are you sick? Do you need me to stop?" Sarah asks.

"I'm okay. I'm scared. Something is going on out here, and we might be walking into danger," I say, grabbing the handle on the door.

"Just up ahead, we'll be entering the property from the front. In the front are the house and the barn. Someone might be there. If they're keeping Maggie there, we could be in danger." I'm shaking and worried about both of us.

"We'll proceed with caution. If Maggie's there, we need to find her. Didn't you say your parents were found on the farm?" Sarah picks up speed.

"Yes, I found them in the barn," I say as fear wells inside me.

"You might want to slow down. Just around this curve is the road that leads to the house." I point to the road.

"We'll proceed slowly, and with caution." Sarah's knuckles are white as she grips the steering wheel.

"Should we call for help?" I ask.

"And tell them we think Maggie might be here?" Sarah's voice cracks.

"The turn is just ahead, but maybe we should park at the edge of the road and walk to the house," I say. I know this area, but I need Sarah to give me directions and reassurance.

"If we walk to the house, will they be able to see our approach?" Sarah asks.

"They can if they're looking. I'm just trying to think of the best way to do this," I reply. We're alone and have no protection.

Sarah pulls to the side of the road and puts the car in park.

"Rebecca, something bad is happening—or has happened—here. It could be that they found another body. It could even be Maggie. If someone is hiding out here, we could be next. I'm not sure what to do, but right now, we could be in danger. Sit tight and let me think." Sarah's hands are shaking.

I want to say something, but she's trying to think. I want to slide out of the car and walk to the house, but if someone is there, it would be a mistake. What if someone is there and has Maggie?

"I'll walk to the house, and you stay here. Call the police if I don't come back," Sarah says.

I shake my head.

"What do you mean?" Sarah asks.

"You stay here and let me take the tree line to the house. If I don't come back in fifteen minutes, you call the police," I say.

"I don't know. Let me think," Sarah says.

"I'll go while you think. It's the only way. I know this land and the path to the house. I know the house and the placement of the windows," I assure her, reaching for the door handle.

"Rebecca, someone could shoot you. You're putting yourself in danger," Sarah tells me.

"Sarah, someone came to this house and got my parents out of bed. They took my parents to the barn and shot them. I was there in the house sleeping.

If they wanted to kill me, they would have done so that night. Maybe I'm wrong, but let's pray that I'm not." I step out of the car.

Sarah nods at me, and I run for the tree line. My stomach is tied in a twisted mess and hurting. There's a knot stuck in my throat, making it difficult to breathe. I run along the tree line, heading straight for the back of the house. My legs are shaking as I try to run. I reach in my pocket to make sure I still have my cell phone. I'm nearing the house when I notice some buzzards circling above. Looking up and watching them circle, I leave the fence line and run into the open field and over the ditch in the center. Something is lying in the ditch.

I'm out of the tree line, I think. *If someone at the house is looking outside, I could be spotted. I'm putting myself in danger.* In the ditch, I expect to find a wounded animal, but it's a person lying there. I blink to make sure that I see it correctly. It's not just a person but a girl. Could this be Maggie? Why would they bring her here? I run into the ditch and kneel next to the body. It's a girl with wheat-colored hair and a slender body. I turn the person over, and to my surprise, it's Maggie.

"Maggie," I say in almost a whisper, not wanting anyone to hear me.

Maggie isn't moving, but her body is warm. I let out a breath, so relieved that she is still alive. I sit down on the ground next to her and reach to feel for a pulse. My own heart is pounding, but I can tell that Maggie's pulse is weak and I have to get help. I can't physically carry her out of the ditch, so I run back to get Sarah.

I run as fast as possible and stay along the tree line.

I have to get help. I can't move Maggie by myself.

I'm praying under my breath that we found her in time, and that she'll survive this ordeal.

I reach the car. Sarah is looking at me with a puzzled look. "I found Maggie," I says. "I think she's hurt or unconscious. I don't know how we're going to carry her."

"Did you see anything else? Was there any sign of anyone?" Sarah asks, looking toward the house and back at me.

"I never got to the house. She's lying in a ditch. I didn't see anything else," I say, out of breath and gasping for air.

"Well, let's go and get her," Sarah says, jumping out of the car.

"I don't know if I can be of any help. Amanda sliced my shoulder open. I have thirty stitches."

"I have a folding lawn chair in the trunk and a blanket from a picnic recently. Maybe we can carry her on it and divide the weight. Maggie isn't very big, so the two of us should be able to manage even with your hurt shoulder."

"Mr. Everman lives just up the road—maybe he can help us," I say, waiting for instructions.

"Rebecca, we can do this. We don't even know if Mr. Everman is at home. It could end up being a waste of time. Time is crucial. Let me open the trunk," Sarah says.

She opens the trunk and takes out the lawn chair and blanket. All I can think about is if we will make it in time. She slams the trunk and we crawl through the fence and into the pasture. We run along the fence line. I'm sprinting and gasping for breath. I trip and fall, but I pull myself up and keep running. I turn, and Sarah is running a short distance behind me.

I can hardly catch my breath by the time I reach the ditch. I bend at the waist and grab my sides that are hurting. I desperately need water, because my throat is parched. I stand at the edge of the ditch, waiting for Sarah to catch up.

"Girl, you should be on the track team. I can't believe how fast you run. You looked like a deer sprinting away from a hunter," Sarah says, gasping for air.

I point into the ditch, and she nods her head. Together we walk to Maggie. Sarah places the folded chair on the ground next to Maggie. We cover the chair with the blanket and roll Maggie onto it. Together we lift the chair and Maggie.

"What do you think, can you do this?" Sarah asks.

"We've got this, but it will be slow moving her out of the ditch," I say.

We struggle to lift Maggie out of the ditch, and eventually we return to the car. Several times we had to lay Maggie on the ground and catch our breath. Our hands grew tired of the grip on the chair, but we remained strong. Both of us are tired, thirsty, and out of breath.

"I don't know why Maggie's here, or who the woman was who took her," I say.

"What's going on?" Sarah says.

We lay Maggie on the back seat and get into the car. Sarah starts the car and starts driving. She calls the police station and tells them that we found Maggie, and that we're on our way back to the hospital.

We drive to the hospital. Sarah is speeding and trying to get there quickly.

"I hope she'll be alright," I say, turning to check on Maggie.

"Has she even moved?" Sarah asks.

"She hasn't moved at all," I say, hoping that she survives.

"I want to know who took her, and why," Sarah says.

"I want to know that too. I wonder if this has anything to do with the death of my parents," I whisper. My mouth is dry and parched.

We pull in at the Emergency entrance of the hospital, and I run inside to get someone with a stretcher.

Minutes later, Maggie is in the trauma room with the doctor, and Sarah and I are in the waiting room.

The sheriff comes into the Emergency entrance door.

"Thanks for calling me. How's Maggie?" Sheriff Webster asks, taking a seat across from us.

"We don't know—the doctor is with her now," Sarah says, grabbing her wallet out of her purse. "I'm getting sodas after all that running. We need something to drink."

"Yes," I respond.

"Rebecca." Sheriff Webster leans forward. "How is Maggie?"

"She's going to be okay—hopefully," I say. "Sheriff, why was Maggie at the farm?" I ask.

The sheriff shrugs. "The State Police have been at the farm. They caught a woman there who had broken into the house."

"Maybe she was holding Maggie there," I say with a shrug. I'm wondering why they were at the farm. "I guess Maggie managed to escape. She just didn't make it very far. I wonder what that woman did to her." I shake my head.

"When all the police cars got to your property, the woman tried to run, and the police caught her," the sheriff tells me.

"So, you have the woman who kidnapped Maggie?" I turn to the sheriff.

"I certainly do," the sheriff says.

Chapter 32

"I'm going back to the station." The sheriff stands. "Rebecca, come with me. I'll take you home."

I shake my head. "I can't leave now. Not without knowing—"

Sarah returns with sodas and interrupts. "Please, Rebecca, you look tired. I think you're only surviving on nervous energy."

Webster frowns at me and reaches for my hand to pull me up out of the chair. "It'll give me a chance to go over some things with you."

I shake my head. "That's my sister lying in there. I can't leave until I know about her condition."

"Keep your voice down. We don't want anyone to hear you. Remember, Maggie doesn't know about you and her," Sarah says, staring at me.

"I'm sorry, but it's true." I brush a stray hair from my cheek.

"I promise to call you when I know something." Sarah pats my arm.

"No matter what time, you'll call me?" I ask, looking at her. Her deep, green eyes are the same color as Maggie's.

"I promise. Now go and get some rest." Sarah stands and extends her hand to help me get up.

I stand. "But the doctor can tell us something at any time."

"Or it could be hours. No need for both of us to wait," Sarah persists.

"Okay, but promise you'll call me. I'll sleep with my phone," I say in protest.

Sheriff Webster grabs my arm and leads me out the door. It's strange that he insists on my leaving with him. Why didn't he call Bess to pick me up?

We get into his car, and there are other police cars parked in the parking lot. Officers are standing outside and inside the hospital. It all seems strange for our quiet little town, where everyone knows each other.

It's quiet on the short drive to Bess's house. I wonder why the State Police are here. I want to ask, but I'm afraid that he won't tell me.

Turning the car onto my street, Webster asks, "What made you go to the farm to search for Maggie?"

I swallow hard and realize that my mouth and throat are still parched from running. "I didn't know she'd be there. I heard you found Mr. Mosley on Gil's property. Something has been going on out there."

"You'd make a great detective."

"I don't think so. You see all kinds of ugliness in your line of work."

"You've got that right," Webster says, turning into the driveway. "I'm going inside with you. I want to speak to Bess."

"Am I in trouble? Did I do something wrong? Has something happened to Bess?" I blurt out.

"Nothing's wrong." Webster steps onto the porch and rings the doorbell.

Footsteps approach from inside, then we hear the deadbolt being disengaged, and the door opens.

Bess's eyes grow large, and her mouth flies open. "Sheriff," she says, "I wasn't expecting you. Is something wrong with Rebecca?"

"No, she's fine, and she's right here with me." He nudges for me to enter.

I step inside, and Bess throws her arms around me and gives me a bear hug.

"Oh, Bess, you're squashing me," I laugh.

Bess turns away from me and tells the sheriff, "Please come inside and have a seat."

We walk into the living room and sit down.

Why is the sheriff here? Why does he want to see Bess?

"May I get you something to drink?" Bess asks as she walks slowly toward the kitchen.

At this point, my mouth and throat are so dry that they feel like sandpaper, but I'm not asking for anything. I'm eager to hear what the sheriff has to say.

"No, I'm fine," the sheriff replies. "I have information that I thought you should hear before it's released."

"What kind of information?" Bess stops cold and frowns as she crosses her arms in front of her.

"Rebecca, you need to hear this before its broadcast on the news."

"Hear what?" I'm growing impatient.

"We've searched the rural area with drones. After we found Chuck Mosley on Gil's property, we started concentrating on that area. It was on your property that we made the discovery." Webster waits for my reaction.

"Made a discovery?" I ask, stunned. So there was a reason all those police cars were parked on my land.

The sheriff nods. "On the backside of the property, it was situated just far enough inside the fence that it wasn't visible from the road. That rolling landscape at the back had it hidden."

"What wasn't visible? What was hidden?" I ask. *What they could have found?*

"Are you aware there's a large greenhouse?" He stares for my reaction.

"Oh—I'd forgotten about it," I say.

"So, you knew it was there?" the sheriff asks, sitting on the edge of his seat.

"Yes, when I was just a toddler, my dad and Connor built it. The plan was to grow seedlings and sell them. When Connor left for the service, my dad just stopped using it. It's been empty for years," I explain, sitting back.

"Do you know if your dad ever went back there?" the sheriff asks.

"I don't think so. My dad said that we had more land than we needed. He often mentioned selling it, but he never put it on the market."

"You don't think he ever went back there?"

"I'm pretty sure he didn't. The day my parents were killed, my dad rode the horse to survey all the land. I had forgotten about it until now. He and Mom had said maybe they should finally sell, and Dad said he hadn't even been on that part of the land for years."

"Did he say anything about it after he rode out to look?" the sheriff asks.

"I don't know. I was feeding the animals when Dad returned and went into the house. Why are you asking me all of these questions?"

"That greenhouse is being used. Not only are drugs being grown there, but there's also a lab for making them. There's thousands of dollars' worth of drugs there. There are also markers for graves. Do you know anything about bodies buried on the site?"

"You think my dad was doing that? Whose body? There are graves?" I jump to my feet and begin to pace.

"At first, I thought it was your parents who were operating the greenhouse. But it is currently in use. That could be the reason someone killed them."

"You think my dad found it that day?" I spin around.

"Yes, I'm pretty sure that's what happened," the sheriff responds.

"Who could be doing it? It isn't their land." I sit back down.

"We're still investigating. Do you remember I told you I would take a DNA sample from Chuck Mosley?"

"I remember." I swallow hard, but the lump sticks in my throat. I have a feeling there is more that I'm about to hear.

"The fresh DNA on Bruiser matches Chuck Mosley's DNA."

"What does that mean?" I jump to my feet, and Bess grabs my hand to calm me.

"It means there's a good possibility that he might be the killer."

"Why?" I turn to look at the sheriff, but my vision is blurred by the tears.

"I don't have the answer. I've been wondering if you'd be willing to help," the sheriff asks. Then he stands and walks over to me. He bends down, and our eyes lock.

"Help with what?" Bess intervenes.

The sheriff doesn't take his eyes off of me. "Oscar told me you wanted to see Mosley. What if I allow you that opportunity? What if you know just enough to ask the right questions? You could wear a wire, and maybe he would spill the beans."

"Now wait for a minute, Sheriff. We're not putting Rebecca in harm's way," Bess says, patting my arm and holding my hand.

"She'll be safe—Mosley's cuffed to the bed. There's no way that he can hurt her. There's enough police in and around the hospital. She'll be safe. Once he leaves the hospital, Rebecca won't be able to see him again. If you want answers, this will be your only opportunity." He stands and searches my expression for my response.

The thought occurs to me that if I don't get answers now, I may never get them. Why didn't Chuck keep me? Why did he give me up for adoption? He and Margaret could have raised me together.

"I have questions. I don't want to live the rest of my life not knowing. I need to know why my parents died and I was left." I wipe away the tears.

"Rebecca's a minor. Isn't this illegal? Will the tape even be admissible in court?" Bess asks, and she wraps her arms around me. "I can see you want to do this."

"I do. I want to know if Mosley did it, and why," I say, waiting for her to permit me.

Bess turns to the sheriff. "You'll be near at all times?"

"The tape will be legal. I'll be close and able to reach her instantly," Webster says, searching Bess's face for the answer.

"When do you plan to do this?" Bess asks.

"If you give your permission, we'll do it tomorrow morning. I need time to set this up. I'll pick you up here at eight."

"I'll be ready." I look at Bess for approval.

"I'm going with you. I won't be in the room, but I'll be close by," Bess says.

"Then I'll see you ladies, tomorrow morning. You should get some rest," the sheriff says, walking to the door.

The sheriff leaves and Bess closes the door behind him. She turns to me.

"Rebecca, you're one brave girl," she says.

"Thank you for allowing me to do this," I answer. "My only thoughts are . . . What if Mosley doesn't talk? What if I hear things that are just too hard to hear? Did he kill my parents? What are all the secrets?"

"Maybe after tomorrow, you'll know." Bess puts her arm around me.

"I need something to drink. My throat is so dry," I say, walking to the kitchen.

"I think we should have dinner and then get to bed early. Tell me, did you find Maggie?" Bess asks as she pulls items from the refrigerator.

"Yes, she's in the Emergency room now. She was unconscious when we brought her in." I take a big sip of water.

"Where did you find her?"

I shake my head. "On my farm."

"I'm sorry about that. I know you love that farm, but it seems to be the root of everything that's happened."

"It seems that way, but all I see there is the beauty of life with my parents."

"Bruce was like that—he looked for the good in everything."

"Do you think I'll find out tomorrow who killed them?"

"I sure hope so. It would be nice to have answers," Bess replies as she stirs a pot on the stove.

My phone rings, and its Sarah. "This is Sarah," I tell Bess. "It must be about Maggie." I answer. "Hello, Sarah."

"Rebecca, I've just seen Maggie. She's awake and talking. She wants to see you tomorrow. She said she has a lot to tell you."

"What does she want to tell me?"

"I don't know—she didn't say," Sarah responds.

"I'll visit her tomorrow." I take a seat at the table.

"Great, I'll see you then." Sarah disconnects the call.

I sit for a moment as Bess stands at the stove, and I wonder what Maggie has to tell me. What did she discover at the farm? What did the woman do to her?

Chapter 33

I'm wearing a wire, and I've been briefed. I don't tell the sheriff that I have questions of my own. I walk to the entrance of Mr. Mosley's room and hesitate for a minute, trying to gain confidence. I swallow a lump in my throat, and my hands are shaking. The door to the room is standing open, but the curtain is drawn around the bed to hide the view from the door.

I take a deep breath and release it slowly, hoping to gain courage. I step around the curtain to the bed. Mosley's sitting up watching television. He reaches for the remote and turns it off as I approach.

"How did you get in here?" he asks, staring at me.

"I've been trying for days to come, but there's always someone at the door. I guess they must have slipped away for a minute. I should make this visit short before I'm detected," I say. My knees are shaking, and I grab the bedrails to steady myself.

"It's good to see you," Chuck says, smiling at me. "You have beautiful hair like my grandmother."

I swallow hard and smooth out my pants, trying to stay still so that I don't expose the wire. I want to get all the answers before I leave this room. It's time I hear and know the truth.

"Who shot you?" I'm so nervous I choke on the words.

Chuck looks at me.

What if he won't talk to me? What if he doesn't answer my questions?

"Why do you care?" Chuck asks.

"I do care. I care about you and what happens to you. After all, you're my dad." I almost choke on the words. Somehow calling him "Dad" makes me feel like I'm betraying Bruce.

Chuck's face, now beet red, turns toward me with wild eyes. "How do you know that?"

"Does it matter how I know?" I reply, confident with my answer. "So who shot you? Was it an accident?" I ask, trying to show concern.

"It was Gene Maxwell. We've been in business together for years."

I take a minute to swallow the lump in my throat. Why would Mr. Mosley tell me that? It was Gene they'd caught in Dallas for attempting to break into the apartment. *How could Gene shoot Mr. Mosley if he is in jail?*

"It was good staying with you and Margaret. I enjoyed spending time with Maggie," I say. When he doesn't respond or show any emotion, I continue. "You didn't answer me. Is it true that you're my real dad?" I wait for his response. He nods in agreement, but his expression doesn't change. My heart aches that he doesn't show any emotion.

Does he not have any feelings for me?

"What kind of business did you have, and why would Maxwell shoot you?" I ask. I can feel my knees shaking harder, and I tighten my grip on the bed rails even more for fear of falling.

"We disagreed. I guess you'll find this out soon enough. We had a drug business. It was Amanda who got us started. She even suggested the location. It was the greenhouse on your farm. She said your parents would never find out. It was several years in the making, and it was producing a good income. I mostly stayed out of it except for my trips to dispense to our dealers. Even Margaret enjoyed the trips to Dallas and Fort Worth because she liked to shop. I'd drop her off and then take care of the drugs and then go back and get her. She never had a clue." Chuck shakes his head and smiles.

Rage builds up inside me. I want to scream or punch him. He finds it amusing that Margaret didn't know what was happening. He's a liar.

"Amanda is a lawyer; she has an office in Dallas," I say, and Chuck laughs.

"Rebecca, I know she's your aunt, but there are things about her you don't know. She isn't what you think she is." I'm stunned by his answer, but I try to stay focused on my questions. If she wasn't a lawyer, where did she go? Was she working? Did she even have an office in that building?

"I know she's my aunt, and she's a lawyer." My voice rises with confidence.

Chuck looks away and moves his head back and forth as if I'm a fry too short of a Happy Meal box.

"Rebecca, she's not a lawyer. She never finished school. Her 'job' was running drugs. That's why she left at odd times and wasn't always where she was supposed to be."

Anger floods my face. My heart thuds as the realization of my stupidity settles in my churning stomach.

"Why were you out by the farm? You even told Maggie and me to stay away from the farm, and that it wasn't safe. That was my home." I remembered when Maggie and I had been at the farm and gotten scared when we'd seen the black van.

Was that Maxwell in the van?

"Rebecca, I didn't want you to catch us. That's where we processed the drugs. We didn't want you and Maggie to do any sleuthing."

"But Amanda lived in California," I say, thinking he's blaming her, and that she wasn't even there. Not that I want to defend her.

"That's what she told your parents, but she was renting a house in Silverton." Chuck smiles like he's glad Amanda's secret is not out.

"Did my parents know about it? Did you know about the drug business?" I ask, wanting to clear them, knowing that the sheriff is listening.

"Not a chance, but the day they died, your dad saw us. He said he was calling the police, and then he was going to destroy everything. Well, we couldn't let that happen. We were making a lot of money."

"My dad saw you? He found out what you were doing in the greenhouse?" I ask. A wave of nausea hits me. My dad was so innocent, and he'd lost his life because he'd discovered their secret.

"He saw us, and he was mad." Chuck shakes his head.

"So, you decided to stop him?" I ask, wanting him to spill all of it. I suddenly panic; Mr. Mosley is a criminal, a killer, and I'm related to him. Chills run up my spine. The sight of Mr. Mosley disgusts me.

"Gene was going to shoot him right there on the spot, but I stopped him. I said you don't do anything—I'll talk some sense into him. So that night I went to the house and talked to Bruce. I tried to convince him to keep quiet, and that we'd split the money. But Bruce would have no part of it."

"So you were the one who came to the house that night. It was you and Dad shouting at each other," I say, reliving that night in my mind.

"That's right. I tried to talk Bruce out of destroying everything. We wanted to keep the drug business. Bruce was determined to report us. Gene was going to kill all of you, but I didn't want you to die."

"So you talked Gene out of killing Dad?" I ask, pressing further. I've waited long enough to know what happened that night.

"I told Gene I'd handle it."

"But Gene didn't believe you, and he killed them anyway?"

"I waited until everyone went to bed, and I was sure that everyone was asleep. I eased into the house and startled your parents. They were asleep and never even heard me. I woke them and told them that if they would come with me quietly, that I wouldn't hurt you."

I wait without speaking.

Chuck isn't telling me everything. Maybe if I wait, he will.

"I told them to follow me. I wouldn't hurt you. Your parents begged me not to disturb you. They begged me to leave you alone. They didn't realize that I could never hurt my flesh and blood." He has an evil look in his eyes, and an ugly grin stretches across his face.

I shiver. I'm staring evil in the face. My stomach begins to churn. Will I be able to last long enough to hear the rest?

"We went to the barn, and you know the rest."

"No, I don't know. So my parents went to the barn, but what happened? Who pulled the trigger? Who shot them? Was Gene in the barn waiting? Or was it Mr. Mosley who pulled the trigger?

"You don't need to know the rest," he says, looking away.

"Yes, I do need to know. I've played it out in mind over and over again. But I want to know what happened." *He just might not tell me anything.* A tear slides down my cheek as I wait. There is a long silence before Mr. Mosley's evil face turns back toward me.

"I shot them and left," he whispers, in a voice so low that I can barely make out the words.

The words spin over and over in my head. "I knew it was you," I say. "I found the dollar sign off your key chain lying in the barn."

"So you knew? You knew all along it was me?" Chuck says, staring at me.

"When I was born, why did you give me away? Why didn't you keep me? I have to know." It's not a question the sheriff told me to ask, but it's my only chance to find out.

"Amanda and I had an affair. I was in love with Margaret, and Maggie was still so young. I tried to break things off with Amanda, but she continued to communicate with me. She just wouldn't let me go. I guess that's when I realized that I was in love with two women. Amanda and I had other children, but she killed them. You'll find the graves around the greenhouse. Amanda was fine, giving you up. The thought of my flesh and blood belonging to someone else was just too much. I wanted you and Maggie to be together."

"I have other brothers and sisters?" My legs are now shaking so much that I have to sit in the chair by the bed. "All the years I longed for a brother or sister, and you robbed me of that experience."

"They're buried right there on your property next to the greenhouse," Mosley says, showing no feelings of remorse.

"How could you? How many are there?" I begin to cry. "What would it have been like to have my brothers and sisters?" I'm sure Dad and Mom would have adopted them too.

"There were two boys and twin girls." Mosley smiles like he's so proud.

"I thought you were deep-sea fishing when my parents were killed," I say, wiping my eyes with the back of my hands.

"I left just hours after I shot them. I had to have an alibi. I figured if I were away, it would clear me. I would have left sooner, but your dog attacked me. The dog tore a chunk out of my leg."

"So that's why you were limping. You didn't hurt your leg fishing." I swallow, and he nods. I pause, wanting to finish with the questions and get out of the room.

"Someone took Maggie. A woman," I say, wanting to find the connection. Surely he knows who took her and why.

"That was Gene's wife, Rhonda Maxwell. They took Maggie because I was going to destroy the greenhouse. I figured the police would eventually search the entire farm and find the greenhouse. Maxwell knows that when I get out of here, I'll go back and burn it down. They were going to keep Maggie to prevent me from doing it."

"Do you know that Amanda was arrested for attacking Margaret?" I ask. *Does he know, or was he involved?* I swallow, waiting on the answer.

"That's been years in the making. Amanda hates Margaret. Amanda is one evil woman. I wish I'd never got mixed up with her."

"I think deep down there's something good inside you. But you've tried to bury that good for so long that you've become a cold, heartless man. I'm ashamed to admit that we have any connection. I'm embarrassed that you're my father, and that Amanda is my mother. The Wilds were the kindest and best people anyone would ever meet. I'm proud to say that they're my parents. I'm glad that they raised me to be like them."

"I'm sorry it all turned out this way," he says, reaching for my hand, but I pull it away. I stand and take a step back away from the bed.

"I'm sorry too. And just so you know, I'm wearing a wire, and the sheriff just heard your confession. My greatest regret is that Maggie will discover that you're not the man she thought you were."

"What?" Chuck jerks up in the bed.

The sheriff walks into the room and stands right next to me.

"I got it all on tape, Chuck," he says. "You're going away for a very long time."

The sheriff and I go upstairs to Margaret's room. She's sitting up in the bed.

"This is about Chuck, isn't it?" she asks. "You know the rumor mill has been buzzing. Even the hospital can't keep things quiet."

"So, what have you heard?" the sheriff asks.

"I know Chuck was shot. How is he?"

"He's fine and will make a full recovery. Margaret, I'm sorry to tell you this, but Chuck killed the Wilds," the sheriff says, standing next to Margaret.

"That can't be true. Chuck wasn't here when the Wilds were killed," Margaret says, shaking her head.

"He left right after he shot them. I have his full confession on tape. Amanda and Chuck have been running a drug business for years. He's going away for a long time," the sheriff says, standing next to the bed and watching for Margaret's reaction.

"Poor Maggie, what will I tell her?" Margaret shakes her head again and her eyes water.

I step up to the bed. "How about the truth; I want her to know we're sisters."

Margaret begins to cry, "I think we'll be disgraced in this town."

"You and Maggie are victims just like Rebecca. You'll be fine. People will stop talking and move on to other things," the sheriff says, patting Margaret on the shoulder.

Footsteps come from the hallway. I turn to see Maggie slowly enter the room.

"Rebecca, I heard your voice and wanted to see you. I've been told a lot of disturbing things by Rhonda Maxwell."

"Maggie, you shouldn't be out of bed," I say, rushing to her side.

"I'm going to be fine. I want you to know something. We are sisters!" Maggie hugs me.

"Yes, we are," I say, hugging her back.

"I also know that my dad isn't a nice man. He killed Bruce and Carol. There is a lot more about him that no one knows, but Rhonda told me everything."

"Oh, Maggie, I'm so sorry," Margaret says.

"Mom, it isn't your fault. You don't have to put up with him mistreating you anymore. Yes, I knew that Dad was mean and abusive. You thought I put him on a pedestal, but the truth is; I was afraid of him."

My hands are still shaking when the sheriff turns into the driveway at the house. There's a slight movement on the porch. I strain to see. Blake is standing on the porch with a bouquet.

"Who's that nice-looking young man?" Bess says.

"That's Blake, the boy I met in Dallas." I smile at Bess.

"He certainly has good timing," Bess says, getting out of the car.

I reach for the door handle, and Sheriff Webster turns to me. He smiles. "You're an amazing young woman. I'm so proud of you. If it weren't for you, we might not have solved this case."

"Something tells me you would have. Thank you for allowing me to get the answers I needed. I think I can now move forward in life."

"I'm sure of that," the sheriff responds.

Chapter 34

Two Years Later

I drive up to the farmhouse and park the car. I hesitate; the sun radiates through the tree limbs and makes a pattern of light on the ground. I have beautiful memories of playing under those trees. I slam the car door, and the warmth of the morning sun takes the chill out of the air. I still have thoughts of that fateful morning. I grab the handle to the barn door and shove as hard as I can, and it slides to the side with a loud squeak. *Gee,* I think. *The hinges could really use some lubrication.*

I step into the barn and to the opening where I found my parents. Today there's fresh hay in a large mound filling that space.

"Mom, Dad, it's me. I've come to tell you that the trials are over. Chuck Mosley received a life sentence, and Amanda will probably remain in prison until she's an old woman. It was hard listening to their testimonies, and neither of them regretted their actions. I'm going away for a while, but I'll be back. This is my home. Thank you for adopting and loving me. You are both special to me. And Dad, I remember you said you wanted to name me Jordan, but Mom liked Rebecca. I'll come back soon. I love you both.

Connor is waiting for me outside the barn. "So, is this it? Are you leaving for college?"

"Yes, Connor, but I'll be back for holidays. I hate to leave Bess—she's been amazing, and I've loved living with her. I'm thankful you're living here and taking care of the animals. Next time I come, maybe we can ride Farrow and Velvet."

"I have something I want to tell you before you leave." Connor shoves his hands into his pockets and kicks the dirt. I can visualize him as a young boy kicking dirt.

"What is it, Connor?"

"I've been seeing someone, and I think I might propose." Connor's face reddens.

"Oh, who's the lucky woman?" I lean against the car.

"I think you'll approve. The woman is Margaret Mosley. I've already asked Maggie for her approval."

"What did Maggie say?" I ask.

"Yes! She said it's about time! But now I have to ask Margaret, and that could be the hardest part." Connor crosses his arms and leans against the car.

"Margaret is a sweet lady. She won't make it difficult."

"I hope you're right. I've never been this scared."

"So you bought the ring?"

He slides a little black box out of his pocket and reveals the stunning oval-shaped diamond solitaire.

"Connor, that ring most have cost a fortune!"

Connor smiles and puts the ring back in his pocket. "I hope she likes it."

"She will. Maggie and I are going to share a room at college. She's been a great big sister. Now there's something I have to tell you."

"What?" Connor plants his feet firmly on the ground like he's waiting for the shock of his life.

"Bess and I met with the record company, and I signed with the same label as Dad."

"Now Rebecca, your dad got messed up with drugs."

"Do you actually think that after everything that's happened here and to my parents that I'd touch drugs?"

"No—but be careful. That's a tough industry. Are you going to use a stage name?"

"Yes, it's Jordan Nash. Anyway, I need to go. Bess is waiting for me." I open the car door, "Good luck tonight. Call me and let me know how it goes. I wish I had a video."

"That's the problem with you young people. Nothing is ever private." Connor shakes his head.

"Good things are to be shared! Just remember that." I slide into the seat and smile at Connor.

Connor bends down and props his arms on the side of the car. I roll down the window.

"I forgot to tell you that I hired a farmhand," he says. "This is a lot to take care of when you work a full-time job."

"Who did you hire?"

"Clay. He's one of your friends. He's going to work here and go to the local college part time."

"Clayton? You hired Clayton?" I'm stunned that Clay would be at the farm.

"Hey, he's a good farmhand. He even worked for your dad. He told me how he acted around you."

"Clay told you that he was pushy and obnoxious?"

"That isn't what he said. He told me that he had such a big crush on you he acted like a jerk. He said just being near you made him nervous."

"He might have had a chance with me, but I'd already met Blake. Blake is the only guy for me."

"So, you and Blake are still together?"

"Not really. We're going to different colleges in different states, but we still talk, and I'm not interested in anyone else."

"I just hope you don't get your heart broken."

"Thanks, Connor." I start the car, and Connor backs away.

I look in the rearview mirror and see Velvet grazing in the pasture. I smile. Sheriff Webster was right; you can start a new life.

CPSIA information can be obtained
at www.ICGtesting.com
Printed in the USA
LVHW091305280721
693915LV00007B/263/J